The Flighters - Believe

BYRON JAMES-ADAMS

THE FLIGHTERS - BELIEVE

The Flighters - Believe

This story is fictitious.
Some long-standing institutions, agencies, and public offices do exist.
The characters and situations involved are wholly imaginary, and resemblance to natural persons, living or dead, or actual events is purely coincidental.

Again a big thanks to my beta readers....

Cover Art: Canva and by author.
Internal Book Design: Ingram Sparks.

THE FLIGHTERS - BELIEVE

Welcome to Edi-Aleda

It is the year of The God, 2045

During the mid-2020s, a clandestine team of scientists worked specifically with eugenics: a set of beliefs and practices that aim to improve the genetic quality of a human population.

This team was known as Project GEMSTONE, (Genome Engineering Modification Searching Toward an Overall Network of Eugenics). They were called The Seekers.

In their pursuit of creating 'better humans', they introduced different elements at the embryonic stage, however, most were unsuccessful, as the manufactured embryo would often not make it to full term.

A certain scientist known as Dr Seeker 7, chose to use the element Helium (He) as his muse. Together with his newly developed isotope, (He9), he found that a human could be created with the benefit of this element. He called them 'The Flighters'.

Chapter 1 Carlyle

Thursday morning; 18th December: Today, I am to meet my new friend Zamiro; she is a Ground-Dweller, and I am a Flighter. I do know we should not get acquainted, as it is dangerous for a Flighter to develop close feelings for a Ground-Dweller. She is a Teacher at an Early Learning Centre, and I have watched her from the Adult Learning Centre where I have recently enrolled. Although the two campuses are near each other, I believe she has not seen me watching her.

I am currently wandering through the streets and bergs of Edi-Aleda towards my intended rendezvous. What do I want her to need to know about me? I am of twenty-two summers and, as a Flighter, I may not live beyond forty summers as I may have a built-in life redundancy. I do not yet understand what that means.

There is so much else I want to tell her, too; I live alone, I am lonely, and I had decided to enrol at the ALC as I had missed much of my early learning. I want to know more and read and write correctly. I have made this my quest, my sense of purpose.

It was at the ALC where I first saw Zamiro.

My berg, Munta, where I had spent my early childhood, is across the sea from Edi-Aleda. I was raised on a farm where my family grew amnimates and crops. I was supposed to be home-schooled, but my parents needed my focus to be on the farm. Then, my father was injured during a Carrion Frenzy, and then they were both killed by the AIC. This is why I despise The AIC and hate The Carrion.

I am making the three-hour trek by foot, from my berg to the site where I had elected to meet with Zamiro today. I am still reluctant to use the little solar-powered scooters called Zoops that we all have access to. My uncle, we called him Cowboy, used to maintain the Zoops at our property in Munta. He, along with his wife and their daughter, were killed by the AIC, and even though it was over seven years ago, I still avoid using them as they remind me of them. The supply of fossil fuels expiated long ago, and there have been further advances in the storage and use of solar energy, so all transport operates with solar. Some Ground-Dwellers have also told me that the year is now 2045, and some have lived beyond forty summers, while others have even lived a hundred summers. I find that impressive.

With this bit of gain of confidence and limited knowledge, I can finally feel a change within me as I am sensing a feeling of belonging, and I know this is making me a better Flighter, and a better person.

I have also learnt that as a Flighter, I do not need to be educated or live a life of any structure. I want for nothing. I have learned that it is my gifted way of life. I have everything provided for me by The GOD and am considered to be a chosen one.

I can also choose to save people from The Carrion.

I arrived at the designated place and waited for her. I know she will come as I believe in her, but hope she believes in me. Zamiro wants to teach me to read and write. I also mentioned my need to understand the time intervals, although I am unsure of what benefit. Whilst waiting in the remnants of a derelict residential building in the foothills hills high above the community of Edi-Aleda, I decided to walk closer to the edge of the flat and crumbling cement platform for a better view. I can see the sprawling metropolis stretching out below. I was unaware of how impressive it is, not having seen the view from here before.

I feel maudlin as I am not truly a part of it; I know that I need to be, want to be and should be. During the day, I am free to move around the bergs to work or to visit other groups of Ground-Dwellers that live beyond my berg and vow I must do more for them.

I can also see the cement water channels that snake through the bergs, and these are kept clean with controlled water flushes from higher upstream. There is a siren warning system initiated when The Flush is to commence. Sometimes, I spend hours cleaning the debris from within the water channels to keep busy as there is not much else that I have to do. I still miss my farm. I still miss my family.

I am looking into a western setting sun, which is the direction that The Carrion invades from. As it is not yet dusk, it may be too cloudy for The Carrion tonight as they prefer to use the bold, bright, golden setting sun behind them as their ally to invoke a killing raid. This is called The Frenzy.

I once saved Zamiro from an attack from The Carrion, and I do not think she knows this. I managed to infiltrate the melee without being noticed, and as Zamiro is small and light in stature, I held her in my arms as we floated up and safely away. This was my first and only rescue of a Ground-Dweller, she is unaware of this and likely does not know how she survived.

No one ever survives The Frenzy.

Finally, Zamiro arrived and descended the rubble path leading towards me. I wonder if she is smiling as she meets me, but I believe she likes smiling. She is prettier when she smiles, and I have not known many other pretty things in my life for a long time. Zamiro is likely the only one, although I am unwilling to tell her about my feelings towards her. I hope to one day, maybe today. Maybe not. She called out to me. 'I've found you – you are not so good at hiding after all.'

'Mm, I did tell you where I was going to be,' I replied, trying my best for a clever retort. She looked past me towards the setting sun. 'You do have a great view from up here. Do you think The Carrion will be on tonight?'

I shrugged my shoulders, and she continued. 'Do you know much about The Carrion, and have you ever seen them up close?'

I looked over to her, not quite knowing how to respond. 'I know they generate their power to fly and attack from the solar energy within their golden metallic bodies. They cannot store the energy as they do not have any capacity to do so within their bodies. They use the energy when the sun is out. They cannot operate when it is overcast, or when they are in shadow, or at night. This is their weakness.'

She nodded. 'How do you know all that?'

'I have watched for them from where I live and often tried to figure out what they are here for. I have been watching them for years.'

'Have you ever seen a swarm of them attacking people? Did you know they call it The Frenzy?'

That was a question I didn't want to answer, so I shook my head and tried to come up with something else. It was then I saw she had a green rectangular block in her hand. 'What is that? Is it for me?'

She opened it, flicked through the leaves of the pages, then handed it to me: 'This is a blank book with spaced lines, and it can be your journal.' It was about as thick as my fingertip. 'It's for you to record your private thoughts.'

I was slightly suspicious about why she would do this but nodded anyway. My reading ability is limited due to my upbringing; however, I can recognise signs and know that being able to read and write is very different.

We sat there for a while in a comfortable silence, so eventually, I asked her something to hear her talking. 'So, can you tell me what you know about The GOD.' She looked at me momentarily. 'The GOD is the Government of Day and comprises randomly selected Ground-Dwellers. They become The GOD Panel and oversee the running of society, organising the distribution of food, transport, and demands of the community groups. You are to believe in The God as The GOD believes in you.'

I liked hearing the sound of her voice even more than I thought, so I nodded to let her continue: 'The GOD collects half the value of every transaction exchanged and distributes the collected funds back into the Berg. They provide the roads and other services including fresh water supply and sewerages.'

'OK, but do you know anything about The Flighters?' I enquired softly.

'Well, did you know The GOD provides monthly stipends to The Flighters? If I were a Flighter, I wonder what I would do with myself and all the money.'

I nodded again, hopefully not giving away my secret.

She had stopped talking, so I said: 'See, I know about The Carrion, and you know about The GOD. We do make a good pair, don't we?'

She looked at me. 'Mm, I think we should start on the journal now.' Zamiro proceeded to tell me to record my thoughts and experiences in the book and told me it would be my best friend, but I think I want Zamiro to be my best friend first. So, upon hefting the book, I cynically wondered if *all* my writing in it would add to the weight. I kept that thought to myself but did not know what to write.

Zamiro was standing opposite me, but was now sitting on a stone boulder alongside the makeshift table I had assembled from an old, discarded door.

She is much closer now, tucked a loose curl behind her, revealing the large scar on the side of her face. I know that one of The Carrion managed to swipe at her cheek as we floated up and safely away. The day I saved her life.

I thought about the journal again. It will be interesting to record my thoughts and experiences and read through them later, but Zamiro is now lightly laughing at me as I leaf through the empty pages of the book. I smiled at her and knew I would also need to spell and learn about grammar.

Zamiro removed the back sack slung over her shoulder, dropped it onto the table, opened it and removed a small cardboard box, then handed it to me: 'Happy Birthday.'

It has been a long time since I celebrated a birthday, and missed the sentiment. I have spent so many years on my own after the tragedy of losing my family so many years ago. She continued: 'These are a box of these pencils.'

I looked at the pointed, dark, grey-coloured end of the pencil, held it towards my tongue and licked it. This is one of my memories from my childhood, and it still tastes powdery. I looked at her again and smiled. 'OK then, let's get started.'

After collecting my thoughts, I began to write my first entry, but even that was a struggle:

My Jurnal –dai 1.
Thrsday 18th Decembr
Helo. Ths is mee. I am Carlyle. I dunt no wot to rite.

I was pleased to show her what I had written, and she looked at it. 'We have some work to do here, don't we?' I didn't know if that was a compliment, in that I could do more than she expected, or that she did not understand what I had just written.

Zamiro looked at me. 'Don't worry about fixing anything now; you can return to it once you have learnt to spell and use grammar better. It will be like teaching the young ones at my ELC to write; you are just a little older,' then took the pencil from me. 'I will just underline the spelling and grammatical errors to show you.'

Starting with the heading, she underlined that, then paused, looked on at the remainder of the text, and underlined everything. 'At least you spelt your name correctly.'

Chapter 2 Zamiro

Early afternoon; Thursday 18th December: I am the daughter of Ground-Dwellers and have just celebrated my 23rd birthday with them. I live with my family in a five-bedroom house in our berg called Yelnu. The GOD owns our house, and we are the tenants. I teach young children and work at an Early Learning Centre (ELC) near my home.

I have arrived at my intended rendezvous, having ridden here on a Zoop, and am standing facing my new friend Carlyle. I presented him with a journal. I think he saved me from The Carrion, but I am unsure. I moved around the makeshift table and am now sitting beside him.

We are located within the remnants of a rubble building site and I think it was a home once too. I don't believe it is his home, or he lives around here, and I feel that he is suspicious of me for some reason. I have often seen Carlyle around my home in Yelnu, and have seen him around my ELC too, although he may think that I have not noticed him. He may also be enrolled at the ALC; however, I am unsure of this.

I feel safer when I am around him, but don't understand why. I also think that he may be a Flighter. If he is, he will be the first Flighter I have been this close to. Flighters are suspicious of Ground-Dwellers, and Ground-Dwellers and Flighters are not usually acquainted but think he saved me from The Carrion.

I found myself smiling into the warmth of the setting sun on my face, and closed my eyes to remember the first time I met my new friend Carlyle:

It was around six months ago, and I can still remember it clearly as the warm setting sun that was on my face that day, too. I had completed a late afternoon parent-teacher session at the ELC, and there was a golden setting sun. It was near dusk as I made my way across the assembly area from the school. I only had to cross a road and would be safely at my house. It was then I saw them.

Ground-Dwellers know to get indoors and keep out of sight at dusk in case there is an invasion from The Carrion, as this is the ideal time for them. They also say The Carrion can hide by blending into the golden setting sun when they attack, and they do. This was to be my firsthand experience of The Carrion, and The Frenzy.

I never wanted one, no-one ever wants one and I was now looking into the setting sun and the belly of The Carrion swarm. Looking at my house across the road, then back to the school I realised I had a choice to make as The Carrion was coming closer with every moment. It was then I noticed a small group of students opening the school doors and making their way across the forecourt towards me and realised they were oblivious to the incoming Carrion swarm.

They were waving at me, and I remember trying to warn them, to get them to turn around and go back into the school for safety, then I realised they were not waving at me, rather it was at their parents standing twenty metres before me.

Their parents had their backs to The Carrion, and by now they were all looking at each other, and not at the sky. So, as they met in the middle of the assembly area, I had another decision to make: How can I warn them?

It was all too late, as I heard the noise from The Carrion, and it was then the children and parents also turned to face the fracas. They looked up at The Carrion and it quickly began. The first strike and the first kill. The children shrieked and the adults screamed, but there was nowhere to go.

We have been told never to panic, never to be out in the open at dusk, and never to move amid an attack by The Carrion. We were told a lot of things, but none of them mattered now. The first Carrion had attached itself to the tallest man, then a second Carrion joined in, then a third and a fourth and a fifth.

It was a killing field. It was The Frenzy.

They picked at his head, clawed at his eyes, his nose, his face and picked at his chest. Severed flesh dropped from his torso and blood spurted from his open wounds, and then he fell to his knees. 'Papa' I heard a child call, 'Pap....' The Carrion started their attack on all of them and tore strips of flesh from each kill. It was all a bloodied mess; a bloodied massacre and death was everywhere. It was then The Carrion finally noticed me.

I think I fainted and perhaps this had saved me, but when I woke from my stupor, I remembered seeing a man that I did not know sitting beside me. I did not believe I was injured by The Carrion but do not know how I escaped them. I looked around, but did not know where I was, then realised I was on top of the school. I was on the roof and could see the remnants of The Frenzy below me.

There were no survivors. I remembered feeling nauseous and began to swoon once more. I felt a wetness on my face, wiped it away and my hand was covered in blood. Was it my blood?

I looked at my bloodied hand, then to the man, but he just smiled at me. I remembered asking him how I got away, how I got up here, but he shrugged his shoulders, then he handed me a ragged cloth and beckoned towards a bowl of water in front of me. That man was Carlyle.

I remember shaking from the adrenalin rush, having just survived being involved in a slaughter by The Carrion. I had just seen my friends and some of my students killed in front of me, but all of that was before I fainted. I remembered closing my eyes to avoid the vision from below, and to retain my composure, but when I opened my eyes again, he was gone. How did I survive?

Now, upon re-opening my eyes, I am back with Carlyle at the house on the hill. The sun has almost set, and I am relieved as The Carrion did not come tonight. I looked at Carlyle, and he smiled back at me. Does he know what I was thinking about? I suspect he is a Flighter, which is perhaps why he is suspicious of me, but I do know my new friend Carlyle saved my life.

Chapter 3 Carlyle

Late afternoon; Thursday 18th December: It is almost dark now, and decided that we must move back to town. We are safe from The Carrion tonight, however, there are still elements of the society I must be wary of, as a Flighter.

I closed my journal and leaned towards Zamiro to take the box of pencils, and she suddenly pulled away. I am puzzled by this as I wonder what she thought I was going to do.

'We have to move now Zamiro as it is getting darker. How did you get here?'

'I used a Zoop… How about you?'

'I walked.'

'OK. I think the Zoop should just be big enough for both of us if you want a ride back. I don't know where you live though…are you in my berg?'

'Err…not really, but I will ride back with you and make my way home from there if that's OK.' I was still a little nervous about telling her too much about me, and as we made our way back up the path realised it was much darker now, much too late to walk home from here. Zamiro pulled the fob for the Zoop from her pocket, pressed her thumb on it and the little machine lit up with a chirp.

I looked at the small, flat, rectangular saddle. It was going to be a close fit. Zamiro donned the helmet that slung from the handle, climbed onto the seat, and beckoned me to climb on.

We sat and wriggled to get more comfortable, and she shuffled forward just as I did. I looked down and around the Zoop, then raised my legs to feel for and to find if there were any pedals to rest my feet on during the ride, but at the same time, Zamiro had lifted her feet from the ground, having placed them on the front pedals to get a better position. We now had both of our feet off the ground simultaneously, and the little Zoop toppled over with us on board.

Fortunately, as it was not heavy, I easily rolled from beneath, however, Zamiro was on the ground trapped by the little toppled scooter. She started to laugh, as she rolled herself out from under the little unit.

'We'll have to work together to make it work.'

We tried again, and this time I kept my feet on the ground, so she turned the throttle we moved off slowly with a slight wobble. I had my arms held behind my back holding onto the rear of the saddle and this made the ride a little uncomfortable, but then Zamiro lent her head back to mine telling me it would be better if my arms were around her waist for the balance.

We wobbled a bit more, but once we gained momentum the ride was quite invigorating, albeit a little slow. I have not needed to use these machines for quite some time and am beginning to feel it's my first time in a long time for everything when I am with Zamiro.

We arrived at her house without further incident, and she stopped the Zoop outside her front door, but as we both climbed off, we both let go of the Zoop at the same time again and it toppled over. This time I laughed.

Zamira looked at me. 'Would you like to come in, or do you have somewhere else to be?'

'Yes, and No.' I replied.

'Which is which?'

'No, I wouldn't like to come in, and yes, I don't have anywhere else to be.'

Zamiro considered my reply, then continued: 'My folks live with me, so we won't be alone. I think my two brothers and my sister are home too.'

I considered my options and used the time to look around. I know this place well as I have watched it so many times before. I also knew both her brothers and sister were home as I had passed through here earlier this afternoon hoping to catch a glimpse of Zamiro. I looked down at my feet and then rolled my head around thinking of what I should do next. My neck creaked a little with the motion and from the Zoop ride. 'This is your ELC isn't it?' I stated whilst pointing my head to my left.

Zamiro nodded. 'Yes, and this is where The Carrion came that day too'.

She had briefly told me before of her experience with The Carrion Frenzy, so I decided to move across the road and entered the ELC gates whilst there was not any traffic to avoid. 'This is where it happened hey?'

She followed behind me as I made my way to the assembly area, so I stopped and crouched down gently rubbing my hands across the tarmac on the specific spot I had rescued her from. I knew that any trace of The Frenzy was well and truly gone by now, but still remembered it well. I looked up to see that Zamiro was standing over me with her arms crossed tensely over her chest. She had started to lightly tremble.

'Just how did you survive then?'

Zamiro took a deep breath. 'I had fainted, which meant I was not moving. They are not interested in you if they think you are dead.'

'I understand that, but you mentioned that you then found yourself on the roof of the ELC, up there.' I raised myself and brushed my hands on my jeans, then nodded towards the roof of the school.

'Funny about that, Carlyle.' I felt that Zamiro was sterner with me now. 'I think you know how I got up there. Just what is your game, Carlyle? I have seen you around, I have seen you watching me, I think that you...' but she finished in mid-sentence, as her two brothers had made their way across from their house to join us in the paved assembly area.

'Yo Zee ...you all good?' came the comment from the older one.

I think his name is Kilby, and believe he is of twenty-five summers.

'Yup, she's been out all this arvo and missed us that's all,' came the comment from the other brother. I think his name is Marty and he is of twenty-four summers.

They both put their hands out to shake mine, then enquired who I was and why their sister was out so late with me. 'Kilby,' said the first one offering his hand.

'Marty,' said the second one, nodding once at me.

'Carlyle,' I said taking and shaking their hands separately, but before Marty let go of mine, he rolled my hand over in his.

'Looks like you work out mate. What exactly do you do?'

'Bit of this, a bit of that,' I replied quietly.

'What do you want with our sister then?' Kilby probed.

'Enough boys,' Zamiro interjected. 'I was just telling him that this is where the Carrion attacked me. The Frenzy, and somehow, I ended up alive. Somehow, I ended up on the roof up there.' She nodded toward the roof of the ELC.

They followed her gaze, then looked back at me. I shrugged my shoulders and decided it was time to make my departure as I knew she would be safe tonight.

'So you're not coming in now then are you?' she enquired once again.

'No, I guess three's a crowd.' I said on my impending departure. 'I would like to see you again though Zamiro if that's ok?' I said as I looked over to her.

'Don't bet on it, big fella;' this came from Kilby.

I thought I had heard something else from Zamiro as I was walking away but hadn't entirely caught her comment, then realised what it was: 'Don't be a dumb amminate, Kilby. I like him, and I am just teaching him to read and write. That's all.' I smiled at the comment, and upon returning to the front of their house noticed the Zoop was still there. Should I try? Why not?

Meantime, Zamiro had caught up with me and noticed I was looking down at the Zoop. I assumed she knew what I was thinking of doing tossed me the fob, and then handed me her back-sack containing my journal and the box of pencils.

'Go your hardest big fella,' she said with a grin then added. 'Have you used one before? You need to re-set it to your control.'

I looked down at the fob now in my hand.

'See the small button there, press that, as it re-sets it.'

Zamiro handed me the helmet. I tried it on, and it smelt light of her scent, but as it didn't fit my head properly I attached it to the handle instead. I then sat on the saddle, then turned the throttle on and took off wobbling down the street. They are relatively easy to control and ride, but it has still been a long time since I've ridden one. At the first corner, I almost took out a rubbish bin. Zamiro was laughing out loud behind me and then heard Kilby and Marty laughing too.

I eventually made it home, albeit much faster than had I walked. My berg is called Evoh, and I am currently living in a twelve-story apartment near a beach in the city of Edi-Aleda. It is located on the banks of a large sea, and it is considered a luxury to live in this area. I am a registered paying tenant here although as a Flighter, I do not have to pay rent to The GOD but chose to do so as it helps maintain my anonymity. I also chose to live here as my apartment faces west, faces into the golden setting sun, and can watch for The Carrion. I might be able to warn people and might be able to save people, including my new friends the Ground Dwellers.

I live on the 11th floor, but the lifts currently don't work as sometimes during the change of The GOD Panel, maintenance of buildings gets delayed. I will not use The Rush to get up to my apartment although it is already dark, I used the stairs.

I scanned my wrist to open my apartment door and threw the fob and helmet from the Zoop onto the kitchen bench. My apartment has an open living, lounge dining and kitchen and by habit, I always check the two bedrooms and the three bathrooms; this is a habit I cannot seem to break. Flighters are always suspicious. I made my way over to the balcony, worked the lock and slid open the two balcony doors. The lock is a little sticky due to the salt from the nearby sea, but I don't mind that either, and I looked out into the darkness. Both the sea and sky were black tonight.

I decided to go back in and grab a drink from my cooler. My choice tonight is beer, but it just tastes like bitter water. It tasted good anyway. I raised the bottle in a silent toast to my first real date with Zamiro and then remembered that I hadn't eaten since this morning.

I am not hungry when I am to meet with or see Zamiro, and am yet to fully understand why this occurs. It has been a long time since I have had such feelings for someone, so with her in mind I picked up the helmet from the kitchen counter, placed my face in and slowly breathed in. I feel confused by this woman, and should I be? I am a Flighter, and she is a Ground-Dweller.

The cooler/oven has a Voice Operated Command function so instructed it to cook a meal that I had left in there previously. 'Shelf 2. 90 seconds on high.' Zamiro had said I needed to understand the increments of time, but I hadn't realised what we could demand from it. I finished up my meal, cleaned up and made my way to my boudoir where I sloughed my clothes and showered.

The luxury of warm water cascaded down whilst I reviewed my day in my mind, and I thought of Zamiro again, thinking of her scar, and found myself subconsciously drawing its crescent shape in the misted glassed wall of the shower. I am now thinking of her shape as a young woman.

'Stop it', I yelled aloud to no one. 'Just stop it.'

I quickly turned the tap over to the cold, shut the water off and as I was drying myself, realised I could be writing something more in my journal. I wrapped a towel around my waist headed back into the kitchen, stood at the counter, opened the journal, and took a pencil from the box.

I remembered that Zamiro said it is a private journal, so maybe I should not make it too personal in case someone does manage to find it and wants to read it. I think again about that and realise why it shouldn't matter, as it is only something I had chosen at a time and place to write down. It is not my every thought, it is not a recorder, and it is just a record, so I added to my previous note:

My Jurnal –dai 1. Thursdy 18$^{\underline{th}}$ December

Helo. This is mee. I amm Carlyle.

I dunt know wot to rite.

Marty brutha – 22 summers? Kilby brutha – 24 sumers.

Do they work? Sistr?

Muthar and Father stil alve – yes. What do they think I am? Can I convinc them I am not?

I must lern to driv the Zoops bettr.

I like it when Zamiro larfs. I like it when she smiles. I just lik it.

I stopped there and seeing that it was dark now, finally decided to head off to bed, so dropped my towel and lay down on the futon. I was thinking of Zamiro as I tried to get to sleep.

Chapter 4 Zamiro

Early evening; Friday 19th December: I am watching Carlyle take off wobbling down the street on the Zoop, realising he has no idea how to control it. I think he is going too fast as he is about to turn a corner.

'Just how do you know that guy?' Kilby asked of me with a softer tone now.

'He is just someone I met and am helping him to read and write. It's just something that I liked to do for him.'

'Is he a Flighter? I haven't seen him around here. Do you know much about him? Do you know where he lives? Where does he work? Who he hangs with?' This time it came from Marty.

Just as I was thinking how to respond, we all saw Carlyle almost take out a rubbish bin at the corner as he disappeared out of sight, and we all laughed loudly. It felt good to laugh after reminiscing about my own Carrion experience.

Carlyle has piqued my interest in Flighters, but I do not dare divulge my suspicion that he is a Flighter to Marty, Kilby, or any others in my family. He has gone now, so we all turned and walked up the stoop into the house, we are fortunate in that our house is one of the larger ones in the Yelnu

Berg, as it has five bedrooms and four bathrooms. Mata had prepared our meal, so we gathered around the dining table. There were nine of us dining tonight, including Mata's parents who had come from their Berg.

My younger sister, Tristesse had brought along her new boyfriend. He stood up to introduce himself to us and took my hand. 'Columbus,' he said, whilst shaking my hand vigorously. He then looked over to my Mata and Fata and said rather abruptly: 'Good evening, Bryan and Elizabeth.'

I wondered what that was all about.

'Columbus, as in the old explorer, in 1492 he sailed the ocean blue,' my Fata said grumbling under his breath, whilst taking a fork full of the prepared meal in front of him and shovelling it into his mouth.

'Although, there will be no exploring of our sister tonight.' Kilby stated, then burst out laughing. We all laughed, but Columbus was not amused.

The conversation eventually got around to The Carrion and The AIC. Columbus was saying what he would do if he had to fight them and went on to say that he thinks they are not really that dangerous. Then started claiming that he knew all about The Carrion, and began to lecture us:

'The Carrion's appearance is based on the long-extinct American/African Vulture. The AIC have deemed them the easiest to imitate and manufacture. They are built with extendable and flexible necks; small sleek bodies and they have three sharp talons on each claw. Each has razor-sharp triangles as beaks and are golden in colour and are known to shimmer in the golden sun when in flight.'

By this time, we were not interested in his opinion, but he

continued: 'A collective swarm of Carrion may comprise fifty or more. They swarm into a site and seek to kill anything that appears to fear them. This is known as The Frenzy.'

I wondered if he was ever going to take a breath.

Then he stopped, looked at Fata and said: 'But you know it is mostly crowd hysteria.' And with that comment, I knew he was not aware I had been involved in The Frenzy.

Fata gently placed his knife and fork on the table on each side of his plate. It took a lot to stop Fata from eating. 'Don't talk crap boy as you know nothing!'

This stopped all the conversations around the table. Columbus looked over to him, and I saw that Tristesse had moved her hand over to his arm to stop him from saying any more about The Carrion.

I lightly ran my finger along the scar down the side of my cheek and tucked my hair behind my ear. 'I have been in a Frenzy' I said stoically. 'And I survived. I don't know of any others that have. This is what they did to me. I was lucky.' I turned my head to show him my scar and my thoughts turned back to Carlyle. He is a hero, and Flighters can all be heroes, so why don't we celebrate them? I kept this thought to myself though, excused myself from the table, went to my room, and was soon asleep.

My last thoughts were of Carlyle.

Chapter 5 Marty

Late evening; Friday 19th December: After Zamiro had gone to bed, Columbus started up again with a different topic, as he revealed he wanted to nominate for a role as A Represent. I could see that this was much to Tristesse's surprise as she had mentioned to me privately she thought he was 'the one' and wanted to start a family with him.

I saw Tristesse take a deep breath. 'But, Columbus, a Represent is dangerous work. You can get killed by either a Ground-Dweller, wanting to keep them from being found out, or a Flighter who does not want to be rescued. I don't want you exposed to this risk. Our children would not want to be raised without a father.'

He looked at her dismissively and stood up: 'I want to track down any Flighters being held as prisoners by Ground-Dwellers and rescue them. The Ground-Dwellers are breaking the law and must be punished. A Flighter living with a Ground-Dweller is just stupid.'

Of course, this didn't go down well with any of us. We knew our grandparents were involved in this practice. We knew they had been harbouring Flighters at their home until the search had been completed. It is known as The Forced.

With Kilby's assistance, I tried to convince Columbus that it was not a good career move and even had to mention that the 'new prospective brother-in-law' needed to look after our sister and refrain from such a career move. However, Columbus remained defiant within his agenda. He eventually sat down, but the evening went uncomfortably quiet from then on.

Finally, he got up to leave, and Tristesse, Marty and I went outside with him. Columbus made an overt move to Tristesse to kiss her good night, but she turned her head, so he only managed to give a light peck on her cheek. He then left on a Zoop, however, when he rode to the corner, he collided with the same rubbish bin that Carlyle had only just managed to avoid hours before.

Marty yelled out 'You dumb-animate. You can't even ride a Zoop.' Tristesse didn't comment.

We returned inside and sat down at the table. I asked the others if they knew as much as Columbus did about The Carrion. My grandfather, Dave, spoke first: 'The Carrion appear to cooperate. Their golden colour comes from the access to minerals the AIC has commandeered over time. The shimmering finish of the body of The Carrion is the actual element of gold, but being gold, it could melt off easily. That's why they only attack at dusk when the sun is cooler.'

We looked at him to continue: 'They invade with the golden glowing sun behind them, and it is believed to assist them to become invisible, but the practice simply makes them predictable. Please, never go outside at dusk.' That certainly changed the mood of the room, and then grand-mother Courtney spoke: 'And I didn't know if I should have said something when Columbus was talking about Represents. I know what we are doing is illegal, and are risking you all in our foolishness' She looked over at Dave for confirmation.

'Nope,' Tristesse said, and then elaborated: 'You have taught us that all people great and small make this world better for us all.'

We all nodded in agreement.

Dave sighed, then added. 'Although we must all be careful.'

Mata pitched in. 'We all believe that you are doing the right thing by helping Flighters and Ground-Dwellers live together. If we could all understand that we all need to work together to defeat The Carrion, Edi-Aleda could be a better and safer place.'

'I don't think I will see Columbus again' claimed Tristesse, then excused herself from the table and off went to bed. Grandfather and Mother excused themselves too.

Fata leaned into the table and raised the issue of Zamiro's new friend to us. 'Boys, do you know anything about this guy Carlyle? Do you think he is a Represent?'

'No, Zee is just naive, and Carlyle is a bit guarded for some reason. Although we think we have seen him around our Berg but don't know much more.' I claimed and Marty nodded in agreement.

It was after that, we all retired.

Chapter 6 Carlyle

Early morning; Friday 19th December: I was abruptly woken by a loud and insistent thumping on my apartment front door, and although I felt I had only been asleep for a couple of minutes, noticed that it was now lighter outside, so must be around daybreak. I put on my shorts and made my way to the door, and the thumping started up again.

'Hey, are you Carlyle? I am with The Represents, so open up.'

Someone was calling from the other side of the door and the thumping continued. I opened it and a large man was standing there. He was alone and I recognised the uniform of A Represent. 'Are you Carlyle?' the agent enquired gruffly then added: 'Do you live here alone …. Are you the tenant?'

'I am and yes.' I responded quickly so as not to annoy him and thought as it was still early, he must want something of me urgently.

He responded quickly. 'Are you a Flighter, or a Ground-Dweller?'

I quickly surmised the situation. I cannot tell him I am a Flighter as he would kill me if he knew. It is alleged that some of The Represents are killing people indiscriminately by pushing them out of multi-storey buildings to their deaths. I offered him my right wrist. He will be able to scan my chip as The Represents carry mobile scanners, and will read that I am paying rent. This will be sufficient for him to assume that I am a Ground-Dweller and not a Flighter. He scanned my wrist and it read out that I am a paying tenant of Apartment 1103. 'Hmm,' he muttered. 'I am looking for G-D's that are harbouring Flighters. Do you know anything about that?' he enquired gruffly.

'Nope, I haven't been here long.' I replied, knowing he could confirm this from the wrist scan, and hopefully, his interpretation of long and mine are aligned. I have been here for almost three summers.

'OK,' and with that turned and made his way down the hall, he then stopped, turned and called back to me. 'Hey, is there anyone else living on this floor?'

'I have no idea.' I knew there were at least six other apartments on my floor, however, there are not any other tenants at the moment as the lifts have been out of action for some time and this meant having to carry everything up eleven flights of stairs. You would need to be strong and fit to do this regularly, however, as a Flighter, you could risk using The Rush to get up this high with your baggage. I realised he would be gone soon, and he would have to take the eleven flights of stairs to get down. I smiled as I closed my door.

As was already sunrise, I decided not to visit Zamiro today as she may think I have nothing better to do. The truth is I do not.

Chapter 7 Marty

Early morning; Saturday 20th December: The next day dawned and Kilby and I ate breakfast at the table under the stern gaze of Mata but not much more was said. Every time Mata brought something up we both grunted with 'Mmm can't talk – eating.'

I then went outside and located a duo shuttle to take the ride to the AIC where we both work as technicians on the chip assembly line. We left our own Berg to head for the AIC facility, and I asked Kilby what his level of information access was at the AIC.

'Why?' he replied suspiciously.

'Well, if you have access to the registrations database, you can check out Carlyle?' He ignored me, and we sat there silently. Whilst the duo shuttle is often on full throttle, its maximum speed is around thirty kilometres an hour, and it has taken us about an hour this morning to travel the thirty-five or so kilometres.

We finally arrived at our designated shuttle parking space after we passed three checkpoints, all within the AIC facility itself: At each checkpoint, we had to hold our personnel passes against a black panel, and then each of us was required to exit the vehicle and wait until the other one's verification was completed. Then we climb back in and go through the same process after driving to the next checkpoint.

Each checkpoint also requires facial recognition, so sometimes we hold our heads down to try and get a reaction as it might not be able to screen our faces, but we always seem to get through. The AIC must know that we are travelling together as we are registered to work together, so it assumes that we are together when trying to get through all the checkpoints. We have both quietly considered the whole process may be vulnerable to manipulation if we were ever prompted to attempt it.

Each checkpoint is about five hundred metres from the last one, and the land between each one is sparse. It is believed to contain unstable abandoned land mines from many years ago, so we are compelled to keep to the roads. The checkpoints are unattended, and although they all have cameras, we notice sometimes that the cameras are not tracking our movement as they remain static. We believe this is also an indication of a vulnerable system if we ever need to utilise it.

I had talked to Kilby about this before so thought I would raise it again. 'They don't want anyone else in here, do they?' I remarked whilst shutting the doors of the duo shuttle as we finally made our way towards the entrance doors, 'And what about the cameras?'

He looked at me. 'Sshh not here' he retorted quickly, twirling his index finger 'Everything spoken is heard.'

We entered the facility and then sat at the production line where the computer chips were made. These are inserted into the left and right wrists of every person once they reach the age of fifteen summers. These wrist chips provide us with the mechanisms to buy and sell, to live in Edi-Aleda, everyone has them. The chips are also a tracking system for the AIC - the AIC can keep track of everything and everyone and, in reality, whilst it is still only a machine, we believe it is paranoid.

The work we do is mundane and is not that taxing. It is simply our job to watch for any chip that when created is out of alignment on the sheets of computer chip panels. We are seated opposite each other, are not allowed to speak other than single words, and are not allowed to have unscheduled breaks, but we have a break every fifteen minutes, and a new crew is substituted then in.

We often go through our shifts without having said anything to each other or having done anything, apart from watching the panels of computer chips rolling past us. Our total shift only lasts for fifteen minutes in the hour, so for forty-five minutes we are required to sit in an empty room devoid of any other contact or any other thing, apart from our current AIC partner. Generally, it is boring, but most of the time it is just annoying.

There are only four teams of two that each work on the line and of these eight we are aware that are there only two other personnel within the AIC making a total of only ten within an operation the size of a large shopping centre. The rest of the operations are in the immense facility controlled by The AIC. The teams only have access to one room to rest between the shifts.

There is never a variation. You do not mess with The AIC.

Chapter 8 Kilby

Late afternoon; Saturday 20th December: Our working day had ended after only four hours and four shifts so Marty, and I left without further comments to each other. We made our way back out through the three AIC checkpoints all over again but once outside the AIC campus he decided to raise the issue again with me.

'So, any ideas?'

'Not in here,' I responded quickly, 'the cars have gears'

Marty nodded over to me whilst concentrating on driving.

'Gears? ..don't you mean?'

'Sshh later' I again quickly responded circling my finger in the air.

When we arrived back home Tristesse was sitting alone on the stoop waiting for us, and although it had been raining I could not tell if she had been crying: 'He's gone, Columbus...he told me we were too different. I think I called him a jerk and he said he didn't know what that means...what a jerk!' she said sadly whilst I helped her rise. We entered the house.

'Did anything happen today?' Mata enquired as we all sat around the table.

We each shrugged our shoulders, and then Tristesse muttered softly, 'Columbus has left me.' She put her head into her hands and sighed loudly; 'I never going to...'

'C'mon, sis, if Zee can get a bloke interested in her, there is hope for you.' Marty claimed cheekily, and with that, Zamiro came into the dining room and sat down.

'What did I miss?' she asked anyone who would respond.

Tristesse burst out sobbing, stood up and left the room quickly.

'What did I say?' she asked of us, but we didn't respond.

Chapter 9 Carlyle

Early morning; Saturday 20th December: I made up my mind not to see Zamiro due to the early morning interruption by the Represent, but he made me consider if I should take a break from my daily routine. I decided to take some time away from my apartment.

I had learnt there is a major river about fifty kilometres away from Edi-Aleda and don't think the single shuttle Zoop could make it that far, so I might try one of the larger shuttles and can remember seeing a shuttle terminal in one of the streets in one of the Bergs, now if I can only remember which one.

I chirped the Zoop, climbed on to make my way towards the city and as it is about a fifteen-minute ride in have to stop at a set of traffic lights and happen to notice there is a shuttle bus stopped just up ahead of me. It is going in the same direction as I am and the sign flashes across the back of the vehicle: "Day trips to the Munna Cliffs"

I wondered what a day trip to Munna Cliffs might mean for me, then realised why I didn't just get on that shuttle anyway, it must be going somewhere out of the city, and this is just what I needed. As the lights changed from red to green, I twisted the throttle on the Zoop to take off but soon realised it would not be going fast enough. I needed to get in front of the shuttle to get on board. I will have to use The Rush.

I can utilise the concentration of Helium within my body to initiate a process to float up and away from any perceived danger, but it can also be used to float away from any scenario that I choose. I vividly remember the first time that I discovered this as it was the day that my parents were killed by the AIC.

I had heard the introduction of the concentration of Helium at the embryotic stage meant a body contained the metabolism to generate and accumulate Helium in a single event to gently float - it is a simple and seamless process and involves holding the arms firmly lengthened down against the sides of the body, fists clenched and my head raised. I close my eyes and focus, and this builds up the adrenalin and activates the helium corpuscles to course throughout my veins. It is something that I am still in awe of every time I decide to use it.

The build-up is initially slow and peaks after about three seconds. I can float for only around a couple of minutes, however, this is generally enough to float up and away where I can move then to a higher place, where I can momentarily rest and re-commence the process.

I can continue indefinitely and am limited only by the height of the buildings and other tall structures. Gravity is my enemy, as when I want to come down from a height am still susceptible to the effects during a descent, so a Flighter must develop timing and the technique to utilise their ability to control a drop-float.

I am aware the effect of gravity is roughly ten metres per second squared, therefore, a jump from a height of less than sixteen metres could mean injury or death should it not be timed correctly.

During a drop float, and just before the approach to the ground, I must initiate The Rush to generate enough resistance to slow me down and gently land. It is all about control and I continue to practice the timing. An obvious outcome of this is, should I be injured, or need medical assistance after an attempted drop-float, I would have revealed that I am a Flighter, and this is the reason that I reside on the 11th floor of my apartment. It's not a good idea to reveal your ability as a Flighter.

I considered this for a moment realising I don't have any other option. I alighted from the Zoop, pressed the top of the fob to cancel the ride, and looked to make my way to the nearest building of at least two stories. Fortunately, it was only across the road so I ran across the double-lane road, and scampered up the external flight of stairs to the roof. I looked around but could not see anyone looking up this way, so I held my arms to my side and waited for The Rush.

I began to float up and fortunately the trees along the side of the road provided cover for me. I can now do multi-directional floats as I move from one building to the next. This is something I have only recently discovered, and it still needs mastering. I have been able to move to the taller buildings along the road as I go and am gathering speed after each float. I stopped momentarily on the top of the fourth building, which is six stories high and considered my next leap. I looked up the street for another higher building, then down the side of the building and noticed a small child looking back up at me from down below. He was out on the balcony by himself, and this is not good. Has he seen me?

'Daddy, daddy' he cried out. 'Come and see, there is a birdman on the roof.'

He may have just been seen floating but hope he didn't see me land. I moved back from the edge and moved slowly to the edge to look over, but he was still there.

'Daddy, Daddy he is back again.'

I considered my options and looked back down the street to see the shuttle leaving a stop down the street below me.

'Alright, alright I am coming.'

I assumed his father had yielded to his son's cries and the man looked up. I knew he could not see me although I was still holding my breath for some reason.

'Come back inside, there is nothing up there,' he claimed to his son.

I breathed out and decided to make my move, so re-initiated The Rush and floated up and onto the next building. It was just across the laneway between this one and the next closest one. The boy yelled out: 'I know you are there, bird-man, even if Daddy doesn't.'

That was close.

I am now finally well in front of the shuttle, so made the final leap to a higher building and am on the tenth floor of a building. I landed on an outside balcony and made my way inside the room, Fortunately, as the balcony doors were not locked, I casually exited the room and took the elevator to the ground. The shuttle had not yet passed and was still at least three stops down the road. I made my way to the nearest shuttle stop, took another deep breath waited for it. It arrived and I entered.

They are driverless, so I swiped my right wrist on the console and sat down in the closest seat. The shuttle stopped two more times and announced it had arrived at the terminus. People around me began to descend and then I heard another announcement from within the shuttle: "*You have arrived at your final destination. Please get off.*"

Well, that was worth the risk, I chuckled to myself. I found my way to the enquiry desk within the terminus and saw it was operated by a hologram. Not knowing how to activate it I looked around and noticed a man standing next to a mop and bucket and I assumed he was a cleaner of the terminus. I made my way over to him, and nodded with a polite hello, then asked him about the day trips to the Munna Cliffs. He directed me to Bay 13.

I saw from a digital clock above the bay that there was a shuttle leaving in about forty-five minutes and there was another sign too. It showed they run every hour, on the hour. I realised had I stayed on the Zoop and simply followed behind the shuttle, I would have been there in plenty of time. I missed having breakfast this morning in my haste to find something to do, so interrupted his cleaning again and asked him if there was a place to buy food in the area. He mentioned the markets across the road, I thanked him and he said: '

You're not from around here, are you?

'No, I live in Evoh, in the berg down by the sea.' I also let him know I had not entered the central area of Edi-Aleda previously. It's called the Central Berg.

'Hey me too. I live in Evoh too.' he then claimed excitedly; 'Which building are you in?'

I started to say where then realised I should not be telling people I do not know where I live. I am a Flighter it could be dangerous for me. 'Maybe I will see you down there.' I offered instead.

'Yes, that would be good, I like people.' he said back to me.

I don't know what that is supposed to mean. He offered me his hand.

'I am Creedence,' introducing himself.

'Carlyle'.

I exited the terminus looked across the road saw the markets that Creedence had mentioned, then wandered around the area and brought food and a drink. I placed it in the back-sack I was carrying. It is Zamiro's, so this means that I will have to see her again. I must return the back-sack to her at least. I must do that.

I eventually stopped in front of a shop that had a large clock on the outside and assumed they could sell me a time-piece. Zamiro mentioned I should have one. I entered the store, and the merchant behind the counter remained sitting. He looked up at me. 'We'll be too expensive for you sir'.

I don't know how expensive is, and it has been a while since I had to be concerned about the cost of anything. I told him I could afford it, so he rose slowly from his seated position and asked me if I liked anything that I saw. I wished Zamiro was here to guide me. I stammered, thinking even if I bought a watch, I wouldn't be able to read the instructions very well.

'Do you have any that talks the time?' I enquired, thinking

this had to be the least ignorant question I could come up with.

'Of course,' he said lifting the glass-topped cabinet in front of him and as it opened toward me. He removed one of the timepieces then dropped the glass top and placed it between us on a soft mat of dark blue cloth: 'This is the latest in interactive watches offered by the AIC and is linked to their new satellites too,' as he splayed his hands out. 'It can link to and control your home hub, it has V.O.C., GPS, is 100% waterproof, has a built-in torch, never needs to be charged, will also actually tell you the time and yes, it does speak to you.'

He took a breath and then continued: 'It has a translator, electronic leveller, it measures height, weight, depth and distance, records and plays back and you can use it instead of the fob when using a Zoop.'

I didn't think he was going to stop.

'Oh', he continued: 'It has an interactive encyclopedia as well as a genealogy function.' He then handed me a small book. 'Here, these are the instructions and you must keep this book in a safe place. It is your title to the ownership and has the registered details if you lose the watch. The book is coded to show the location if you lose the watch.'

OK, I understand, the book is important - this little book of instructions. I was going to ask why it needed an instructions book if it was a voice command, but thought better of it.

I flicked through it and noticed that the text was really small. I also saw there was a little black square on the final page. I will never be able to read it, and will most likely never read it. I put it in my pocket and thought perhaps Zamiro could read it to me instead.

I understood nothing of what he had said to me apart from it being a timepiece, and it could speak to me and tell me the time. 'OK, I will take the watch and the book. Can you set it up for me just the time and date please?' I still don't know what he means by a watch though as I want a timepiece, then I assumed he must have realised his guilt given that he didn't tell me how much it was.

'I can find a cheaper one for you.'

I shrugged my shoulders and told him to finalise the sale. I swiped my right wrist over his console and completed the purchase. He pressed a few buttons and placed the watch on my left arm. It felt heavy. He pushed another button and it announced: 'The time is 11.30 am, Saturday the 20th of December 2045'.

He told me I needed to synchronise my voice to the watch, but I kept thinking what do I have to watch? It is a timepiece. What am I missing here?

'For the V.O.C function.' I must have looked confused as he clarified: 'For the Voice Operator Command. Please read this sentence out loud as it will recognise your voice so you can command it.' He referred to a phrase on a card. I asked him to read it to me instead: 'The quick brown fox jumps over the lazy dog.' It was an easy statement to remember.

He pushed another button on the timepiece, nodded to me to make the statement which I repeated three times and then he asked me to say a command to the timepiece. I asked it to tell me the time and it responded: 'The time is 1135 am, Saturday the 20th of December 2045'

'You are good to go, sir, thank you for your patronage.'

I thought... and thank you for making the sale easy for

me, although I was still embarrassed by my naivety. I was about to leave when he made another odd statement: 'Oh if you find that you find it is lost, let me know as I can track it down for you with the help of the new AIC satellites.'

I hesitated at the door to listen, and he managed to further clarify the statement: 'I have to register the purchase with The AIC, but that is not a big concern. It is because if someone steals it or you lose it, I can locate and track it down.'

I called back and waved. 'Good to know, and thank you, again.'

I exited the shop and then realised I was running late to catch the Shuttle to Munna Cliffs. This was my distraction for today, not purchasing a timepiece.

'Find it is lost', I considered that was an odd statement.

I started to run and made my way back into the shuttle terminus and was relieved it hadn't yet left. It was due to depart at noon. I asked my timepiece to tell me the time: 'The time is 1145am, Saturday the 20th of December 2045'.

I realised that I knew the day and date so ask it again. 'Please tell me the time only and not the date.' It announced "11:46 am." That is impressive I thought, and as I passed Creedence he saw my timepiece. He whistled and commented; 'Whoa Carlo nice watch. That's worth at least thirty thousand.'

I shrugged my shoulders, simply said 'thanks;' and wondered what thirty thousand meant. I do get it now after thinking about the last comment that Creedence just made, as a watch is a timepiece, and a timepiece is a watch, but I still wondered why it is called a watch. I look at it, I don't watch it and then realise there is so much I need to re-learn.

Meantime the shuttle had now pulled into Bay 13, and I

saw about ten people wanting to board with me, so my mind turned to Zamiro, and I wondered what she was doing today. She will be most likely teaching at her ELC, and I know I will miss not seeing her today, and it is starting to concern me. I made my way down the aisle of the shuttle and the seating configuration was 2 x 2 with the aisle in the middle. I took a seat about halfway down and as I prefer that no one sat beside me I removed my back-sack and placed it on the seat to my left. I watched as most of the others found their seats randomly around me.

I looked over and saw a man with a young boy sitting near me and an elderly couple of Ground-Dwellers behind me. I realised then I like people too - thank you, Creedence for reminding me of this. As the shuttle was driverless, I looked at my watch and it showed exactly twelve when the door of the shuttle shut.

We started to move backwards but no one but me appeared to be concerned about it moving by itself. The shuttle slowly made a complete half-circle turn, then straightened up and drove forward toward the street. I was fascinated by this and looked around at the other passengers, however, no one else was seeing this with the same fascination that I had. It then patiently waited for a break in the traffic and joined in when there was a sufficient gap. This is crazy I thought, how does it know what to do and where to go?

I decided that I would sit closer to the front of the shuttle so collected my back-sack and journal and standing up made my way forward, but the shuttle suddenly slowed with a jolt. The man with the young boy called out to me. 'Stay still mate, you are not allowed to change seats until we get to the

Eagle.' I sat back down, the shuttle started moving off again and wondered what the Eagle was.

We had been motoring along for about thirty minutes when I saw on the watch it had an elapsed timer function and wondered when you would use that. I must have Zamiro read the instructions to me. I would like that. I then noticed that some of the other passengers had started to collect their belongings just as the shuttle made an announcement: *We will arrive at the Eagle in two minutes.*

We arrived in exactly two minutes, and as the shuttle pulled to an abrupt stop I rose and called over to the man that had spoken to me before.

'Is this near the Munna Cliffs?'

'No, this is the Eagle. We will be stopped here in about fifteen minutes. If you do get off here and want to get back on you better not be late, as the shuttle don't wait.' He started to laugh; 'Hey I am a poet, and I just don't know it'.

I didn't understand what that meant, so I asked him: 'How long until we get to the Munna Cliffs?'

'About another hour but we are going there too, aren't we?' he said rubbing the top of the head of the child sitting next to him; 'We are going fishing. I am taking the boy, it's his first time. I will let you know when we get closer. Oh, and if you want to move to the front better do it now whilst we are stopped.' He then added. 'First time on a shuttle?'

'Yes,' I replied.

I considered it was my first time for a lot of things, and I am making a habit of this. I decided to move to the front of the shuttle, and not having a driver was still a bit concerning, so I tried to relax. The shuttle started exactly fifteen minutes later, so we re-joined the highway. It was very quiet as you only heard the road noise, the rubber of the tyres on the cement plates of the road.

I found the sound rhythmical, and upon relaxing more felt myself falling asleep.

Chapter 10 Howard

Noon; Saturday 20th December: I am taking my boy to Munna Falls today and will have some one-on-one time with him. He is nearly ten summers old and is growing so quickly, my Bernie and I am so proud of him. I had convinced him that we would enjoy fishing for eel and salmon at Munna today, and as I grew up there. I can remember I was around the same age when I first went fishing with my father.

My Father was killed only recently, and I miss him, we both miss him and I am still so raw about his death. There was a terrible accident. We were told he had fallen from the top of the office building where he worked, but I still do not believe it. The Emergency Responders came and eventually convinced me not to worry about pursuing it any further.

I still believe he was pushed as he would have never gone to the roof area by himself, he did not like heights as none of our family do. I think there was more to it, but I was told by them not to pursue it. He had told me that he had recently befriended a couple of Ground-Dwellers and I can recall him mentioning their names, Dave and Courtney. He said they were around his age. I also recalled they mentioned The FOO, but am unsure what that referred to.

We had now taken our seats on the shuttle, and the door closed. We were now moving. I looked over to my boy - he makes me laugh, he is so inquisitive, he wants to learn so much. I looked around and saw that there were not many people going to Munna. I noticed a couple that I had met before, and a man sitting by himself, but I did not know him. He was looking around and perhaps he was impressed that the shuttle was driverless. I will make a point of talking to him when I get the opportunity and will try to make him more comfortable, although he may only be going to Eagle Berg.

Bernie looked over to me and asked me to tell him something nice, but I couldn't think of anything specifically as I was still thinking about the loss of my father, so I started to tell him what I knew about The FOO. I began to tell him about Ground-Dwellers and Flighters. I think he is old enough to know about 'The Talk' that every parent dreads having with their children.

'Bernie, I am going to tell you about life choices and having children. When Ground-Dwellers, male and females, well, really like each other,' I realised that 'The Talk' is more awkward than I thought:

'Well, Ground-Dwellers and Flighters can get together and as we are the same, except a Flighter can float off the ground and all around. Do you know about Flighters?'

'Dad,' he said indignantly, 'I am nearly ten summers, you know.'

I took a breath thinking it was going to get serious, and I wondered if he was ready for all of this when suddenly I felt the shuttle slow down. The man sitting alone had just stood up as it looked like he wanted to move further down the aisle. I told him to stay still as you are not allowed to change seats until we got to the Eagle, and he sat back down.

I started again to Bernie, 'OK…well…Ground-Dwellers choose to have children with Flighters, as there is a possibility of saving themselves and their families. The Ground-Dwellers sometimes live with a Flighter just for the procurement of a sexual relationship, in case the process is successful over time. This is called The Forced. This entrapment of Flighters is generally frowned upon, however, some small groups of opportunistic Ground-Dwellers believe it is for the betterment of society. If Flighters manage to breed with Ground-Dwellers, it may create more Flighters, and this could mean a safer world. Did you know a Flighter can kill The Carrion?' I hoped he never see The Carrion, and we have been lucky so far, but this is still hard for me to talk about:

'Some Flighters decide to accept being sex slaves as a way of life as they will be well looked after by the Ground-Dwellers, but they will have to endure having sex. Being a healthily kept Flighter could mean healthy offspring for the Ground-Dweller. The Flighter can of course use always use their ability to escape if they want to but often choose to stay as it gives their life purpose.' I took another deep breath to gather my thoughts. Bernie looked over at me. 'My life will have a purpose. I will make sure it does.' I smiled and noticed we had arrived at The Eagle.

The man moved again, and he asked me if this was Munna, so I assumed he must not have been on this trip before. 'No, this is The Eagle, and we will stop here for fifteen minutes. If you do get off here and want to get back on you better not be late, as the shuttle don't wait.' I laughed, then added, 'Hey,

I am a poet, and I just don't know it.' He didn't respond, I thought it was funny, and noticed Bernie was grinning at me.

The man then asked me how long until we got to the Cliffs, so I told him it was another hour. I introduced him to Bernie and told him that it was the first time we were going fishing. I then said to him: 'I'll let you know when we get closer, and you wanted to move to the front, better do it now whilst we are stopped'. I also asked if it was his first time on a shuttle. He confirmed this, and then he moved to the front and left us both alone.

As I was still on a roll with my in-depth conversation with Bernie, thought I would continue and, although it was a bit one-sided, I felt it was cathartic for me.

'Did you know that Flighters live alone and spend much of their life alone?'

'Don't they get lonely?' Bernie asked.

I thought, good question son, 'Yes, that is why they stay with the Ground-Dwellers as it provides them with the sanctity of a family, and this is precious to a Flighter. It is a feeling of belonging that forms part of their sense of purpose.'

Bernie nodded understanding it all so far. He is such a smart boy although it still sounds to me that I am boring him. I don't often get to have him so close to me without distractions and want him to learn so much from me. I once overheard him tell his friends that I am such a great Dad, and this made me so proud, so I continued:

'This could ultimately mean fewer people are working the land and helping out with The GOD. There was a recent decree to declare The Forced was an illegal practice and those partaking are in breach of the law, so a group of selected agents were appointed to monitor and deal with the Ground-Dwellers involved in such behaviour. They are known as The Represents. They search for, investigate and ultimately rescue the Flighters from The Forced, but some Flighters refuse to move or be rescued.'

I took another breath, as I was about to tell him something that I had only just become aware of myself. 'Bernie, some The Represents have become so arrogant in their pursuit of The Forced and developed a sense of self-righteousness. They believe in their commitment to support The GOD, it allows them a sense of empowerment, and some are even resorting to killing. Represents believe that it is within their authority and part of their mission.'

I looked out of the window and saw the man who had moved forward was now asleep. I would have to wake him as we will be a Munna Cliffs soon. I leaned closer to Bernie. 'A Represent does not carry anything that can cause death, but they can still be dangerous. If you ever meet one of them, don't upset them, and be respectful. I know you can do that.'

He nodded intently and was still so engrossed in all of this but upon starting the next part I knew I would have to be careful in case others were listening. 'Bernie, A Represent kills by Pushing. They push Ground-Dwellers out of build-ings and push them from and into moving shuttles. It is known as The Push.'

I looked at him, and he was just watching me talk, taking it all in: 'A Flighter can always escape though as they invoke their ability to float but a Represent is aware of this so they will make sure the Flighter is too close to the ground to initi-ate this process and will try and push them from the level of a four-story building instead of five. From this height it may be too low to initiate The Rush and the act of such violence is rarely investigated by The GOD as they do not expect this trait from A Represent. The GOD naively believes the premature death of Ground-Dwellers only comes from The Carrion'.

I had finally stopped talking, felt mentally exhausted, and upon realising that we were nearing Munna Cliffs, called out to the man upfront that we had about two minutes to go. I looked at Bernie, and he was wide awake himself.

'Dad,' he said quietly. 'Yes, mate.'

'Do you think that your father was pushed off the roof by A Represent? He always told me never to go onto a roof by myself as it was too dangerous and too scary.'

'I don't know Bernie; I don't know, but certainly hope not.'

Chapter 11 Carlyle

Early afternoon; Saturday 20th December: I was woken by the man calling out to me again: 'We are almost here, about two minutes to go.'

I noticed I'd been asleep for about fifty minutes, so rubbed my hands briskly over my face to wake myself up. I had completely missed the trip, but hopefully can stay awake on the way back. I do not know what lies beyond Edi-Aleda as I have not ventured here before, nor have I ventured anywhere in a long time. The shuttle entered a slip road and I assumed we must be getting closer to the Shuttle Terminus at Munno Cliffs, then the shuttle came to an abrupt stop and announced: *We have arrived in Munna Cliffs.*

'Been here before?' the man that spoke to me before enquired.

'Nope.'

'What are you here for? Do you fish?'

'Nope.' He looked at me. 'Would you like to join us? I have extra fish rods and the boy will likely get bored easily.'

I decided I might as well, as I didn't know what else I was planning to do whilst I was here and had no plans. I wanted something to distract me from Zamiro.

'OK sure, if you don't mind'.

'Nope', he said grinning at me then re-introduced himself as Howard and thrust out his hand enthusiastically. 'Call me Howie, and this is my boy, Bernie'

He looked down at his son. 'Formally introduce yourself to the man, Bernie.'

Bernie held out his hand.

'Carlyle', I said shaking the boy's hand. 'Nice to meet you.'

I saw the boy's eyes suddenly light up. 'Wow, look at your watch,' he said noticing my timepiece. 'I haven't seen one in real life. May I look at it please?'

'Sure,' I say holding out my left hand.

'Do you know what this is Dad? It's the latest Phillipe Patek. It's amazing!'

I looked at Howie and shrugged my shoulders.

'Do you know what it does?' Bernie asked me.

'Not really, I bought it this morning'

'No way!'

'Way,' I replied.

'Can I ask it a question?'

'Sure.'

'Oh, I can't as it needs your voice to work it,' he realised disappointingly.

I nodded. 'OK then, ask me the question then and I will ask the watch.'

Bernie hesitated then said; 'How tall am I? ...Hang on it doesn't work like that; may I have a look at the instructions book, please? Do you have it?'

I pulled the instructions book from my pocket where I had placed it before and handed it to him. He was smiling whilst he concentrated and began to flick through to pages, then pointed towards a single paragraph.

Howard looked at me, 'Bernie wasn't this excited when I told him we were going fishing today' he claimed with a smile.

'Found it,' Bernie claimed having now located what he was looking for. 'Oh right, it says that you need to introduce me to the watch before it can read me.' He continued: 'Hold the watch towards me, then say to it let me introduce you to Bernie.'

I held out my watch, pointed it towards him and said to it; 'Watch. Let me introduce you to Bernie.' It instantly responded, 'Hello Master Bernie. You are a Ground-Dweller'.

'Whoa,' Bernie remarked; 'Can I ask how high I am now?'

'Sure'

'Nope, I won't, I want to ask something clever and better,' so he stopped and asked: 'Where am I?'

'Good question Master Bernie' it replied quickly, then went quiet momentarily and after a few seconds, responded: "You are currently standing with your father; Howard and he is standing with Carlyle. You are in the Berg of Munna Cliffs. You are going fishing today. You will need to walk down the path to your right for five hundred footsteps where you will then find the river. The fish are running today."

I looked at Howard and said, 'Didn't it say Bernie was standing with you?' Howie looked at me puzzled. 'How does it know that?'

'Dad, it has a genealogy programme.'

Bernie continued, 'It knew I was here, and it knew Carlyle was here, so it deduced the third person here was you.'

'What about the fishing?'

'When it scanned me it would have seen the slender poles I was holding and had assumed, as we are near a river that has fish it would have known this is where other people fish.'

I thought that was impressive, and wondered what else it does, then I realised it had recognised Bernie as a Ground-Dweller and considered I will need to be careful what I say to it, and what I do with it myself. We followed the path the five hundred steps as it had suggested and whilst the river was wide here, the bank was too rocky and ready for us to find an area to unload the rods for baiting.

Meantime, Bernie had insisted on reading the book of instructions as he walked, but after stopping to bait the rods and casting off nothing was biting, so we sat there for about thirty minutes. We didn't have much to say to each other as I still found it difficult to create conversation. Bernie was so engrossed in the watch instruction book that he didn't want to talk to us anyway.

'At least he is reading,' Howard commented looking over at me.

They eventually decided to move along as Howard mentioned he knew of a cement channel that ran parallel to the river was used for irrigation, and carried fish.

I decided to leave them alone and go for a walk by myself. I nodded to Howie and moved off. 'Thanks, Howard. Great day. Great boy.'

Howard called back to me. 'Are you going back tonight? The last shuttle is about five o'clock and leaves from the terminus in the centre of town but don't be late as the shuttle won't wait!' and laughed to himself again for some reason. I moved away from them looked around for another path to follow, and saw one that would take me up the cliffs to a position high above the river, so I headed up there.

About halfway up, I turned and looked down to the river below and could see Howie and Bernie walking towards the cement channel below me, another fishing spot. I saw a large deeper pool of water at the end of the channel where the water flowed and watched as Bernie moved towards it. He began to remove his shirt and shorts, so I assumed he was going for a swim, but he suddenly stopped as Howard must have called out to him. I could just make out his call from up where I was, so I watched as Bernie turned around and dejectedly made his way back to his father. Howard then handed him a fishing rod, and they both sat down by the cement bank dropping the lines into the channel.

I re-assessed my position and realised had about another ten metres to get to the plateau at the top, so decided as there was no one around, and as Howard and Bernie were fixated on their fishing, I would use The Rush for the final climb.

I felt The Rush course through me, then gently floated up to the plateau where I landed safely. The view from here was amazing. I could see across the other side of the river, and behind me, Munna Cliffs.

It was a beautiful warm summer day and pretty here, and it reminded me there are other pretty things in my world as well as Zamiro. I looked down again at Howard and Bernie could just make out that they had caught some fish as they were neatly piled beside them. I knew that Bernie was finally going for that swim as he began to take off his shirt and shorts, and was now barefoot. He made his way to the pond at the end of the cement channel.

I drop-floated to where I had been watching them previously and was enjoying the view when I noticed the pond in front of Bernie. He was contemplating how to jump in. It was then I saw the ripples across the stillness of the pond. I knew he could not see this from his position. I also saw movement along the top of the water. It was being made by a couple of large snake fish. I remembered they are called eels. There were about four or five of them and they began to scatter. I wondered if something was chasing them.

It was then I saw it.

I had to strain my eyes to focus on whatever it was as I was too far away. It looked like a large floating log, but it was moving. It appeared to have scales or shingles along its sides, was very sleek, was very large, and moving quickly. As it was just underneath the top of the water I could not calculate how big it was.

I looked again and saw that Bernie was about to jump into the pond. He moved back a little as he started his run-up, and as he jumped he tucked his arms under his knees. I knew he was most likely to land directly on top of the river monster and realised then that I was useless to warn them from up here. I needed to get down.

I called out, 'Stop! Stop Bernie!' but it was futile as he could not hear me.

Howard looked up at me and waved, but he didn't heed my call or my warning. It was all too late, all left unheard. Howard stood up and started to collect the fish and rods together. I then realised Howard was not looking in the same direction as the pond. He dropped the fish into a bucket, and moved the other way, away from Bernie, and away from the pond. Bernie jumped into the pond with a 'Whoopee' to which Howard then turned just managing to catch and wave to him.

From my position, I saw that Bernie had landed directly on the back of the river monster. It reared, and it was then I saw that it was not a fish at all. It appeared to be metal, and it appeared to be made of the same golden shimmering metal as The Carrion. It was much bigger than I first thought.

I watched as Bernie rolled off its side further into the water. The monster turned and with jaws wide open swallowed him whole. Bernie did not surface and the pond water had returned to being still. Howard was now looking up, and started to move towards the pond, he then moved just a bit quicker and started running.

I drop-floated from my position and managed to control my descent enough to land safely, but it was a hard landing, it took too long and now I am too late. I started running towards Howard, toward the pond.

He was now yelling at the water as I caught up to him. 'Where is he, he hasn't ...where is? Bernie!'

'I saw it, it took him. I think it was a Carrion,' I said with a heavy breath.

'What Carrion? Not here, not in the water, not Bernie.....Bernie. Where? How?'

'I saw from up there, I tried to warn him, yelled out. You heard me.'

'Yes, I heard you and I heard Bernie too,' Howard replied. 'It didn't ...you didn't...Bernie!' he cried out louder this time in frustration and fear, and started to take off his shoes and shirt. 'I am going in.'

'No don't', there is nothing…Don't!'

He then turned to me, 'How did you get down so quickly?'

I feigned an ache in my leg, 'I ran down, slid down and fell, but I still didn't make it in time. I couldn't stop him. I was too late. I am so sorry.'

He looked at me, looked at the pond and there was nothing but stillness now.

'What do we do? Can we…we should call the ER.'

I said to him. 'I don't have anything to call them on. Do you? No one knows we are here.' I realised my watch had GPS, so I exclaimed excitedly. 'Bernie told me it has a tracking system.' I needed to find the book and then realised that Bernie had it. I looked down at his discarded shorts. They were on the ground with his shoes.

I looked at Howard. 'The instructions book… it is in his shorts,'

He turned solemnly, looked at them, looked at the pond again, then at me. 'Just ask it' he said annoyingly.

Of course, I realised, 'Watch. Call the Emergency Responders'.

"They have responded. They will attend within seven minutes."

It was the longest seven minutes of my life.

I could not console Howard as I could not remember how. I looked at him and he looked destroyed and I began to feel his pain. I don't often feel this way, it was so sad, it was terrifying and wonderful. It was emotion. I had missed so much of everything, hiding away from it all for so long.

The Emergency Response Team arrived and interviewed us. Wanting to know how I saw what was happening, and why I did not stop him. I felt ashamed. I felt hopeless.

They talked about draining the pond and other options but decided as the pond drains back into the main river it would be pointless unless they could dam it off somehow. They also did not believe that we saw, what I saw, and did not believe The Carrion would be in the water. I could not convince them.

A female ER came over toward me after leaving Howard standing over the pond and her nameplate was visible on the shirt. It read as 'Aya'

'Can I do anything more to help, Aya? 'I asked her.

She looked at me, 'No, I don't think so, nothing more to do here.' Then she looked up at the cliff face and asked me to explain again how I got down so quickly from such a height. I sensed she was getting suspicious, so I kept quiet, and she continued: 'You haven't been saying much,' then added softly: 'The Carrion hey, and in the water?'

I shrugged and she defensively crossed her arms over her chest. 'Don't you trust us? We are not The Represents. We are ER,' she said probing for more commentary. I kept quiet, so we stood there a little while longer. 'Are you recording this?' I eventually asked.

She tapped her right wrist with her left hand, and I could see there was a leather guard that was glowing a light shade of blue. 'I don't need to as this does.' She held a wrist plate towards me and explained that the Wrist Logger, she called it, records everything.

I realised that I must be careful what I say and do around the ERs.

The woman sighed. 'I was wondering when the AIC would get around to this.'

'The AIC?' I queried her.

She responded with her own story about The Carrion and The AIC, and after she had finished, I shrugged my shoulders again, and the other ER representative, Axa, I think his name was, made his way over to us and updated us. 'We are not going to do anything more now so we will call it finite and you can go back to Base. I will wait here with Howard until his family comes to get him.'

Howard came up to us and looked at me, but I didn't know what to say or what else I could do so I held both arms for some reason. I don't know why. He stepped into them, and we stood there holding each other. After he pulled from the hold, he told me the last shuttle would most likely be leaving in the next twenty minutes, and I would need to get the Munna Terminus if I wanted to go back home tonight.

I could see how much pain he was in, and could now feel how much pain he was in. He then mentioned he had family here in Munna Cliffs, so they would collect him as he would stay with them. He also said he would come back here in the morning. He wanted to be with Bernie and wanted to say his goodbyes.

I thanked him again for the day and wanted to tell him it was one of the best days of my life since leaving Munta, but I couldn't, as I knew it would always be the worst day in his life, the day he lost Bernie.

The female ER officer offered me a ride back into the

Berg and along the way, she prompted me for more about the events of the day and started talking about the AIC facility again.

'Where is it' I asked her, 'Can I go there?' but I didn't know what I would do if I could, as I just thought it was the right thing to say.

'All over, everywhere' she replied 'The AIC are using whatever metal the drones collect for them and put them together. I want to destroy them all if I could. I hate them and they kill us for nothing. Nothing.'

I thought about my own previous experiences with Emergency Responders so long ago and convinced myself that I needed to confess my reluctance to talk to her, after all, she might understand. I took a deep breath.

'What?' she queried looking over at me.

'This is not the first time that I have had to …. meet…deal with you people.' I blurted out angrily.

'Oh,' she said in reply.

'Yes. The ER was there the day my parents were killed. Murdered by the AIC.' She looked over at me again and looked back to the road ahead.

I continued: 'It was about seven years ago. The AIC brought my parent's plane down out of the sky and killed about a hundred people. They blew up the plane and killed my girlfriend, Mel. It's been a long time since I have said anything about this to anyone.' I took another breath looking out to my left of the window of the small shuttle we were travelling in, and continued speaking towards the window: 'I was only a child, a juvenile. I was in Edi-Aleda to get my wrist chips put in. I was fifteen summers.'

I noticed in my reflection there was a small line of water on my face and raised my hand to my eyes as they felt wet. Flighters don't cry and I haven't for such a long time as I don't do emotions. Maybe I should.

'I only survived as I happened to be watching the plane and no one else appeared to be. I was in the middle of a wave to them, to my parents and the plane and saw it all happen. I was there. We had come across by boat from the other side of the peninsula. My Berg is called Munta, and they brought me to Edi-Aleda to have my wrist chips installed. There was a group of us, my family had a farm on the other side of the sea, and we grew crops and livestock.'

I felt anger rising through my body. I couldn't stop talking. I wouldn't stop talking: 'It is a small community of around five hundred people, where everyone knew everyone. I remember it so clearly even now. The plane took off, banked to the left, slowed down, and then it dropped like stone.'

I took a deep breath and continued: 'There was a second fireball after it blew up, and this meant anybody who survived was killed in the second explosion. Debris, people, planes and body parts were expelled into the sky. It was raining chunks of burnt flesh, raining blood and raining plane parts'.

I stopped talking momentarily to gather my thoughts: 'I managed to turn and hide behind a large tree as the explosive cloud came towards me. I thought that I would be immune to the falling debris and as it turned out I was, as a large, damaged panel from the side of the plane had landed in the tree canopy above me and bore the brunt of the descending mass. I watched Mel running towards me with her arms stretched out. I was willing her to make it. Willing to run faster, but a falling dismembered half body of pulpy mess got her instead, and she was killed instantly. I sometimes close my eyes, and even now seven years later, I still see her.'

I looked over at Aya and as she was all business listening to my story, so I continued. 'I still don't understand how I survived, but the tree trunk saved me from the horizontal cloud and the tree canopy and damaged plane panel lodged above me saved me from the vertical cloud. I was unscathed. Then The Carrion arrived, but as soon as they came they were gone. I remember the ER coming in and looking around and as it was so close to the airport, they had arrived relatively quickly.'

The expression on her face hadn't changed, so I continued: 'I remember going up to them, wanting to tell them what I saw, what I experienced, but what did happen was no one believed me.'

'Oh,' Aya finally said, 'Why not?'

'I was clean, my clothes were unstained, and my shoes whilst a little bloodied, showed little other evidence of what had just transpired. Only one ER even bothered to interview me, only one said why do you look so distraught? I had just lost my parents. I just lost Mel, and my family.'

I sat in the shuttle reflecting on what had I gone through that day, but kept this next memory to myself: I had been standing behind the tree holding my arms firmly to my sides to avoid everything happening around me. The tree was protecting me. I remember closing my eyes and clenching my fists. I wanted it to stop, wanting it to go away and when I looked saw the plane panel in the canopy above me. Then it happened to me. The Rush. I first felt a tingling sensation in my feet which rose through my legs, through my groin, and into my chest. I felt lighter and was slowly moving off the ground. I floated upwards. I am a Flighter. I also realised my parents were most likely not my true mother and father as they were both Ground-Dwellers. I am a Flighter but I didn't get a chance to tell them. The supple branches and soft leaves had given way to me as I rose through them and towards the underside of the plane panel. I had to put my hands up to prevent myself from crashing into it but when I softly collided with the panel it held. I was safe. I was about five metres off the ground but was prevented from going any higher by the damaged panel. Then I saw the carnage all around me. Once I saw the ER had arrived I climbed out of the tree. This is why The Carrion missed me. It was why I was relatively clean, and how I had survived.

I pulled out of my reverie, and Aya was still sitting beside me in the shuttle. She didn't dare ask much more after that, and I didn't dare tell her much more. I noticed we were at the terminus, so climbed out of the shuttle duo. Aya came around to firmly shake my hand once again and promised she would get back in touch with me. I told her where I lived, as I thought that was the right thing to do.

We had arrived in time at Munna Cliffs for me to catch the last shuttle back into Edi-Aleda. On the return trip, I thought about Howard, thought about Bernie, thought about The Carrion, thought about what the ER Officer had said about The Carrion and wondered if I could ever make a difference. I could not sleep on the shuttle trip back and vowed not to sleep as now I knew I must defeat The Carrion. I once wanted to believe that I could *help* to defeat The Carrion, by myself if I had to.

Upon arriving back at the City Terminus I waved to Creedence as I disembarked the shuttle, but could not bring myself to tell him about my experiences today. I took a Zoop home using my watch as the fob, just as the watch salesman had told me. Bernie is, *was* right, the watch is impressive. I made it home safely and as the lifts were now working, took one to my apartment. I thought I was too exhausted to write in my journal, but what could I write about today anyway, so decided to add one word:

<u>My Jurnal −dai 2. Friday 20th</u>

Love.

Chapter 12 Aya

It is mid-afternoon; Saturday 20th December: My ER
partner and I had been arguing over who was the oldest as I
was almost twenty-eight summers, but I didn't let him know
that, and I was also talking about all the specialist fields that
ER can get into. We can elect to attend the simple call out,
to locate missing animals known as the Amninates, or to
attend to full medical emergencies. We are also authorised
and qualified to handle matters of state, including making
citizen arrests and performing ad hoc medical procedures,
and we both have stories to tell from our past. I have not
yet mentioned to him I used to work at The AIC facility in
Edi-Aleda.

This station at Munna Falls, like most Bergs, also provides services on a 24-hour rotational basis and has a medical
centre attached, so I can choose to train in all fields related
to ER. I am happy to be based here, at least for the short
term pending anything drastic happening. The call that came
through directing us to the large pond at the end of the
cement channel near the Munna Cliffs River, had come via
an emergency request from a Phillipe Patek watch. This was
new for us as those watches are not very common in these

parts. We looked at each other, climbed into our duo shuttle and headed toward the directed site of the call. The watch has a built-in GPS, so we know where to go.

When we arrived the path from the road was wide enough to drive down, but we didn't know what to expect here. What we found was two men standing close to the edge of the large pond of dark water. This is where the cement drain flowed into, and it was away from the main river. They looked at us as we climbed out of the shuttle and I instantly saw that one of them was looking particularly distraught, the other not so.

I knew instantly something bad had happened here.

'I'm Howard,' the first one said introducing himself to us, 'And my son is in there,' pointing to the brackish pond water. 'He jumped in…he hasn't come up.'

The other man then looked at us and said: 'And he won't.'

This second man however did not offer his name, an introduction or an explanation, but I will get it out of him. I also noticed the one who called himself Howard had a finger-band on his index finger. It was an unusual three-ring gold and silver band.

I looked over at the other man's hands and noticed the Phillipe Patek watch on his left wrist. This was where the emergency call must have come from. I noticed these simple things and wondered too if they were life partners, and if the missing boy was theirs, but didn't think so. It was a feeling I had. My ER partner asked him to elaborate, and the quieter man responded with two words. 'The Carrion.' I looked over at my partner. 'Axa, I think we need to find out what is going on here,' and directed him to separate the two men for questioning so I took Mr No-Name, and my partner took Howard.

'Mr. No-Name' introduced himself as Carlyle, and told me that he had not known them before today, Howard or Bernie, Benny?? ..the boy-child. They had only met on the shuttle on the way up from Edi-Aleda. He had never been to Munna Cliffs before and had stayed with Howard and the boy as they had asked him to. He also admitted he had nothing else to do today, nothing planned and I thought that sounded plausible, but I felt there was something he wasn't telling me.

I could sense it.

He went on to tell me he had left them fishing together to take a walk and had made it up to the plateau above the river. I looked up to the cliffs and to the path that he allegedly took and then back at him I thought that is quite a way. He then told me that he was resting up there when he saw Bernie running towards the pond and saw The Carrion as it was in the water and watched as Bernie jumped in landing on it and he was sure it swallowed the boy whole.

I believed him, but I was not going to give it up that easily as there was something else going on, so I asked him again just how he got from halfway down the cliff face so quickly. He told me he ran down, slid down and fell, and that he didn't make it in time and again he said he was sorry. He began to rub the side of his leg as if trying to validate his response so looked at where we were standing, and where he allegedly ran from. 'That was quite an achievement in such a short time' I said aloud to him this time, but he kept very quiet, so we stood there a little while longer in silence. He then asked if I was writing any of this down, so I tapped my right wrist with my left hand and explained about my Wrist Logger.

'It records dialogue, takes pictures and sometimes it even catches people out if they are lying.' I said to him with a slight suspicion; 'I always wear my Logger as it automatically relays every observation, and every conversation is immediately sent back to the ER Base for archiving.'

What he was saying seemed plausible, so I thought I'd throw out a spontaneous statement to see his reaction about The AIC. I then explained that The AIC are building bird-like flying robots, The Carrion, and I have seen them. I also mentioned I used to work on the campus where they make the chips, the ones we put in our wrists. I told him I could not take it anymore, and joined the ER.

I knew something else was going on here though, and now this, so said to him that I agreed with him that The Carrion could be in the water too, trying to gain his confidence. He simply shrugged his shoulders.

Axa then came over to us and said that nothing more was to be done here tonight, then Howard came up to us and embraced Carlyle, and this gave me the impression that they had known each other much longer than Carlyle had just said to me.

Maybe I am too suspicious.

Axa also mentioned we wanted to meet up with Howard again in the morning to review the events of the day. I told Axa I would take Carlyle to the terminus in Munna Cliffs so he could return to Edi-Aleda tonight. I thought it might be an opportunity to find out a little bit more about this mystery, and this mystery man.

During the ride, Carlyle was initially quiet so I decided to bring up the AIC again, so I mentioned I used to work there and this seemed to pique his interest, as suddenly he blurted out that The AIC had killed his parents, had brought down their plane and he despises the AIC. Don't we all? I thought.

He then began to tell me a story about the time at the airport around seven years ago, when he had dealt with the Emergency Responders. I looked over at him but tried to maintain my composure. ERs often talk of the day in our training sessions of this day, but we were never told there were any witnesses. The ER has always categorically denied there were any witnesses or any survivors. We were always told that once the plane was brought down, The AIC then brought in The Carrion to kill anybody left alive. This was the first time the AIC showed its capabilities and it showed to mankind that it was planning to take over, this was also the day the planes also stopped flying. The AIC had won round one. I looked over at him again as he was now looking out through the window on his left, and I thought he was crying.

I dropped him off at the Terminus and told him I would be in touch. I was surprised that he told me where he lived in Edi-Aleda so thanked him for that, but I felt there was something else, something he hadn't told me. What I didn't tell him, was that the ER would have archived those statements, and I could listen to them now, if only I could find them.

Chapter 13 Creedence

Mid-morning; Saturday 20th December: I have been able to live a life of anonymity and in five days it will be December 25th. It will also be my 40th birthday and I am not looking forward to it. I am a Flighter so it means it will be my death day too.

As a Flighter I am also not supposed to have a job either as The GOD already provides me with a monthly stipend, but I have been fortunate enough to have been a cleaner at the City 33 Central Shuttle Terminus for over ten summers and this has helped maintain my anonymity. I currently live in an apartment on the 5th floor in the Berg known as Evoh and life has been good to me. Today met a man in the Shuttle Terminus where I work. He called himself Carlyle.

When we spoke it felt good to communicate with someone who didn't appear afraid, whilst he may have been suspicious of me, he wasn't afraid. I found that unusual, and felt I had seen him before somewhere but could not recall where.

We talked briefly about the places we live in and work in and noticed he wasn't used to being in the Central Berg, but I didn't ask where he works, or what he does. He also told me he didn't know how to use the hologram to find his way or where to go so, I offered to help him. He then told me that he wanted to go on the shuttle to Munna Cliffs so I showed him where to catch it from and he mentioned he had not been on the bigger shuttle before.

I was also happy to direct him to the markets as he was also looking for some food for his trip today. He told me there were a lot of things about himself, and that he had not experienced much in life, he wanted to do more, and I thought he needed to, as we all need to do.

When he returned sometime later he passed me again, and I noticed that he had since purchased a timepiece, as I had not seen one on his wrist before. I knew it to be the latest model Phillipe Patek, and knew it to be expensive, but as a Flighter I did not need to worry about my expenses. I whistled and commented about the price of the new watch, and called him Carlo to see if there was any reaction, but there was none.

The day went slowly as usual and I had to finish my cleaning work late as there had been an incident somewhere. I happened to see Carlyle was arriving on the last shuttle from Munna Cliffs, so went to call out to him. He looked exhausted, saddened, and drained, and I wondered what happened, but he did not respond to my calling.

I rode a Zoop home and rode the lift to my apartment. I was thankful The GOD had finally completed the scheduled maintenance. I had been carried everything up the five flights of stairs, and have often used The Rush, but have not yet been caught.

It was dark tonight and as there was no moon, and stood on my balcony looking out to the darkness. The sea and the sky are both dark tonight. I had chosen this apartment as it faced west into the setting sun. The Carrion attack at dusk, so I might be able to warn people and might be able to save people. I decided to carry my trash downstairs, and although it was late, there would be no one else around at this time of night. I looked at the bag of trash, looked at the balcony, and decided to use The Rush to drop-float down to the ground.

I climbed over the balcony, jumped off and am now freefalling one, two, three, then I felt The Rush invoke and I safely controlled my landing. I had mastered it many summers ago. It was dark by the trash receptacle area as the lights were due to be replaced.

Suddenly I saw movement to my right. There was something there, and I saw a shape. It was too late for The Carrion, maybe A Represent? I saw the shape of a man in the darkness, and he then moved toward me. Did he see me land? Did he see me control my fall? Did he see that I am a Flighter?

I saw it was Carlyle.

'Hey,' he said softly to me.

'Taking out the trash,' I replied casually, and he moved out into the light.

It was Carlyle, but I didn't know to be relieved or frightened.

'Creedence,' he said as he nodded at me. 'You live here too?'

Chapter 14 Carlyle

Late evening; Saturday 20th December: I can't sleep and have missed Zamiro today as there is so much that I want to tell her and am devastated about the loss of Bernie and the loss to Howard. Did I say too much to Aya? Did I say too much to Creedence? The Carrion?

They are no longer just in the air. Doesn't that mean that they can contaminate our water supply and control our water supply? Have they found another way to meet their objective - by cutting off the water supply they control the growing of food?

I decided to leave my apartment, to go down for a walk and although it was late and dark, I should have been safe. I made my way down the 11 flights of stairs and exited the door on the ground floor. It opened outside by the trash receptacle area and is still dark here. The overhead lights have not been replaced in months. Suddenly I saw movement to my left and sensed something, then saw the shape of a man in the darkness. I realised it was Creedence and he moved towards me telling me casually he was taking out the trash. I asked him if he lived there too. I didn't recall hearing the ping of the elevator and may have missed it, although I was certain he wasn't in the stairwell. How had I missed him?

I was still pondering that as we both moved closer to the light emitting from the ground foyer area, so we walked to the elevators together. I assumed he was suspicious of me, or maybe he was too tired to talk. I felt I was too tired to talk to him too.

We got into the elevators together without comment. He pushed 4 and I pushed 9, and now we may know what floor we live on. He alighted at 4, said goodnight, and moved away as the doors closed on me. I alighted on 9 then took the stairs up to the 11th floor where my apartment is, and considered he may have done the same.

Flighters are very suspicious.

Taking my clothes off and climbing into bed, and felt I could finally get to sleep.

Chapter 15 Zamiro

Mid-morning; Sunday 21st December: It is a non-work day for me today and I have no plans. Marty and Kilby had left for work and Tristesse was still sulking in her room. Columbus had told her he wasn't coming back, and we don't think he will either.

Mata was busying herself in the kitchen and Fata was reading an old fiction book sitting at the dining table as I sat down with him at the dining table. He looked up at me. 'You know this guy is quite good, Michael C-onn-lly' he said to me placing it face down on the table and reading from the back sleeve of the book. 'The lead character is named after the old drill set I have seen in your grandfather's work shed...Bosch. Fancy that.'

'Where did you find the book? I haven't seen one around for ages. Not a fictional novel like that anyway?' I said nodding over at it.

'I was in the Central Berg the other day as Mata was in the markets, so I went for a walk. Did you know they have re-opened the Book Storage Archive Building? I thought it had been closed years ago.'

I nodded. 'I often send my ELC children there, if they want extra reading.'

'Oh,' he said nodding in confirmation. I then told him what I knew of the building, 'It was almost destroyed by the AIC about seven years ago and no one understood why The AIC specifically targeted that particular site and many of the rooms were destroyed as well. The AIC used multiple incendiary devices, and many Ground-Dwellers were killed.' I remember that I was still at my ELC, and knew I was well away from the danger.

Fata continued: 'The GOD told us it was the beginning of the end, but no one from The GOD was prepared to say what that was supposed to mean, and fortunately, within the building, there was a huge impenetrable cement bunker where many old records had been accumulated over the years. Whilst these were saved, there is not much use for ancient history these days, as we have moved on from the past.'

I paused in reflection on that comment and he continued: 'The Building still contains hundreds of thousands of books and there are archived old newspapers, old encyclopedias and many instruction books on how to manufacture almost any-thing, and there are the old micro phish records from even early times.'

I had considered that I should get Carlyle to go there with me one day as think he would find it fascinating. He wants to know more, and I liked this about him.

Fata broke the silence. 'You seem to be deep in thought?'

'Yes, just thinking about the Library, that is what is called, the building that holds the books.' A muffled ringing then interrupted my reverie, and we looked at each other across the table. The noise continued: 'Bring, brrrring,'

Mata came out from the kitchen brushing her hands on the apron in front of her, 'I know that sound. It's our new telephone.'

I looked at Fata. 'We have a telephone?'

I didn't know we had one installed, but I had noticed a new hip-height cupboard in the foyer next to the front door. The cupboard doors were closed. 'Well, at least that explained the muffled ring,' I stated as I made my way there.

It had been ringing for quite some time by now, so I opened the doors, reached into it and the ringing was coming from a round box, with a square handle on top. I lifted the handle and held it to my ear and mouth. 'Hello, this is Zamiro. Who is calling?' I stated into the unit.

'Hello.' came the reply and was intrigued by this as it sounded like a man's voice. 'Hello.' I replied and there was a pause.

'Hello Zamiro' came the hesitant reply. 'This is Carlyle. I just wanted to ring up to say....... hello.'

'OK,' I said back to him, 'But why did you call on the telephone? How did you call on the telephone? Where are you?'

'I am in my apartment. I had a telephone installed. I don't know anyone else that has a telephone.'

'How did you know we did?'

'I bought a timepiece yesterday, and it found your number for me.'

'A timepiece can do that?' I was surprised at that, and also that he'd bought a watch. I only mentioned in passing that he should get one.

Carlyle continued: 'Yes, and it does much more than that. I would like to show it to you. Are you busy today? If you are, what time can I see you?'

'OK,' I replied and went on 'but don't you want to know if I am not busy instead?' I corrected him.

'Oh,' he then paused. 'As you are busy? Sorry, I interrupted you.'

I held the telephone handle away from my ear and mouthpiece. 'No, I am not busy today. Do you want to come here?' I said back to him.

He paused again and said with more hesitation this time: 'I would like to show you where I live.'

OK, I thought, that is interesting, I wasn't expecting that.

He told me how to get there: 'Catch the shuttle from Stop 6 in my Berg, alight at Stop 9 at the Evoh Berg. Take a Zoop from there and make your way down to the beach area. I'll meet you by the Special Stones Jeweller halfway down the street facing the water at noon.'

He then abruptly disconnected.

I turned to my Fata, who was again engrossed in the novel, and summarised to him what was happening, and I would be going out. When I mentioned the Special Stones Jeweller, Mata suddenly came out from the kitchen, this time albeit hurriedly.

'You are meeting who, to go where?' she said brightly. 'A Special Stones Jeweller?'…and a man is meeting you there?' She clasped the palms of her hands together in front of her face excitedly.

I looked over at Fata, and he looked back at me rolling his eyes.

So, I am meeting Carlyle at a Jeweller? This will be interesting...

I caught the shuttle, rode the Zoop as he instructed, and eventually found my way to the jeweller. I was early so waited outside and noticed several gold finger bands in the window. I did begin to wonder what was going on as these ring bands are used when individuals decide to become a couple, and, a young couple came out through the door next to me. They were looking at each other and then looking at a finger-band on her index finger.

'Your turn next!' the young man said looking at me.

I was horrified, then calmed down. Don't be silly I thought, wait, just wait, there must be a valid reason why he wants to meet me here. I then looked at my watch and realised Carlyle was late, so maybe he did not know how to read his time-piece. I turned around and looked towards the sea with my back to the jeweller's window. It was a bright shimmering blue - the sky was a paler blue, and the sun was shining bright yellow. It was a beautiful day, and have missed seeing days like these as I have to work inside the school. I vowed I must make more of an effort with the children to get them out of the classroom.

Carlyle was now coming towards me, and he was smiling. He doesn't often smile, and I often wonder why not. I think he is handsome when he smiles, and I must tell him one day, but certainly not today, and certainly not standing in front of a Special Stones Jeweller shop.

He was closer, and not slowing down. He held his arms out to me and we held each other. He has never done this before, and I wonder why now, why here? The hold seemed to linger on, so eventually I pulled back and noticed he was looking a little sadder.

'Ok... why here?' My curiosity has finally got to me. He looked at the finger bands in the window, then turned to face me. 'I would like to ask you a serious question.'

'Oh no', I dreaded.

He hesitated and then leant down to his side. Oh no....is he going to get down on his knees??! No, no, no! Not here! Not now! We haven't known each other long enough.

He rubbed his lower leg instead. 'What?' he said looking up at me. 'I bought this yesterday,' and he held out his left arm for me to inspect. I recognised it as a Phillipe Patek watch, and they were very expensive, but I'd never seen one this close. 'And?'

'Well, I have lost the instruction booklet and need to get another one. I think they sell these timepieces here.'

'Phew', I let out under my breath.

We entered the store, and I thought the trader was disappointed as we only wanted a replacement instructions book for the Phillipe Patek. I suspected he was still on a natural high from the couple that had just left the store as he kept probing us regarding finding a suitable finger band. The vendor grinned. 'You let me know what you want as I am sure we have it.'

Carlyle didn't tune into what the merchant was alluding to as he just kept saying we just wanted the timepiece instructions book, so eventually, the merchant we were not a couple, and the book was all that we needed. 'Not today, anyway,' he managed to mention a few more times. He then admitted that the instruction book was not necessary as it was only required if the watch was ever lost. The Phillipe Patek agents have them supplied to the traders to understand the functions. He went on to explain that as it was such an expensive watch, they preferred to sell it new, in the box. The book was only to be removed to show the features, and to track a watch if it was lost.

'I didn't buy mine in a box.' Carlyle stated to him.

'You must have them as we are not allowed to sell them over the counter without a box …where did you …Oh, never mind. You do know it has V.O.C. You don't need the instruction booklet as you just ask it anything you need.'

Carlyle looked sheepishly at me. 'I do know that.'

I softly punched him in the arm.

'You are a couple', the vendor added, 'Are you sure I can't get you a nice finger band instead?' I grabbed Carlyle's arm and quickly helped him out the door.

After walking around his Berg, then along the beach, Carlyle suggested we go to his apartment, and it was only a short walk from where we were. I noticed he had been very quiet today, even quieter than on the days I have been with him previously. I felt that he wanted to tell me something, something was troubling him, and something had saddened him.

As we walked we talked about him living in this Berg, so close to the sea, and he told me that he had been here for about three summers. He mentioned he had met someone who also lived in his building, although he didn't say much more about her/him. I don't know why, but felt a pang of jealousy and hoped it wasn't her.

We crossed the street stopping at doors leading into a foyer of a modern building. It was twelve storeys and he looked up telling me that the lifts hadn't been working so I groaned. I was not walking up eleven storeys and then back down again to go home.

Just as we went inside the foyer though a large man approached us hurriedly, and I was a little taken aback by him. 'Have you seen any G-D's with Flighters?' he barked at us.

'Nope,' Carlyle quickly replied' 'You asked me the same thing yesterday morning.'

'Oh right, Carlyle isn't it? 11th floor, Apartment 1103. Did you know you are the only one living on that floor?... As if you didn't.'

Carlyle nodded; 'This is Zamiro, She is a Ground-Dweller;' introducing me to the man.

'Harrumph' was his reply, 'Hawke, A Represent', shaking my hand, then he said to us, 'and the elevators are working now.' I was relieved to hear that comment.

'What has that all about?' I asked Carlyle as The Represent made his way out of the building behind us.

Carlyle shrugged, then he selected the 11th floor, and we began to rise. 'I met him yesterday morning, well, he knocked very loudly on my apartment door and scanned my wrist to check I was a paying tenant. Flighters don't pay rent, and he wanted to know if I was harbouring any Flighters. It is all part of The GOD's investigations into The Forced. The Represents have been known to throw people out of buildings to prove they are Flighters and not Ground-Dwellers?'

I looked over at him just as the lift then pinged as we had arrived at the 11th floor, and he continued as we stood outside his apartment door:

'Well if you are a Flighter and you are far enough off the

ground when they throw you out you can control your fall and safely land, but you will reveal your ability to save your own life. If you are a Ground-dweller you die from the fall.'

'You're kidding?' I said in shock.

'No, apparently most Flighters tend to live above the fourth or fifth floor so they can survive the fall.'

I thought about that and trying to hide my suspicion of him said, 'You live on the 11th floor don't you?'

He looked over at me. 'Yes, and did you also know The Represents drag the suspected Flighter to the third floor, just to throw them off there instead?'

Good answer I thought. 'And people say The Carrion are the only ones we need to look out for.'

He nodded. 'I assume that people will start to move up here now the elevators are working, but no one is on this floor as yet.'

We finally moved to the door of his apartment where he swiped his left wrist over the door scanner, the lock clicked open, and then he hesitated a little and turned to me. 'I have never brought anyone else here. You are the first.' He opened the door and I saw that the apartment was very impressive.

I live in a five-bedroom home with Marty, Kilby, Tristesse, Fata & Mata and this place is much bigger. 'Wow,' is all I could manage.

'It's only two bedrooms and three bathrooms though. This is the living, dining and kitchen area,' showing the open space before me. 'Would you like to go to the bedroom.'

'Whoa,' I thought what have I got myself into? But why not? I thought. I trust him and know he saved my life. I followed him to his bedroom, and it too was massive. There was a king-size futon bed that looked towards another balcony, and a large bathroom was behind the bed wall. I went in there and noticed the bathroom too had a view of the sea. I finally got my bearings and realised every window, every balcony, every view was of a westerly direction. 'It all faces west.'

'Yes, and if I am home at dusk I can see The Carrion coming from every view.'

I entirely understood his need to do that.

As we hadn't eaten as yet I asked him if we were going to, but he told me that he wanted to wait until the sunset as there was a golden sun tonight which was ideal for an invasion by The Carrion. So we waited and watched. He served me some wine, and I had not tasted wine very much, then he told me there was alcohol in the wine, but not in beer if I preferred that. I stayed with the wine but felt my head beginning to feel a bit fuzzy even though I had only had one glass.

We watched the sunset and sat out on the balcony and then we saw them, The Carrion. We had almost missed them, as they were high in the sky, flying high over the Berg, high over us. I pointed them out. 'Not coming in here tonight. Too high.' I hoped that they were not going anywhere.

A look of concern came over his face. 'I think I know where they are going. They are heading for Munna Cliffs. Do you know where that is?'

'Yes I do, and why.'

'I was there today and saw The Carrion in the water, in a pond, it took a boy.' He then told me everything that happened to him, and sometime later, after one more glass of wine for me, he stopped talking.

I was horrified when he said The Carrion is now in the

water. 'Does this mean that they can contaminate our water supply, cut off the access to the water and kill us by starvation too?'.

He said softly. 'Yes, that was the very same thing I thought of.'

'But what can we do?' I asked him.

'I don't know yet but I will think of something,' then he said; 'First we will eat, but after that who knows.'

I wasn't quite sure what he meant by 'but after that who knows'. Did he mean tonight? After eating tonight? I wasn't game to ask him.

He then told me that he had purchased meals before meeting me that afternoon and brought them back to the apartment, and that was why he was late meeting with me. He called out to the Cooler and instructed it to cook the meal. We don't have a Cooler at home, as we have Mata.

After eating I went to get up from the dining chair, but the alcohol in the wine had taken some effect, so I sat back down abruptly. I realised I wouldn't be able to get home tonight without him helping me.

'Do you think I could stay here tonight?' I asked him quietly, not knowing if I wanted to, but felt I needed to be safe. 'Maybe I can use your spare room or I can sleep on the couch whatever is easiest?'

He didn't answer immediately, but then said; 'Of course, you can. Would you like to shower before retiring?'

'That would be good.' I then realised the bathroom was behind his bed in his bedroom. OK, I thought if I could handle surviving The Carrion, I could handle that too. He looked at me. 'There is a bed already made up in the second bedroom and it has its own bathroom if you are wondering.'

That is good I thought, and after saying goodnight I made my way toward the second bedroom. I closed the door and noticed there was no lock. I disrobed, stepped in the shower to let the warm water cascade over me, and used the soap dispensers in the wall alcove within the shower space.

After drying myself off, felt I had sobered up a little and noticed a robe lying on the bed that was not there before. Carlyle must have come in and left it there whilst I was showering, but he hadn't come into the shower. I did not know whether to feel disappointed or relieved.

I opened the bedroom door to see if he was still up, or had gone to bed himself, however he was standing over the kitchen counter. He had a robe on and I could see he was looking at the journal I had given to him and thought he was writing something as he had the pencil poised over the book. I said hello to attract his attention. He turned around saw me and smiled so I thanked him for the robe. He then asked me if I wanted to see what I had written in the journal so far, and said I would as long as there was nothing bad written about me. He smiled again; 'No, well not yet anyway.'

I moved over towards him, and he stepped out of the way I could tell that he had showered too as his hair was damp with the aroma of the same lather that I had used myself. I then saw his robe was gaping a little and didn't know if he was wearing anything under it.

I didn't know what to feel about that too, so I tightened the sash around mine and started to read. I saw that he had added to yesterday's entry, but the spelling and grammar were still atrocious.

My Jurnal –dai 1 18<u>th</u>

Helo. This is mee. I amm Carlyle. I dunt know wot to rite.

Marty brutha – 20 summers? Kilby brutha – 24 summers? Do they work? Sister?

Mother and Father still alive – yes. What do they think I am?

Can I convinc them I am not? I must lern to driv the Zoops better.

I like it when Zamiro larfs.

I like it when she smils. I just lik it.

My Jurnal –dai 2 19<u>th</u>

Love.

I finished reading as there wasn't much there and wondered what he meant by the phrase, 'What do they think I am,' on Day 1…and why one single word, 'Love' was written on Day 2 and wanted to correct the sentence about.

'What do they think I am' to 'Who do you think I am.' I mentioned this to him.

He told me though that is what he meant. I thought that was odd as the grammar is incorrect. 'Nothing yet in Day 3?' I said looking at him.

'Nope, today is not over yet and neither is the night' he answered as he looked back over to me and smiled.

Just what was that supposed to mean? I thought but said: 'You intrigue me, Carlyle.'

I turned back into my bedroom closing the door behind me, looked again at the handle on the door and confirmed my initial realisation there was no lock. He must have realised what I was doing as I heard him call out: 'There is no lock on the door if you are wondering.'

I gathered my clothing from where I had left it on the floor and piled it up against the closed door. I slept very well as I felt safe with Carlyle.

When I woke early the next morning the sun was not quite up, so I crept out of the apartment, took the stairs down all eleven flights, grabbed a Zoop and arrived home at Yelnu Berg before my own family had arisen.

Chapter 16 Aya

Early afternoon; Sunday 21ˢᵗ December: 'Hey Axa, do you know how I can access archives from seven years ago?' I asked my ER partner as we had just finished reviewing the database of downloaded reports into yesterday's events at the pond. Whilst the boy's body was not recovered, it was concluded that he had drowned. The case file will remain open/unsolved until such time it can be proven otherwise.

'I met with Howard up there again this morning,' Axa said back to me instead and I didn't know if he was ignoring my last question or just didn't know.

'Oh, how did that go?'

'The boy did indeed jump into the lake. That was a given, but what happened from there is anybody's guess.'

'Was The Carrion in the water then?'

'We don't know, but I did find small traces of the metallic substance around the edges of the water. It could be a co-incidence as it could be traces of a previous Carrion Frenzy, rather than something newer.'

'Any record of one up ever up there though?'

'Well no, but that doesn't mean it never happened.'

'So Carrion could be in the water then?' I followed up with. He responded. 'I guess, but we will never know.'

'Maybe we should just drain the pond to see what turns up.' I thought to myself, then said it out aloud.

'I've thought of that, and yep we already have the approval,' He continued, 'I am going back there later this afternoon if you want to come, also have an ER Recovery Team coming with drainers as we are going to pump the water out of the pond, divert it around and then run The Flush through the cement drain.'

'Sounds like a plan.'

I stood up and decided to grab some lunch as it was going to be a long day, When I returned we drove back to the river together in the duo shuttle, arriving a couple of hours before dusk. It was a cloudless day; the sun was golden in the sky and we stood next to the pond, watching The ER Recovery Team setting everything up.

They had blocked off the pond where it drained back into the water, and four large hoses had been dropped in the water at various intervals. The sunny day meant the generators running the pumps would be more effective. More sun meant more power.

One of the ERs came over to us saying it should take about an hour depending on what was in there. I looked into the western golden sun, and I thought that it should mean we would be finished just before dusk. I mentioned this to my partner.

'Whatever, but there are no Carrion in these parts anyway,' he responded.

'I hope so,' muttering to myself.

The pumps then kicked in, the water began flowing through the hoses, and then the ear-piercing siren from The Flush started sounding. I yelled over the noise to my partner. 'I forgot about that.'

He yelled back at me: 'Me too.'

The draining process was taking longer than expected due to the thickening of the water as we came closer to the bottom of the pond, and there was a flurry and flapping of fish and eels, but nothing resembling The Carrion monster that Carlyle had mentioned.

As the siren from The Flush was giving me a headache, I indicated to Axa and the other crew members I was going over to the shuttle to be away from the noise of the pumps. I climbed inside and the noise lessened significantly.

After taking a swig from my water bottle I closed my eyes. I had fallen asleep temporarily, and upon opening my eyes noticed the pumps had stopped, but the siren was still sounding. The ER crew were all assembled within the drained pond itself. I considered that could be dangerous, as I was the only one up here on the lookout for The Carrion.

'Over here', I heard one of them call out from down within the drained pond but when I climbed out of the shuttle just happened to look up towards the western setting sun. It was nearing dusk and I knew it was dangerous for us to still be outside. Then I heard another noise above everything else. The Carrion had arrived. They were flying in on the golden western setting sun and were a long way from where they had ever been seen previously.

I climbed out of the shuttle but slipped on the ground, and found myself face down in the slew from the pond water that had muddied the surroundings. I tried to get up but went down again. I tried to get up again, but it was futile, it was hopeless. I must get to the pond to warn them. I couldn't move, so rolled over onto my back on the ground, and with my back in the mud yelled out loudly in frustration. The siren from The Flush was still blaring so they could not have heard me.

I lay on the ground and started thumping at my Wrist Logger, hitting it as hard as I could - perhaps someone in the pond would notice that I managed to activate my Emergency Responder, or perhaps someone, somewhere else would too. I managed to roll onto my stomach and rested on my elbows, then looked over to the group of men standing in the pond. I could just see their heads, but they were yet to look up, yet to see they were in danger, yet to see The Carrion flying within the western setting sun towards them.

I had to make my own choice as I could die here today, so I scrambled, sloshed and slithered my way back into the shuttle and closed the door, shutting my eyes tight. I held my hands over my ears and kept perfectly still. I had heard The Carrion can sense movement.

The seven were trapped in the pond. I saw them all look up at the noise. They'd finally seen The Carrion, and then it started. The Frenzy.

I could hear muffled screaming above the noise of The Flush siren, and The Carrion swooped in and out of the crater left by the emptied pond. Any hope of them surviving had been thwarted by the soft muddied pond floor and slippery sides.

The Frenzy lasted about twenty minutes.

I eventually opened my eyes and watched The Carrion fly away through the window of the shuttle, and waited another fifteen long minutes before I willed myself to move. As I climbed out, I noticed that the slurry around me was stained red with the blood of the ER crew and my friends. I looked down and saw a nameplate in the mud a couple of steps away. 'Axa' it read. There were chunks of body mass and flesh everywhere. A bloodied severed arm, and what appeared to be part of a head was lying on the ground above the drained pond.

I slowly made my way over there. It was the longest thirty metres I had ever walked.

I took a deep breath and looked down. It was a bloodied massacre and there were no survivors as I had suspected. I heard a noise behind me and turned quickly thinking that The Carrion may have returned, or that The Carrion were still here, but was relieved as it was a new group of ER who had intercepted my distress call.

I felt my legs gave way and collapsed to the ground.

A little time later I had composed myself enough to make it down into the crater left by the drained pond. I could not leave just yet and had to look for myself. I wanted to know what had they all seen, and why had they all climbed into the empty pond.

Why do they all have to die today?

It was darker now and the second team had set up lighting all around the pond and plugged into the generator, and whilst the bloodied body parts had mostly been removed, a blood-red mist had settled over the bottom of the pond.

I made my way through the muddy, bloody pond floor

to where a flag had been placed by one of the second team, and then I saw it. Carlyle was right, it was a Water Carrion. It was in the pond and had the boy in its maw. I could see from the composition of the head of the Water Carrion that water would flush and flow through it. The boy's feet were still visible in its throat, his torso was visible further down its gullet. I assumed The Water Carrion was dead as much as a robot could die.

'Did it drown?' I heard someone say behind me, as a couple of the ER Recovery Team had now climbed down into the pond with me.

'Nope,' I said grimacing. 'It looks like it suffocated, choked on the boy.'

'Nope,' came another voice from behind me, 'It can't choke as it is a robot. It looks like someone zapped it with a Taser, they used the electrical current.' The other Responder stated solemnly.

I looked down into the mud and could see what he was referring to. It was Axa's Taser. This is the only weapon that ERs are permitted to carry to defend themselves against a threat. The Tasers only provide enough of a jolt to slow down a Ground-Dweller and are ineffective against the Am-nimates, as the beasts are too large. I do not yet have one as I am not yet senior enough.

It appeared Axa had used the additional power from the generator to create an electrical pulse to kill it. I followed the muddied snake of a power extension line across the ground and into the pond. Good idea I thought - whilst these little Tasers are not powerful enough to stop a Carrion, the more senior ERs have begun to manipulate the circuits within the

Taser unit to enable it to generate a stronger electrical pulse. It is dangerous, but effective.

'At least we know how to stop them now.' I said to the men standing with me.

One of them looked at me and said softly 'But only if they are already on the ground and in this case stuck in the mud.' To which we nodded in agreement.

As I went to move off felt my foot had become stuck in the soft mud, so I pulled my foot out with a little effort, and as I began to turn around noticed something pink next to my boot. It appeared to be a muddied severed hand.

'Do you have a baggie?' I called over to the nearest ER man, and he threw me a folded waxed bag that we use to collect evidence. I pulled tongs from my breast pocket and squatted down to collect it, and upon raising it from the mire recognised the three-ring golden and silver band. It was Howard's severed hand.

We then climbed up and out of the pond by using the ladders that had now been set up for access. I finally went home and cried for Howard, Bernie, Axa, my team, and the challenge that now lies ahead of all of us.

The Carrion can fly and are now in the water.

Chapter 17 Marty

Mid-morning, Sunday 21st December: 'Another day at work another day closer to....do we get paid enough to do this?' I said looking over to Kilby as he climbed out of the shuttle at the first checkpoint on the way into the AIC.

'Shush!' he quickly retorted twirling his pointed finger in the air. He remained sitting in the shuttle having to watch me go through the routine of getting out, holding my pass on the black panel, smiling for the camera, and then getting back in to drive along to the second checkpoint.

'They see all, they hear all!' he said with a deadpan face.

We then went through all the other checkpoints, entered the AIC building and positioned ourselves on the assembly line as another shift started. The setup of the assembly line meant that we never saw the previous team as we arrived through a door at the top of the assembly line, and the other team immediately exited through a door at the other end.

There is no need for communication between the teams either as The AIC takes care of everything here, and we had even tried leaving notes on scrap paper just to say hello, but this was a breach of the AIC rules too and if a note was ever found it would mean instant dismissal. I noticed an anomaly on one of the chips on the plate coming towards Kilby as it appeared to be doubled up and out of alignment, so I nodded at him.

He motioned for me to take a tool from the box by my side. It is here in this section that Kilby could manipulate the speed of the line, so it slowed, and I carefully plucked the chip using the tool and placed it in my hand. We were supposed to report these anomalies as there was a strict procedure to follow, so I looked over to Kilby.

He then casually looked up and around as he had noticed earlier that the one camera on us had not been rotating on its usual axis today, and normally he would need to report this too. I expected he would later. He again motioned to me to close my hand on the chip, then said simply, 'Stretch.'

Some words were allowed while working on the line, never sentences, single words as sentences were against AIC policy too. I understood what he meant. I stretched, raised my arms simultaneously above my head, clasping my fingers together and surreptitiously dropped the chip into the gap between the nape of my neck and my shirt. I felt it stop somewhere in between the shirt and my lower back. I moved slightly sideways, then to and fro in the chair, and nodded in confirmation back to Kilby.

Our shift ended without any more incidents or misaligned chips, and we casually made our way back past the checkpoints. We did not dare say anything to each other about the discovery.

There was a shuttle swap-over station not far from home, so upon delivering the duo shuttle there, we made our way back on foot making sure I avoided any sudden moves in case the chip shifted. It was still stuck to my back.

About halfway back home Kilby told me to stop, and I realised we could not take the chip home with us as it would be dangerous for our family, especially if we were caught with it in our possession.

'We need a sanctuary,' Kilby said quietly to me, 'Somewhere safe, somewhere The AIC cannot hear us or see us.'

'Any ideas?'

'No.'

'OK, how long do you think it will stay there? In your shirt?'

'As long as I don't take my shirt off, it will stay there.' I rolled my shoulders and muscles in my back, 'Nope it is not moving.'

We made it home, entered the house and sat down at the dining table but as I had sat down gingerly Fata noticed. 'Something happened at work today boys?' he asked looking over to us.

'Nope', replied Kilby quickly. 'Why do you ask? Has someone been here?'

'No, it is just Marty has not slumped back into his chair like he usually does when he sits down and looked like he may have hurt his back.'

'No, I'm good', I said, trying not to look guilty.

Fata continued. 'OK then. I went back to the Book Storage Archive Building in the central Berg today. Did you know they have managed to rebuild it as well and many of the books were since The AIC tried to destroy it way back when?'

We looked at each other, big deal I thought.

'And the cement bunker saved a lot of the oldest stuff too.'

'Bunker, what bunker?' Kilby said.

'In the Book Storage Building…..you know the library, that building near the markets. I was reading about the bunker.' Fata continued. 'It was impregnable by The AIC. They could not get anything through the walls and there aren't any cameras in there. Nothing but old books and stored stuff.'

I lifted my head towards Kilby and nodded, then he beckoned me to follow him out of the room, and when we stopped in the foyer area. 'I think we just found our sanctuary.'

We decided that we couldn't wait, so a little time later made our way into the city Berg and knew where we were going, as we had both been to the Library years ago as school students. We found our way in and saw the entrance to the bunker.

I was still walking a little awkwardly in an attempt not to dislodge the bounty when we ventured into the large cement space. I looked around. There were rows of books, rows of shelves and separate rooms off the main corridor, it was huge, was solid and was perfect.

We knew it was what we were looking for, but what do we do now?

Chapter 18 Carlyle

Early morning; Sunday 21st December: I wanted to spend the day with Zamiro. I needed to feel that there was something better, that there was something that made everything better, and for me, she did although I going to spend the night with her that still scared me a little too.

I learnt from Ground-Dwellers during the 2030s when the implementation of Artificial Intelligence was in its infancy, the machines were infiltrating the communication networks and taking control of the communication satellites.

The AIC wanted to rule by eliminating knowledge.

It had learned knowledge is power, and it wanted to dominate the access to knowledge, so it was decided by The GOD around that time, to completely disassemble the integrated communication networks. All mobile communication systems were shut down, all the communications satellites were destroyed, and wireless communication was being phased out. Edi-Aleda was returning to the old format of cables and wires. I have also learnt since that The AIC have launched their satellites, and to what end they had no idea.

I arranged for an old-style telephone installed in my apartment, as I needed to do something to keep busy. The installers were not associated with The AIC and told me The AIC was the bane of their existence. They told me they had teams of specialist working on their systems to ensure every firewall was impenetrable.

I had no idea what that all meant, but they sounded convincing. I just wanted it installed as the telephone would give me access to Zamiro when I could not meet with her. The installers told me there is a list of Berg households that have a telephone, although it was against their policy to disclose contact details due to privacy issues. I didn't understand that either but convinced them that she was related to me and that I would be provided with the number. I also mentioned it enabled them to test the implementation.

It had worked on them, and the telephone call worked too, as when I called Zamiro, was surprised she answered. I didn't know what to say to her as it was confusing to talk to someone so far away as you could not see their reaction. I fumbled my way through the conversation and eventually terminated the call.

I remembered hesitating when I asked if she would like to see where I lived, so I gave her directions to follow from her berg to mine and hoped that it too was not confusing for her. I don't think I said goodbye at the end of the call, and this is expected it is protocol and good manners. I know there is so much for me to learn even about the new telephone. I thought about what I could do with Zamiro today.

I want her to be near me and want her to help me make decisions that we can make together so thought about what would impress her. I hadn't thought of anything specific so asked her to meet me at a Special Stones Jeweller halfway down the street that is near my apartment complex.

We could meet there as I might be able to replace the watch instructions book that the ER had retained as evidence yesterday but realised as the timepiece operates by V.O.C, I didn't need the book. I went to the Jeweller shop to make sure it was open, then purchased some food and took it back to my apartment just in case Zamiro decided to dine with me.

Perhaps we could look for The Carrion if she stayed long enough.

I decided to purchase some wine too, as the sugar in the fruit ferments creating the alcohol, however, alcohol can make a person lose their inhibitions. I might have the opportunity to learn more about her. I wondered if she had had much experience with wine. I was a little late getting back to the Jeweller after dropping the wine and food at my apartment and hoped that she hadn't left.

I saw her from across the road and could not resist smiling at her when I got closer, and could not resist embracing her either. I remembered the feeling when Howard and I did yesterday. It felt warm and safe and made me think that everything would be alright, even just for that one single moment.

As we went back to my apartment we were accosted by The Represent I had met yesterday, he mentioned his name was Hawke when I introduced him to Zamiro, but he was dismissive to us as he was only interested in finding Flighters. I showed her my apartment, to the view, and she realised that when I am home I can see into the western sun every night and can watch for The Carrion.

The Carrion did come tonight but were flying high. I felt I knew where they were going, and suspected they were going to Munna Cliffs. This was the first time I saw them going beyond the environs of Edi-Aleda. This was new and also meant that The AIC had started going somewhere else to reign down their terror.

I hoped that Howard, Aya, Axa and any other Emergency Responders would not be outside this late, although Howard had told me his intention of going back to the site today to say his goodbyes to Bernie. I had no way of contacting them and assumed they were not contactable by telephone.

We ate dinner and Zamiro realised that she was not feeling sober enough to make it home safely, so I offered to accommodate her in my second bedroom. She agreed, and I think she was relieved when I informed her the second bedroom has its own bathroom. Whilst she was showering, I realised that unless I provided a robe for her she would be getting back into the same clothes she wore today. I hoped she would stay as there was much I wanted to tell her. I want to tell her about me, and so much more I want to know about her.

I snuck into her bedroom and fortunately, she was still in the shower room, I placed the robe on the bed. I hesitated momentarily as the bathroom door was slightly ajar. I could just make out her naked form silhouetted in the glass-walled shower and this unsettled me. I should not be in here uninvited. I moved quietly back out of the room, back into my bedroom, showered myself and gathered my robe. I went back into the kitchen and was contemplating writing

something in my journal when she called out from her bedroom door.

Zamiro came over to me and I noticed that my sash had
loosened around my waist, would this entice her or get a reaction? Perhaps it was the wine, perhaps I don't know why at
all, but think she noticed too as she tightened the one around
her waist.

Together we looked through my journal entries but there
still wasn't much in there, and she wanted me to correct the
sentence; 'What do they think I am' to 'Who do you think I
am' but when I told her this is what I meant, she told me that
the grammar was not correct.

I then tried to say something clever when she asked me
about not having an entry for today. 'Nope, the day is not
over yet, and neither is the night.' I cringed after realising
what I had just said to her. I felt ashamed and wanted to take
it back immediately.

Upon hearing that comment, she replied, 'You do intrigue
me Carlyle', then she turned and walked back into the bedroom closing the door behind her. I then heard noises at her
bedroom door and assumed that she was still trying to work
out if it locked realising what she was doing.

I called out: 'There is no lock on the door if you are
wondering.' I then heard her gathering her shoes and saw the
shadow of clothing piled up against the closed door. I didn't
sleep well knowing that Zamiro was so close yet still far from
me tonight.

In the early morning, as the sun was not quite up, I
decided to stand out on the balcony off the living room to

gather my thoughts. I closed the balcony doors behind me to keep out any noise in case Zamiro was still sleeping.

I wanted to apologise to her in the morning once she woke.

I happened to look back in through the glass doors at her bedroom, then saw her creep out of her bedroom and make her way across to the apartment's front door. The door does not lock from the inside as a fire safety measure, so she silently closed it behind her. She must have taken the stairs as I didn't hear the lift arrive. I looked down and saw her exiting the building. Zamiro fobbed a Zoop, climbed aboard and I watched her disappear into the morning mist.

What have I done?

Chapter 19 Creedence

Mid-morning; Monday 22nd December: I am still thinking of my meeting with Carlyle the other night, still wary that I had given up my secret to him but am not sure as I have been so careful to hide that I am Flighter for all my life. I do not want to give it up being so close to my 40th death day, so made a point of using the lifts and stairs, and vowed not to use The Rush at home for the time being.

On the way to work this morning, I noticed a young woman exiting through the stairwell, it was not yet dawn. I had not seen her here before but did mention to her that the lifts were now working. She gave me a little wave as she climbed aboard a Zoop and drove off into the morning mist. I thought she was pretty, and hoped that she lived here now, and as the lifts are now working, it will bring in more tenants.

I also noticed another large man skulking around the apartment block and wondered if he was a Represent, if so, I must avoid him as I wouldn't be able to substantiate I am still not a paying tenant and wondered how I can do this. I also spent time this morning on the roof of the apartment complex finalising the re-aligning of the cameras to point in different directions. They no longer face west. I floated across the building gap opposite and re-aligned those cameras away from my building, allowing me to use The Rush without it being seen. I anchored the cameras with slender metal poles that had been scrounged from my work site and this would prevent the cameras from a complete rotation along the axis. I also calculated a triangulation to disrupt the view to the alley behind the apartment and was convinced I could now safely drop-float without being noticed.

Finally, and almost exhausted, I rode a Zoop to work and arrived around 8 am to start the day. The first shuttles began around that time, so I kept busy cleaning the foyer areas and surrounds. Generally, as Ground-dwellers are proud people there is not much-discarded material or detritus, but when some of the younger Ground-Dwellers get access to alcohol or the Hell of a Nite, that is when the issues are created. The serving of alcohol is strictly governed by The GOD but somehow they manage to get access to it, and they somehow access Helium and Nitrous to create the Hell of Nite concoctions.

I have to also initiate the Shuttle Centre Hologram, and as there is only one other person that cleans the Centre, I often go for days not having seen them at all, however, they might be avoiding me too as I have been told I do not take my role as a cleaner seriously enough. Who knew?

Being a Flighter, I do not need to work but this vocation is just my alibi. I take great delight in turning the operating functions off and on when initiating the Terminus Hologram as it causes something called buffering. It is not supposed to happen to this type of unit, but it means the Hologram starts with a stutter and stammer and it is comical to see. I have not yet been caught doing this.

I kept telling myself I prefer to deal with people, and that I must start taking longer work breaks to meet more of them. I am entitled to fifteen minute breaks every two hours, plus one thirty-minute break during the 12-2 time period, so this means I can accrue the hour in a single period. I justified it to myself and will do this today.

Most patrons that use this centre ignore me entirely, but I am still intrigued as to why Carlyle spoke to me the other day despite his reluctance to use the Hologram. I felt there was something more I needed to know about him. I know he also lives in my apartment block and will endeavour to find out.

I have been busying myself enough to while away the time and notice it is now noon. 'Lunch' I announced loudly but no-one was listening, no-one noticed, and no-one cared. I walked out into the sunshine into another glorious summer day. I had heard they had re-opened the Library, so I headed over there to see what this all meant and what I could learn while I was there.

After purchasing some food, I headed to the newly renovated library but as I was about to enter two men hustled and manhandled me out of their way. 'Sorry,' one said to me, 'We're in a hurry!' I waved them past me with a bow. 'Certainly, and after you', wondering why anyone would be hurrying to get into a building full of books. The books are not going anywhere, and you are not allowed to take the books out of the building.

A little time later I had only partially made my way through the expansive space and noticed there was a corridor leading down to another area, so made my way down there. I saw an open large metal door. It resembled an old bank vault door. I recalled having seen one of these a long time ago when I was a child. It was expansive, floor to ceiling, roughly six metres across, six metres high, at least half a metre thick and also solid steel. I tested it for resistance, and it moved easily on the fulcrum. I looked up at the time disc on the wall above the door and it showed 12.45, and although have been in here for almost an hour I have seen hardly anything.

I decided to venture inside the vault. It is a cement cavern, it is huge and there are rows and rows of stored boxes, so venturing a little further in I saw boxes marked May 2020, June 2020, and July 2020, so moved through the shelving and looked higher up and along them. There were boxes much older, some as old as 1960, 1950, and 1940 and looking a little closer at the boxes saw they were all sealed and was disappointed I could not get access to the contents.

I wondered how I could or if I ever needed to.

Whilst standing by these boxes I heard voices that would not have been audible before as they would have been silenced by my footsteps, so I paused and listened closer. I could make out two voices, but could not quite hear what they were saying, so I crept closer to them. I suspected it was unusual for people to be down here as there is nothing here but sealed boxes. Perhaps there was something else in here?

As I rounded the end of the aisle saw them both as they were sitting opposite each other at a small table, and recognised they were the two men who pushed past me at the entrance. Why were they rushing to get in here? Into this area?

One of them had his shirt opened to the waist, and the other was holding something in his hand. It was small and square. I recognised the colour as he rolled it through his fingers. I wondered where I had seen it before, then realised it was a wrist chip. I had seen a few over the years after a Frenzy. I have found them on the ground when the victims' wrists have been severed, and the chips have been expelled during the carnage.

I watched them as quietly as I could but still wondered why they were there and what are they doing with them. My hand suddenly slipped on the box I was leaning on and it made a noise, then the one holding the chip looked up and at me. I froze.

Chapter 20 Kilby

Around noon; Monday 22nd December: Marty and I decided to heed our advice and headed towards the Library. It was an ideal solution as Fata said it was impenetrable. We would be safe from the prying eyes and ears of the AIC and going to the library would be innocent enough I thought as no one would care. In our haste to get in though we roughly bumped into a man as he was trying to enter along with us, so he waved us both by with a bow and polite hand gesture.

We located the bunker, and Fata was correct in that it was cavernous. There was a solid thick steel door at the entrance, and we assumed that is why The AIC could not destroy the records it contained.

I looked over to Marty as he was still walking awkwardly in an attempt not to dislodge the chip we ventured into the large cement space and looked around for a table or somewhere to sit and eventually moved further to find a suitable option.

'Turn around and unbutton your shirt', I told Marty, 'slowly' I reminded him again, 'Slowly, as we don't want to lose it now.'

Marty sat on the chair to reduce the chance of the chip

falling and carefully peeled his shirt off. It remained in position stuck to the sweat and hairs on his back. I carefully extracted it from him and holding it in my hand sat down on the chair opposite. Marty put his shirt back on, leaving it unbuttoned in case we were interrupted.

I was rolling it thoughtfully and gingerly through my fingers and heard a noise sounding like a scratching along one of the storage boxes. I looked up and another man was standing at the end of the aisle behind Marty. I saw him and froze, and the man froze too.

I nodded to Marty. 'There is someone behind you.'

'Now what do we do? Marty said quietly to me as the man moved towards us.

'What have you got there?' the man said looking at me. 'I know what it is so don't worry about telling me anything otherwise. I have seen them before.'

I stood up and raised my hands in front of Marty to indicate to him I wanted him to stand, and I moved to be by Marty's side. 'What are you going to do about it then?' I asked him, readying myself for a confrontation. Then he did something unexpected, something I had never heard anyone say to me before, as he said: 'It's OK, I am a Flighter and want to help.'

I looked at Marty, who then shrugged and spoke. 'Show us.'

The man pushed his arms down to his sides, clenched his fists and raised his head just as we had heard they were supposed to do but nothing happened. We kept watching, then he began to float slowly from the floor. We watched him rise and he floated to the top of the shelving, then he held onto the top shelf lid to prevent him going any higher and promptly sat down. 'The view from up here is amazing', he said smiling down at us from his makeshift citadel, then he added 'And this place is huge.'

I looked at Marty as the man then climbed down, and held out his hand. 'I am Creedence' he then said introducing himself.

'I am Kilby, and this is my brother Marty.' I was reluctant to give up too much more information about us, but Marty wasn't quite as guarded. I wanted to tell Marty to keep quiet, but Marty told him everything:

He told him that we work in The AIC, told him we work on the assembly line and told him we even go through three checkpoints every day to get in and out. I tried to stop him and maybe I should have, but when he started telling Creedence our Grandparents were harbouring The Forced, I decided that was too much and told him to stop.

'Enough, Marty, enough.'

I looked over at Marty and he looked back at me and said, 'Oops.'

Creedence then looked at both of us. Had he been taking all of this in? He finally said 'I think I have to get back to work now. How can I reach you and what are we going to do now?'

I still didn't know, but he did say the word 'we', so we followed Creedence out of the bunker, but as we neared the steel door by the entrance he asked me to show him the chip again. I was still reluctant. He already knew so much about us, and we already knew so much about him, so I handed it to him.

'Watch this', as he waved the chip over his right wrist, and the chip in his wrist beeped, he then waived the chip over his left wrist and that wrist chip in there beeped also.

'What does that beep mean?' Marty said.

'What it means my new friends, is that I just became someone else.'

I looked at Marty as if we didn't understand. 'Explain.'

'Well, my wrist chips that are currently in here', raising his forearms to us; 'are programmed specifically to me and were just wiped clean. I've just re-set them.'

We looked at each other. 'How do you know that?' Marty asked.

'I have been around many years, seen many things and learnt many things. I'm nearly forty summers,' he replied and continued. 'I've learnt I can virtually disappear for about twelve hours or so, can go off-grid so to speak, then the wrist chips re-set somehow, then goes back to normal. So, by waving someone else's chip over your wrists, one that has been recently implanted, or not implanted as in this case, it seems to temporarily interrupt the circuits.'

'And…when? How did you find this out?' I looked at him suspiciously.

'I discovered this when I once saved a young Ground-Dweller from The Carrion, The Frenzy. He would have barely fifteen summers and would have just had them imbedded into his wrists and the chips had been partially expelled as his both wrists were split open by The Carrion. He died in my arms.'

He went on a little quieter; 'I had used The Rush and carried him out of the Frenzy. I thought he would live, thought I could save him, but I had to leave him to die on an apartment balcony. As I left, I noticed his wrist chips had fallen out during the float and were stuck to my wrists. He had bled out and my arms were covered in his blood. I tried to enter an ER station nearby to let them know but found that my wrist chips were defective. I could not enter the building. I could not get in as the doors did not open. Eventually got someone's attention, but I could not be identified when they scanned me either, so I couldn't be verified. Then I remembered hearing the beeps when I collected the boy, so went to mention it to the ER officer, but realised that this may not be a good idea. I then hesitated and decamped the ER station without offering any explanation. It is dangerous to disclose to even the ER that you are a Flighter, and I realised that I would no longer be tracked by the AIC.'

We were in awe of all of this, and he continued: 'Apparently, the chips can still maintain a charge even though they are outside the body, and even though the fusion between our blood and the chip may be lost, they keep operating. I think this lasts about twelve hours. I don't yet know how or why.'

'Wow,' I said. 'Just how can we use all that?' Marty asked him.

'I don't know yet.'

I hesitated momentarily and realised we had to decide between the chip, my safety, and our family's safety looking over at Creedence knew what to do, I told him to keep the chip. He nodded and said thank you. I trust him with it and I would trust him with my life as he is a Flighter. I believe he may also be a FOO-Flighter.'

We then moved onwards and outwards, and as we finally exited the bunker he turned around to us. I thought he was going to say something, but he simply looked up as there was a clock on the wall above the bunker door and it read 2.45.

'I guess I might need a new job' he said as he began to jog out of the library and left us alone. Together.

Chapter 21 Creedence

Early afternoon; Monday 22nd December: I arrived back at the Shuttle Terminus and noticed it was already 3 p.m. and assumed someone or something would have noticed I had been absent for so long, but no, I was still invisible. I tried to make myself busy, but was distracted by the meeting with Marty and Kilby, and then realised in my haste to return didn't find out how I could get in touch with them.

I found a secure place to secret the bounty on my person as the chip must not be discovered in my possession and must be kept safe. I will keep it safe and vow I will die before revealing how it came to be with me, but I hope it does not come to that. I am no one and no one notices me. I am anonymous. Then I realised that someone does know me, know that I work here, he knows where I live, and that someone is Carlyle. Given that he has found me, will anyone else? The day dragged on and eventually, it was time to leave, nothing and no one contacted me about my absence for those three hours.

Around 7 p.m. I took a Zoop home, but was in a dilemma, what was I going to do now as I had just re-booted my wrist chips and wouldn't be able to get into my apartment? I stood there not knowing what to do. Carlyle happened to be in the foyer of the apartment, and it looked like he had been for exercise somewhere, so I asked him if he had seen The Represent around today.

He said that he hadn't. I was then going to ask him if he knew the pretty woman on the Zoop that I had seen early this morning, however, realised I had other things to deal with.

'You are a tenant aren't you', I said to him.

'Why?'

'How did you register to get an apartment?' then I added. 'It's for a friend if they wanted to become a tenant?'

'You find an empty apartment, hold your wrist chip over the door, and it if opens it is not tenanted, if it doesn't it is.'

'That easy hey?'

'Not quite, as once you have unlocked the apartment door you have to get downstairs and run your wrist chip over the front door entrance panel as it is then it synchronises the apartment that you have moved into.'

I nodded. 'So, I will recognise you as a tenant and then charge the rent to you?'

'Yes, that's about it, but sometimes the process takes over-night to update, but otherwise, it is done.'

I thanked him, and we then went into the lifts together I knew my new chip would not work as it was no longer synchronised to my apartment so asked him to select Floor Five for me.

He looked at me. 'I thought you lived on four?'

'Nope Five.' He looked back at me, 'I must have had it wrong then.'

I stopped on Five and exited the lift. So how do I do this I thought?

I could get into a new apartment easily enough but now can't get back into mine, so I chose another apartment further along the western side. It was Unit 503 and I used to be in Unit 507.

I waved my chip over the lock fortunately it opened, and I was relieved, entered and saw it was the same configuration as my apartment but thought it was a bit bigger. I turned around and went out and down to Apartment 507, tried the lock but it did not open. My re-set chip would not recognise me and not allow access. I stood there wondering what I could do when behind me the elevator chimed open, and a young couple came out carrying boxes.

'Moving in?' I inquired.

'Yes, it's our first apartment together', the female said excitedly; 'Apartment 506 is ours. What about you?'

I introduced myself, 'Creedence' and said was 507 but have shifted today to 503. 'Silly thing though I reset the door lock at 503 and cancelled 507 without realising I could not get my stuff out.'

'Easy peasy our new neighbour,' the young man said looking at me. 'Just use our balcony, it might be dangerous though, moving between the two so don't look down.'

I didn't tell them I would have to break in through the balcony door, but at least I had a plan, and it worked as I managed to get in through the balcony door and then they even helped me relocate.

Once I was inside I went to the apartment door and let myself out. I went downstairs to the foyer to synchronise my wrist to the new apartment, but it did not work exactly as Carlyle had suggested. He had mentioned there may be a time delay, so I went back to my old apartment by stepping across the balconies and climbed into bed.

I then realised I still had the new chip embedded between my bottom cheeks as this is where I had secreted it earlier today. I found a very small metallic case that was ideal for the chip which fitted perfectly. I was able to secure it in place with a small piece of adhesive tape used for repairs at the terminus, so I carefully removed it and placed it inside my pillow. I finally went to sleep wondering how we could use the chip to our advantage, but could not come up with anything.

Chapter 22 Hawke

Early morning; Tuesday 23rd December: I am currently standing across the road from the apartment block where I know that the man known as Carlyle lives and am suspicious of him as he may be a Flighter, but he is a tenant and that confuses me as Flighters do not have to pay to be a tenant. I am a Represent and like the power it gives me. I like that Ground-Dwellers must obey me, but have not yet used The Push to kill a Ground-Dweller, nor have I yet dropped a Flighter from a building to see if they can float or die.

Maybe today is the day.

I kept watching the entrance and noticed a man waving his wrist across the panel unit. It does not seem to be reacting, and this may mean two things: that he might not live here, or that he might not have his chips correctly embedded. This can happen sometimes, but it is rare, but not rare enough to lose my interest in him.

I made my way across the road and thought I recognised him as a tenant, although I had never scanned his wrist for confirmation. He may be a Flighter, so I quickened my stride and made my way across the road. Unfortunately, a shuttle suddenly turned the corner almost running into me. I had to wait for it to pass and as it is taller than me, I lost sight of my quarry. Its passing took longer than I hoped, and when looked for the man again he was gone. I didn't believe the elevator door had opened, as he could be my first Flighter, my first Push.

I moved towards the foyer area and looked upwards. Did I see something high above me? I looked again but it was just a curtain moving in the wind. I entered the foyer and looked around to see that he was only just now entering the elevator. What had delayed him?

He had his back to me, so I called out 'Oi' and he turned to me and looked panicked. He looked at me again, then turned his back and started pushing the elevator buttons again. They were not responding, so he stepped out of the foyer area. I was prepared for him to make a run to try to avoid me, so I casually made my way backwards to the entrance doors, leaned against them and was standing across the only exit. He was trapped.

'My chip does not seem to work this morning', he claimed.

'Well, if you are a Flighter it would let you into the build-ing, but not into the elevator now would it?' I said to him whilst crossing my arms over my chest. I even widened my stance to appear overbearing to him. 'Your move', I then said to him with a grin. I have finally got one, but then he came over to me and put out his hand.

'Creedence, Apartment 503.'

'Oh yeah sure. I have not seen you here before, and I see your wrist chips are not working.' I shook his hand anyway. He looked at his wrists. 'I don't know why.'

I looked at him thinking good try, so I reached behind me, and he looked even more anxious as I pulled my mobile scanner from my belt clip. He looked at it, then I grabbed his arm quickly, scanned it and nothing happened.

I scanned it again, again nothing. 'OK, Creedence looks like we are going for a little ride.' I wrapped my arm around his neck and held him in a headlock, but he tried to move anyway. 'Keep trying', I said to him as I ruffled his hair with my other hand. I pushed Level 5 and it chimed as we arrived. We stepped out. He had not tried to move again.

'Apartment 503 hey?' as we made our way towards it.

'I can scan, it will…it will let me in', he said with a muffled voice from under my arm. I let him go, but held the back of his shirt whilst he tried the door, but when he scanned it opened. I was surprised and opened the door. He was still trying to evade me though, so I stepped in and followed closely behind him.

'Nice place, Flighter', I said to him.

'I am not!' he replied quickly.

'So how can you afford a place like this then? A Flighter doesn't pay rent. A Flighter is not a tenant. You cannot spend The GODs money quickly enough?'

'Try again,' he says offering up his wrist again to me, so I do, and nothing happens again. I was again surprised as we had managed to get through the door. He moved around in the apartment, so I maneuvered him towards the balcony and got the balcony doors open by moving around him. He then moved towards the balcony too and I was not expecting that. I manhandled him closer to the rail.

We both looked out to the sea, then down to the ground, and I realised that as we were five floors up, he might survive if he could drop-float. If he is a Ground-Dweller, I will get the mop and bucket when I get down there. Not my problem.

He looked down now too and must have realised what I was thinking. 'Over,' I said to him, 'Climb over, or I throw you over. Your choice.' He looked at me and started to climb the balcony rail. 'What did you say your name was, Flighter?' I said pulling my notebook from my jeans pocket.

'Creedence.' He said.

'So, do you reckon you will make it?'

'I don't know.'

He was now over the rail and his feet were tucked into the railing holding him there, has arms were bent back behind him, and it looked like he was holding on for his life. I guess he was, and he looked genuinely scared.

Maybe he is a Ground-Dweller after all, so he waited, and I waited too. 'Got anything to drink?' I asked him as I turned around and went back inside. 'We might be here a while' I said, grinning at him, 'so don't go anywhere'.

'Yes I have, and no I won't.' He said.

I headed over to his cooler, opened it and saw he had wine and beer, it was fully stocked. 'Nice.' I grabbed a pancake from the shelf and folded it into my mouth, however, as I turned around to ask him if he wanted anything he was gone.

'Shit!' I exploded into a sprint towards the balcony, looked up and could see movement above me. I realised I was right as he was a Flighter and got away. I then saw movement below me and saw Creedence climbing down onto the balcony below. He had swung himself inwards from the rails and dropped onto the next floor level below.

'Nice try smart guy,' I called down to him, 'and unless you can break in through those doors you are not going anywhere.' I rushed through his apartment, ran down the passage into the stairwell, and took the steps three at a time to burst out the fire door to Level 4. I have been through this building many times and know which apartment he is in, and just as I got to the door of Unit 403, he opened it.

'Badman. Breaking and entering, I said smugly. I grabbed him again but suddenly his wrist chip beeped. I stopped, then he stopped. 'Try now, smart guy', he said smugly back to me.

So, still holding him by his shirt I extracted my mobile scanner from my belt behind me and scanned him and it scanned and read: 'Creedence, Tenant Unit 503.'

I had to let him go as he is a tenant, and a Ground-Dweller, but I was not letting him go that easily, so we then rode the elevator back down to the ground, and I left him there alone in the foyer as I hurried from the building.

Chapter 23 Carlyle

Dusk; Monday 23rd December: I had slept most of the morning and had walked around my Berg most of the day just trying to wrestle with my thoughts. I am so disappointed in myself for having commented to Zamiro, what a stupid thing to say to her, 'The day is not over yet, and neither is the night' and am not sure if she will reconcile with me. If my every waking moment and most of my night dreams are spent thinking about her, when will I see her again now? Why do I feel this way when she is near?

It must mean something and am not sure if it is love, but it is my love and does hope it is love as it is a wonderful feeling, although a Flighter does not get to fall in love with a Ground-Dweller. It is not supposed to happen as we are too different, but we are still so much alike.

I made my way onto the roof of my apartment; the sun was golden in the sky and an ideal time for The Carrion tonight, so I would sit and wait. I looked around and noticed something peculiar about the roof cameras; none of them were now facing west. They were either facing inwards or facing east. I looked to another and this one was facing downwards to the alley between the buildings and not into the alley, so as

I got closer saw the others on the top of the building across across the way were not facing west either. Had The AIC done this? I wondered why.

I then saw something jutting up against the side of the camera nearest my location, it was a slender steel rod, so I moved over to it find that it was firmly wedged against the camera struts and to the roof edge. I attempted to pull it from the position, then realised it was preventing the camera from doing a full rotation along its axis. It also meant the camera was not able to point downwards into the alley below.

I wondered why that would be.

I decided to leave them as they were and moved to the western edge of the roof and look out to the sea. It is a beautiful blue, and the sky is clear. I believe I can almost see across the sea to the land on the other side, the land I left so many years ago as this was my Berg Munta. This was where I used to live with my parents, my family and friends.

Now they are all gone.

I still miss them, miss the farm, miss my friends and this is when I met my first and only girlfriend, Mel. I looked down at my wrists: Why did they all come across the sea that day to see me receive my wrist chip implants? Was this why they all died? The AIC killed them. The Carrion killed them. It was my fault.

I was interrupted by a noise from down below me, it was a soft scraping noise and sounded like someone was scaling the building, so I peered over the edge and could see some-one slowly floating upwards to me. They must be a Flighter. They had their back to the wall of the building, and it was their back against the building stucco making a soft scraping noise. They were looking to the western sun and were probably looking for The Carrion too. It was amazing to see this as I have never seen another Flighter in action. It was then I realised it was Creedence.

I kept still as hopefully he didn't see me, and he was now getting closer. He raised his arms above his head but still, he didn't look up to me or the roof. I assumed he'd done this before as he got closer to the roof, he went to grab the rail pipe running along the edge. I stepped quietly out of the way as he came closer to the rail, but he was still not looking up, he still had his back to the building, looking westward.

As he came closer to the rail I thought his timing was a little off as his hands were not quite aligned. He missed the rail and softly floated past it, the rail was now by his waist, then past his knees, and he was looking behind him, but it was all too late I thought. He still hadn't seen me.

He tried franticly to bend down to grab the rail, but it was out of reach now. He started to panic and tried to slow his float, but there was nothing you could do. I have almost been there before myself. There were no more structures above us.

It was then I decided to move forward and grabbed both his legs with my hands. He stopped floating, stopped moving, and looked down at my hands around his shins. I think he just realised someone had just saved his life. I pulled him down to the roof platform and moved him towards one of the air conditioning units. He looked at me.

'Hello Creedence, it looks like I just saved your life.'

'I, yes…thanks, I guess,' he stammered in response, then sat down next to me.

'I guess you know that I am a Flighter.' he then said quietly.

'I would say so', smiling at him, although I didn't know what he was going to say or do next as I have never known what to do myself had I ever revealed my ability.

'Thanks… but I have said thanks already though haven't I?'

'Yes, you have.'

'You know I am nearing my 40th birthday. I have never been caught. I have always been careful…. damn that stupid Hawke….Damn, his stupid attempt to throw me off the building.'

'When?'

'This morning. I followed your instructions and unlocked the door, went down and synchronised my chips to the apartment but the chips didn't work properly so he grabbed me in a headlock and pulled me through the apartments. He then took me to my balcony and was willing me to use The Rush. I disappointed him when I didn't. I climbed down the balcony to the apartment below, into 403 but he beat me to the door on the way out. Then my chip worked.'

'Why did you do that? Are you saying you became a paying tenant just to confuse The Represent? Just because you pay rent to The GOD is enough to fool them?' I said to him already knowing that is exactly what I am already doing.

'Yes. It worked too, so if you know any Flighters, they could use it to fool The Represents. I am a Flighter, so I don't have to pay rent.'

I nodded. 'Mm, if only I knew a Flighter.'

We sat there quietly for a little while longer, and he eventually asked what had brought me up to the roof. I explained I like to watch for The Carrion, but I didn't mention the misdirected cameras.

'Good night for it, ideal for The Carrion', and no sooner had he said it than we saw them in the western golden setting sun, but there were not many tonight, probably only around ten or so.

I nodded to them. 'Smaller swarm. I wonder why?'

'A recon swarm. They do this sometimes when they want to look at a site before they come back with the bigger one.'

'So, what is on tonight that they are going to?'

We both stood up and moved over to the eastern side of the roof scanning the area below, then he scanned the horizon. 'I think I know; it is the new arena; The GOD is building it for the games on the 25th but it is not finished. I was there last week',

He pointed over towards it. It was due east, and if The Carrion attacked there tonight they still have the sun behind them.

'Why there then?' I asked him.

'The lights are on.' I pointed to the large banks of overhead lights shining downwards into the arena and I could now see the light poles in the distance.

'Someone must be rehearsing something'.

'How far?... Do you think we can get before them and warn them?' I said looking towards the arena.

'Maybe twenty minutes, but we will not beat The Carrion there. We might be able to warn Ground-Dwellers that are still out in the open, so we have to go there, he said with determination. 'Are you in?' he then said looking at me.

'Yes, but how can we get there quickly?'

We made our way downstairs via the elevators, and on

the way down he looked at me. 'I will use The Rush, but you will have to take a Zoop. Can you use them?'

I looked at him, 'Yes', but thought maybe I might use The Rush too.

We exited through the foyer doors and made our way into the alley running alongside the building and he said to me 'See you there.' He then initiated The Rush and floated to the building across the street, and I realised why the cameras on the roof were not pointing into this alleyway. He uses The Rush from here, and this explains why he hadn't been caught.

I could see that he was a veteran, using his ability as he ducked and weaved around trees. I was in awe. He also kept himself much longer in the air as I could, and soon was well out of sight. I looked around, do I risk it myself? I moved out of the alley back to the street but could not see a Zoop so waited a bit longer realising The Rush was my only option, and began to initiate it, but suddenly there was a silver flash coming round the corner at me and it was a young boy on a Zoop.

He looked at me and I was fortunately able to stop the process. 'Yo bro', he said, 'beach', as he dumped the Zoop on the ground in front of me waving his pointed finger towards the sea, as he walked out of the alley.

A Zoop I thought, great, but it wasn't as I then realised the boy was too young to have been able to wrist hire the Zoop as you need to be over fifteen summers. I looked down at the motor-less scooter, placed one foot on the metallic plate and began swiping the ground with the other. At least I was moving, but it was too slow. I had moved only about five hundred metres and realised it was not going to get me there in time.

I needed to use The Rush.

I stopped, looked around re-initiated it and thought about the manoeuvres that Creedence had used. They too were working for me as I could now speed up and slow down as I needed to. It was such an achievement. I was moving so much freer than I had done before and arrived at the arena much quicker than I thought. I wasn't seen either, so I drop-floated down to the entrance area and could see The Carrion was now circling in the sky above. I had not seen them do this before and as I looked up noticed Creedence sitting high above me on the roof watching them.

I could also see that although the sides of the arena were incomplete, the big metal sliding doors that would be enveloping the arena were not yet in place and the roof that was supposed to be fully sealed was still half open. The 25th was still days away. The electrified canopy net that was to cover the roof was not in place either, and this meant the arena was not yet able to be fully sealed.

I hoped The Carrion would not use all of these deficiencies to their advantage.

Creedence then saw me and drop-floated down and he landed gracefully next to me. 'You made it, found a Zoop then?'

'Yep', I nodded assuming he was too distracted to notice that there was not a Zoop anywhere near me. 'What now?' I asked him.

'We go inside and wait.'

We went inside, and his assumption was correct, as there

was a rehearsal event tonight, but fortunately, there were only about twenty Ground-Dwellers in there including nine children. As we made it down the cement central aisle that led to the grassy field, he nodded up to the second-tier level. 'I wonder what they are doing up there?'

He pointed to a ring of men and women standing within the tiers around the arena above and around us. They were surrounding us, up above us and all up above the grassy pitch where the Ground-Dwellers were going through the impromptu rehearsal routine. Creedence and I further studied the inside of the arena and could see that the roofing had large hexagons of transparent glass. I realised they would allow the light from the massive light towers to shine through once the roof was sealed.

The light was then refracted through glass hexagons of large prisms contained within them. 'Clever', I said to Creedence then continued with my observations: 'The glass prisms disburse the light to most of the stadium and that also means that The Carrion will not be using the roof to come in and they will have to enter from somewhere else.'

I focused in on the skylights high above me and could see that blinds were running across them as well, which also meant the sunlight could be shut completely if required, and also meant that the whole arena could be kept in darkness, in shadow when needed. I motioned to Creedence.

'Do you want to check them out?' and pointed upwards to the skylight. 'You could see if they are toughened enough to withstand a Carrion onslaught.'

He looked at me. 'You want me to use The Rush?'

I shook my head. 'Yes, but maybe later.'

Creedence nodded. 'I've seen something else up there too', and then he told me about glass-walled sentry boxes that are scattered around various parts of the roof. 'I assume they are there to watch for The Carrion.'

I nodded in confirmation. 'So, if we can see them coming how can we stop them from getting in?'

'Don't know, but we can limit their access options into the arena when they do.'

I looked around and then saw that there was a gap of about fifteen metres below us where the rays of the golden setting sun were streaming through, and that's not good I thought, so we made our way down there. The massive doors were still open and I went over to one and tried to push it. I realised there was a roller track at the top of the door, and one below was embedded in the cement flooring. It moved very easily; just as large barn doors do. I realised that there were currently only two doors in place, and the expansive gap would need four doors to fully seal the space.

We then went outside and heard the noise from The Carrion, so we rushed back in and stood on either side of the cement passage entry opposite each other, and waited. Then it started. The Frenzy.

The Carrion had peeled from their circle high above the arena and split into two groups, half flew straight down, and the other half flowed down flying past us through the open corridor next to us. They flew through the golden gap of sunshine left by the gap of the un-sealable, open doors that we had just come through ourselves. The children saw them first and then the adults, but it was all too late, then we saw movement from the ring of men and women up in the tiers.

They began drop-floating towards the field. They were all Flighters, most likely FOO and The Flighters retaliated. They worked as a team and began fighting back. Flighters are all working with each other.

I had never seen this, and it was working they were winning as many of The Flighters knew instantly how to kill The Carrion: One foot on the neck and holding its head in their hand, they made the wrenching movement to sever the electrical impulse to its robotic brain.

Some of the children were being saved by The Flighters albeit one at a time, but it was happening too slowly. I wanted to do something. I wanted to help so went to move but Creedence held my arm.

'Don't... unless you're a Flighter you would not survive. Are you a Flighter Carlyle?' he asked. I nodded slowly, and hopefully, he read this as my agreement that I was not able to assist, rather than my admission that I am a Flighter.

I saw one of the men grab two children at once and hand them to a Flighter. They clung onto her, but the weight was too much though as she could not float up. I could see she was trying to initiate The Rush as she rose a little off the ground, but then landed flat back on her feet.

The Carrion saw this too, so they attacked her splitting her head open with a swift swipe of their beaks, and then as their talons split her chest open, she collapsed to the ground. The children too, were soon consumed by The Frenzy. I noticed then a cluster of The Carrion not moving, not getting involved and they were simply standing idle so I nodded to Creedence showing him.

'What are they doing? Are they waiting for something?'

'No, they are in shadow, it is the arena, the tiers and the roof, they are casting a shadow over those three Carrion. I have seen this before, but not for a while though. The Carrion need the sun as they are solar energy users generating their energy and power from the sun. 'It has to be', he exclaimed excitedly.

We watched as two of The Flighters made their way over to the three stricken bird robots. These three robots didn't even react as each of them was terminated. They remained there as if obediently waiting to die. It was so satisfying.

We then saw another Ground-Dweller run over to a Flighter and pull at the child she was carrying, and he wrapped himself around the Flighters waist, but they were too heavy to gain height, and soon The Carrion we all over them.

The grassy field was now bloodied and red, and there was death everywhere. We still hadn't moved, so I moved forward.

Creedence leaned into me. 'A Flighter has to choose carefully who we save as it is dangerous to be a Flighter. Everyone wants to be saved, but we cannot save everyone.'

I nodded as I knew this, having only ever chosen to save one person so far in my life, and that was Zamiro, but earlier today however I had saved Creedence.

That was different somehow.

We waited a little longer and what was left of The Carrion stopped and rose up and away, going back to wherever they came from. We then made our way down to the field. I counted thirteen dead Carrion.

It was a good win for the good guys.

I started counting the dead Ground-Dwellers, the dead

children, and the dead Flighters and there were too many deaths at fifteen. I stopped at looked over at Creedence. 'All this has got to stop,' I said angrily to him.

Creedence went over to a group of Flighters, the ones from the tiers and they recognised him. They too were looking around shaking their heads in disappointment. I heard one say, 'We told them the arena was not ready. It wasn't even sealed, the doors were not on, electric nets were not yet installed on the roof or the windows, but they didn't listen.' Then the group of Flighters began the gruesome collection of their two dead Flighters and moved away from us. I looked over to Creedence. 'I think we should go now.'

We went out of the arena, collected a duo shuttle and went back home.

I still don't think he knows how I got to the arena so quickly, although he commented on the way: 'A Zoop hey, must have been a fast one?'

As went through the foyer he called for the lift and looked at me. 'Are you a Flighter, Carlo?'

I didn't react, and he grinned at me upon exiting the lift on Level 5.

Chapter 24 Carlyle

Night Monday 23rd December: I had said goodnight to Creedence and was beginning to suspect he thought I was a Flighter. I will eventually need to tell him. I am to again meet with him tomorrow at the building he called a library, and have seen it on one of my many walks around the Central Berg although I thought it was called the Book Storage Archive Building.

I know it was also almost destroyed by the AIC many years ago, but that is all I know about it. I don't remember what a Library is used for, or why he wants to me meet there. I went out to my balcony after pouring a glass of the wine from last night looking at the tumbler thought about Zamiro. I walked back into the kitchen, tipped the liquid into the kitchen sink, took the bottle from the cooler and flushed the remainder of the wine down too.

I then went back out onto the balcony, and it was dark now, it was night, and it was safe from The Carrion. I looked back at my journal on the kitchen bench so moved back inside and opening it thought about today's events and what to write. Upon re-reading my previous entries, realised they were minimal and was horrified at the poor spelling evident even though it has only been a few days of entries. I found a very old, published broadsheet newspaper during my walks and will be able to use some of those words to refer to as I can read and use the words in the correct context.

There is so much happening now so thought do I still need to write at all? I then knew it was something else that reminded me of Zamiro, so I began again:

<u>My Journal –Day 3, 23rd</u>

I saved someone today. He is a Flighter.

I would say that he is now my friend. I think he is on the same journey as me.

He is much older though. I think he may be the FOO too.

I must offer help too. I miss Zamiro. What did I do? Does she love me?

I stopped realising it was too heartbreaking to think that I may not see her again and knowing she has changed my life for the better. Does she still want me to be a part of her life? This was my last thought as I sloughed my clothes, climbed onto the futon, and quickly fell to sleep.

Chapter 25 Aya

Mid-morning; Tuesday 24th December: I decided yesterday that I would go to Edi-Aleda to try locating Carlyle and was surprised he had a listed telephone. I was wondering how I could meet with him. I was able to obtain his number from our database, so called him and he answered quickly, but he still sounded like he was unsure how to use it as he was talking so loudly into the mouthpiece.

He told me he happened to be standing next to it when it rang and also mentioned it was just installed yesterday. I wondered why he would need a telephone. He also said he would wait for me to arrive and would meet me in the foyer of his apartment block. I trusted him and knew he would wait, but I did not tell him anymore.

I did not tell him about the death of Howard or The Carrion Frenzy yesterday afternoon. He had previously given me his address, so I was able to use an ER shuttle for the journey. It took about fifty minutes, and I arrived just after 10 am. He was waiting for me as I suspected, so I asked him to walk with me along the beach and was surprised how quickly he agreed. He also seemed to be distracted for some reason. We arrived at the beach fairly promptly as he indeed lived close to the beach, and I wondered why. I looked behind me and saw his apartment had an uninterrupted view west, so I mentioned this to him.

'I watch for The Carrion every night, and they came last night.' He told me, then added. 'We went to the new arena. It is not yet finished and there were many deaths.'

He stopped talking and crossed his arms over his chest looking at the water, and I could tell he was saddened. 'We?' I thought sitting down on the warm sand whilst he remained standing, and he looked down at me. I heard him sigh heavily.

'Did you know they need the sun for their energy and cannot operate when they are in shadow? We killed as many as thirteen last night.' He then went quiet again, so I beckoned him to sit on the white sand with me and then he went on much slower and quieter this time.

'I, we, were there. I, well, we saw then come in on the western sun. They flew over us. Went straight to the arena. We think they were on a reconnaissance mission. There were fifteen of them and we destroyed thirteen.'

There was that '*We*' again I thought. I know only Flighters are willing to kill The Carrion. Just what are you, Carlyle?

His soft tone continued, and he kept looking down at his hands. 'I was there with my friend Creedence. There were about twenty Ground-Dwellers and children. They were rehearsing for the event on the twenty-fifth. They didn't need to die.'

'So you and Creedence?' I wondered if he was a Creedence was a Flighter too.

'There was a group of Flighters there too.'

'Oh', I acknowledged, and that comment deflated my suspicions.

'The Flighters could save a few Ground-Dwellers, but not enough of us.'

'Us,' I heard again. So he is a Ground-Dweller, not a Flighter? I was getting further confused. He then kept quiet again, and I don't think I wanted to tell him my news now but began anyway.

'The Carrion came to Munna Cliffs on Sunday afternoon.'

'Oh no, was anyone? Howard, was he there?'

'Yes,' I replied, quietly this time. 'Everyone was killed, and you were right, as it was a Water Carrion. We drained the pond, and we found the boy, Bernie. You were right he had been eaten, swallowed and he had drowned.'

'What about Howard?'

'There were no survivors, he, they were still in the pond. They all were. I lost so many friends. It was a bloodbath. It was The Frenzy.'

He looked over at me again. 'You survived though.'

'I was lucky. I couldn't stand the noise from the pumps, so I went back to sit in the shuttle. All the noise. I was still sitting in the shuttle when they came and then I heard the screams. I still hear the screams now, Carlyle.'

I began to cry, and he put his arm around my shoulder and held me softly. 'Wow,' I thought, a sensitive man too.

We sat there looking at the sea and I leaned my head into his shoulder for some solace. After a little while he started to stand up. 'I have something else to do today,' he said to me softly shaking my hand. 'Thank you for letting me know. It has made me more determined to fix this. We must stop them, and I think I know how.' He then mentioned he was meeting his friend Creedence at the Library in the Central Berg.

'Can I call you again? You intrigue me, Carlyle.'

'Funny that', he replied, 'I seem to do that with other Ground-Dwellers too. Maybe it is just what I do.'

He walked away and left me there sitting on the warm sand, and as I watched him go back to his apartment, realised he had certainly left an impression on me.

Chapter 26 Creedence

Noon; Tuesday 24th December: I met Carlyle again in the foyer early this morning as he was coming back from doing exercise as he likes running along the beach. I had asked him to meet me at noon today at the entrance of the Book Storage and Archive Building and he had mentioned he knew where it was as had seen it on one of his walks around the Central Berg.

I left the terminus just before twelve and was still surprised that no one had noticed that I was absent the other day for so long. I don't know how long I will be away today either, so I ran over there this time which took me about ten minutes. I saw him waiting in the foyer as we had arranged, and he was looking down at his timepiece. I think he was talking to it.

As I got closer I realised he actually was, and it was answering him back, so I went up to him and he nodded to my presence. 'What were you saying to it?' looking at his timepiece.

'I was asking it if it knew there was a way to kill The Carrion.'

'Did it answer?'

'Yes.'

'Oh…What did it say?'

'Use the shadows. Use your knowledge and power.'

I looked at him, 'What is that supposed to mean?' but thought perhaps we both already knew. We then went into the Library. 'Have you been inside this building before?'

'No, what does it have? What is it for?'

'Books, references, storage, reading, learning but that is not what I am here for today. I am meeting two men. They are Ground-Dwellers and might be able to help us.'

I led him through the aisles and corridors as we made our way into the cement bunker and discovered that the doors open at 9 a.m. and close at 9 p.m., but we will be out before that I hope. I showed him to a chair, so we sat down at the desk where I had previously been and waited.

He looked at me. 'Please tell me something Creedence, something you think I do not know.'

I thought about that and walked over to the foreign language section of the shelving and took a book down. I think it was in Chinasian, a language I did not know or could not read. I dropped the tome on the desk where it landed with a thump. 'Can you read that?' I asked him.

'No, what is it?'

'It's a book from another part of the world,' and as I opened the book told him to scan his timepiece over the pages, so he did, then told me to tell his timepiece to translate Chinasian to English. It began a narrative: 'China was part of the Asian landmass before the great ice melt. It was flooded when the Himalayan Mountain range melted. Climate change came too quickly, and mankind was not prepared. Mankind did not heed the warnings.'

Carlyle looked at me and told the timepiece to stop the narration. 'What is China?'

I opened the back of the book and there was an old map of the world in the back, and he was astounded. 'I didn't know.'

He then mentioned his lack of education as a child on the farm at Munta, and he reminded me of loneliness since, so I told him this was a place full of information, full of research material and full of knowledge. He nodded. 'But my Phillip Patek knows information and likely knows all of this already as it has an encyclopedia built in. The trader told me so,' looking for my confirmation.

I sighed. 'Not exactly. The timepiece only knows information that it has stored in its memory. This could be the same as this library, but as the AIC controls the information that it allows to be stored in the timepiece database, it can manipulate the information and keep secrets. This is what the AIC does. In this library, my new friend is so much more and finding out other information yourself from the old books and text is what we can do here. It is very different.'

I then realised why the AIC attacked this building all those years ago, it wanted to destroy the information that is contained within, prevent the research, prevent the learnings, and prevent those seeking an alternate future without the need for The AIC and The Carrion.

I looked over at Carlyle again. 'The AIC cannot control what we keep or put in this Library as it can't get in here, so we can use the all information, then research the knowledge and use it to destroy The AIC.'

We then suddenly heard voices behind us and as they

were getting closer, we could hear two voices coming down the aisle.

'Are we supposed to be in here?' Carlyle asked me quietly.

'Our wrist chips have trackers in them, and so does my timepiece.'

I looked at him and he continued: 'But the AIC cannot infiltrate the cement walls as we are too far within the bunker, so it should be OK.'

The voices came around the end of the aisle and I watched as Carlyle moved to get out of sight. I recognised them.

It was Marty and Kilby.

I moved over to them and shook their hands. 'Glad you could make it.'

Chapter 27 Kilby

Early afternoon; Tuesday 24th December: 'Do you think we got away with it?' Marty asked me, referring to our early departure from AIC today before the last shift started as we are simply not permitted to exit early.

We are expected to remain at the AIC until all the entire shifts are completed just in case there is an issue with the other workers. Each team is then expected to remain isolated in separate chambers just in case we are required again for some reason. Our shift finished half an hour before, but we had left anyway and as there was no one stopping us on the way out if we were challenged, we were going to say we got the time wrong, but it never came to that.

We then headed straight to the library in the Central Berg as were too excited anyway. We were meeting with Creedence again today. The anomalies on the plates of computer chips were still occurring, and we have gathered at least six other clean chips just today. These were all supposed to be reported, are supposed to be destroyed, but we continued to collect them and smuggled them out of the AIC as we had done before, although it was routine but was very dangerous. We believed it was our new mission. We were a little late getting to the library and were hoping Creedence was still there, as we were walking through the bunker, we could not control our excitement.

'We're almost there', I said to Marty, 'We can make this work.'

As I rounded the end of the aisle I noticed two men were standing by the table that we had been at yesterday, one was Creedence, so I hesitated and held back Marty by thrusting my arm out behind me. I looked at the second man and although was still cautious, realised it was Carlyle, so I dropped my arm and Marty followed me to the table.

Creedence came over to welcome us. 'This is Carlyle, and he wants to help too.'

I saw that Carlyle did not move.

'We know him.' Marty replied.

'Why, how?' Creedence responded with some confusion.

'Err', I offered back, then Marty spoke again. 'He has the hots for our sister, Zamiro.'

I then looked over at Carlyle and he was horrified, well I had to guess that was his reaction as he generally doesn't show any emotion. He then looked at us both. 'I don't know, well the hots….it's not like that. I …oh, I give up.'

Marty nodded at him, 'Told you so, Kilby.'

Creedence looked at us. 'What's going on?'

Carlyle explained it, about the meeting with her in the hills, about knowing her from the ALC, about seeing her, about knowing she works at the ELC, but when he started to say how he met her he hesitated and said: 'I saved her'.

I looked at Marty, and Marty looked at Creedence, then Creedence looked at Carlyle. 'From The Carrion?' Marty said.

'Yes.'

'But she told us she fainted, she told us that she somehow ended up on the roof of the building of the ELC and didn't know how she had survived.'

Carlyle responded softly, 'It was me. I saw she had fainted. I was there. I was watching her and saw The Carrion, The Frenzy. I chose to intervene and held her to me, and we floated up and away. I saved her.' Creedence looked at us and then at Carlyle. 'I thought so and hoped so. You are a Flighter, aren't you Carlo?'

'I am,' he replied then finished with; 'but don't tell Zamiro yet, please. I will tell her when the time is right.'

'OK,' the three of us all nodded in agreement, then Creedence added 'Let's get down to business. Did you get any more of them?'

I looked over to Marty and knew I had to trust them both now as we had come this far. 'Yes,' and opened my palm. 'I have three and Marty has three.'

Carlyle looked at them. 'Chips, these are the ones The AIC puts in us. How are you getting them?'

'We work there,' Marty continued: 'On the chip assembly line, all day. We've been there forever, and it's finally paid off, finally been worth it.'

I looked over and explained that a couple of days ago Marty picked off a chip that was out of alignment, which we then had secreted out of the place and it was here in the Library we unintentionally met Creedence.

'That's when he told us he was a Flighter.'

I looked over to him and he nodded.

Creedence then started up. 'I knew what it was and how

dangerous it was for them to have taken the chips out of the AIC, so I wanted to help. It was an easy decision and was the least thing I could do.' He went on and explained about a new chip being able to wipe the existing chips and being able to temporarily interrupt the circuitry.

Carlyle nodded. 'So, the thing you had with Hawke yesterday morning at our apartment block, that was the chip re-set wasn't it?'

'Yes, I was lucky, he almost threw me off the balcony and I would have given away my ability or collided with the ground and ....'

'Died?' Marty said looking at him.

'Yes, that is what The Represents are doing now.'

Carlyle stated, 'It's fight or flight, fly or die.'

'But Represents are Ground-Dwellers like us,' blurted out Marty.

'Us,' I said, 'not them,' nodding towards Creedence and Carlyle.

We looked at each other and Creedence spoke first: 'What's next then? What can the chips help us with? How can they help any of us stop The Carrion?'

'The Carrion.' Carlyle said. 'Did you know they can now live, and operate in water?' He then told us about his news from Munna Cliffs, to which we all listened. 'We will need more help,' Creedence said with a defeated tone. 'And we will need more Flighters. I don't know many others apart from the ones we met last night though.' He then told us about the FOO-Flighters that had assisted during The Frenzy at the arena last night.

We all nodded. 'There has to be a way and there has to be more of us that will help. Just how do we find them?'

I looked at Marty and assumed he granted his permission, so I told them about our grandparents and that they were part of The Forced and they would know how to get in contact with Flighters, as they have been saving them from The Represents. 'At the moment they are heading towards our house at our Berg as they are having dinner with us again tonight.'

We collected our bags, and I handed the chips to Creedence as we exited the library. We took a four-shuttle and arrived back at our home just as Zamiro was coming across the road from the ELC having finished for the day.

'Keep it a secret please.' Carlyle said softly to us, as we all gathered around the front door waiting to enter the house when she arrived, kissed Carlyle in front of us.

Chapter 28 Carlyle

Early evening; Tuesday 24th December: It was already getting dark as watched Zamiro walk across the road towards us. I didn't know what I was going to say. What if she ignores me? What if it is over between us?

As she was getting nearer, she was looking only at me and smiling and approached with her arms out wide. I thought wow this is in front of her two brothers too. Then she did something even more unexpected as she kissed me lightly on the lips.

'Hi Carlyle.' she simply said to me.

I saw that Creedence went very quiet, but he was then the first to speak as he looked at Zamiro. 'I saw you Monday morning leaving our apartment block in Evoh. You waved and then drove off on a Zoop. It was very early though.'

I looked over at him. He hadn't mentioned this before and then Marty and Kilby looked at me, and Marty commented: 'You live in Evoh don't you Carlo, and you told us today that you and Creedence both live in the same apartment block.'

I looked at Zamiro as she was now standing next to me, and she went a pale pink colour in her cheeks, I think they call it blushing.

'Oh no,' smiled Kilby, 'our sister does the walk of shame.'

I looked at him wondering what all that meant. Zamiro shrugged her shoulders and finally spoke defiantly. 'Well, I was late for work.'

Creedence interjected, 'But it was five in the morning, it was still dark. What work do you do?' And to that she replied quietly, 'I am a teacher, across the road at the ELC.'

'Early lessons then?' blurted out Marty.

They all laughed, and I didn't understand why. Creedence looked at me, 'What?' I asked, but he didn't reply.

We then all went inside, and formal introductions were made to Mata, Fata and Tristesse although Creedence and I were still suspicious of meeting new people, as Flighters are always suspicious. I however was comforted in the strength that my feelings for Zamiro were being reciprocated, so we sat around the dining table and waited for the others.

When the grandparents arrived a little later, it was when things became intense as they were going to be asked to divulge everything they knew to two people they didn't know. It was going to be a challenge to convince them that we could be trusted. I caught Creedence's eye and moved around to be closer to him whispering to him I thought that we needed to show them that we were genuine and needed to prove we were worthy of their trust, so told him that we would have to bring them outside as we need to show them. I moved around the dining table to where the grandparents were sitting.

'Dave, and Courtney can we have a word?'

They both looked up at me. 'Outside please.' I asked the others to stay where they were.

Creedence and I showed them to the backdoor and the

four of us made our way outside. Dave looked at us. 'Now tell us why you think we are so important to your cause, Carlyle.'

I then told them that Marty and Kilby had let us know they were a part of The Forced, and they looked shocked. 'Why would they give us up?' Courtney then said quietly, 'Do you know how much danger they have put us in? We don't even know you. For all we know you could be Represents.'

I looked at Creedence, and he acknowledged what we needed to do, so we both initiated The Rush, and they kept watching us suspiciously. We began to float and directed ourselves to land on the roof of the house just above where we had just exited, and they watched us in awe as we then drop-floated down gently and arrived back down next to them.

'We do need your help', I said to them both and they nodded listening in agreement.

Dave asked. 'So what can we do? Does everyone know you are a Flighter?'

I told them Marty and Kilby do but the others don't, and Courtney quietly asked me if I had told Zamiro. I said no. They nodded.

'How can we help?' Dave asked.

We explained about last night at the arena, of what we suspected The Carrion knew about tomorrow's opening ceremony, and that The GOD is making it an all-out affair. It was as if The GOD wanted to challenge The Carrion and there was to be a Ground-Dweller gathering scheduled to start at dusk.

'And, as the weather is expected to be clear the sunny day, it will be ideal for an attack by The Carrion.' Dave added.

I continued: 'We want you to put the word out and

arrange as many Flighters to make themselves available to be in the crowd tomorrow. It'll be dangerous for them as they might have to reveal they are Flighters they might even be killed by The Carrion, but they might get a chance to kill them too.'

'How many people are expected?'

'The arena seats five thousand, but there will be another fifty or so in the opening parade'

'So what is your plan?'

'The roof will be closed and there is also an electrified canopy net across the entire roof section. We don't expect they will try to come through there, so we leave the doors open to the west as they already know this is an access point.

As soon as they come in we close the doors behind them and if we then block out the sun they will be in shadow, as they need the sun to draw their energy. They operate on solar, like everything else.'

'How will you get the doors closed behind them?'

'That is the difficult part as we will have to get the Ground-Dwellers to continue the parade as if nothing is happening and pretend that they are safe.'

'So you are not going to tell them about the possibility of a Carrion strike? And that's the plan?' Courtney said looking at us both.

'Yes.' I then saw movement behind Dave and Courtney, and it was Zamiro and Marty coming through the backdoor. 'We thought you had all got lost.' Marty commented sarcastically. 'What's going on?'

I told them that we suspected The Carrion would strike tomorrow night at the opening ceremony. 'Why?' asked

Zamiro coming up to me and wrapping her arm around my waist, rubbing my shoulder tenderly. Creedence then explained about last night and what we had seen about The Carrion not being able to operate in shadow.

Zamiro commented: 'There are children from my ELC involved in the show. What do I tell them?'

I looked at her and said, 'Tell them to stay away.'

She looked and me I could tell she was thinking of how she could help, and then told us she was going back inside to make some calls. I assumed she meant on the telephone. Marty stayed outside with us and came over to Dave and Courtney.

'Did they show you?' he said.

'Yes.'

'I knew that telling them that you then would be able to get in contact with other Flighters could help.'

Dave and Courtney nodded.

We decided there was not much else that could be done standing outside, so we made our way back in and gathered around the dining table again as there were now twelve of us in the room. It was noisy.

Someone then mentioned the arrogance of The GOD, and the hubbub from the conversations quietened down a little. Fata then interrupted us above the noise then spoke louder. 'Sshh...I have to say something. I have been listening to all of this and I can help too. Are you very sure that The Carrion will strike tomorrow evening?'

We all nodded.

'OK...I am about to tell you something that is not to go beyond these four walls, and that quietened us all down further. 'I am on The GOD Panel, and this means that I might be able to, no, I *will* be able to get them to delay the opening ceremony for at least half an hour, at least until the sun goes down.'

We all looked at him, but Zamiro spoke first: 'Sorry Fata, you will be too late as The Carrion will still come anyway.'

She then moved out of the room, and when I looked for Zamiro they told me that she was on the telephone to start calling people, telling them not to come to the ceremony tomorrow, and had she had a large number of calls to make.

After being away for a while, and after about the tenth call, she came over to us at the dining table and sat down exhausted. 'Mata, I need you to take over for me and start making calls, please. Here is a list of numbers that I have with me. There is another list in my office over the road.'

She then looked at me. 'Come with me Carlyle and we will get the list from my office, then we go back to your place. I will make calls from there. Your telephone is working isn't it?'

I nodded, then thought if she is coming back to my place now, I won't be bringing her back tonight. Creedence then said he would meet us tomorrow at our apartment and left on a Zoop.

Zamiro and I then headed over the road to the school, and she was holding my hand as we walked through the courtyard. As we passed the spot that I had collected her from during The Frenzy, on that day, I stopped. She leaned up and kissed me again.

'I don't think I have said thank you have I?' We held each

other for a while and then moved on into her office, collected the telephone registry, and chirped a Zoop, but she insisted that she drove for some reason.

When we arrived home it was about ten, and I thought it was getting too late to make any more calls tonight, and as we went inside the apartment she resigned herself to my suggestion, and went over the cooler.

'All the wine gone?' she said looking through the contents.

'Yes. I gave it to Creedence. We had some after we came home,' then I thought I am not going to lie to her, why do I need to?

'Actually, I tipped it out' and I went on to tell her that I did not like what the alcohol in the wine had made me do. It put me in a place I did not want to be, and I felt the need to apologise to her for my comment the other night.

'Oh, which one?' she replied coyly.

I believe I said, 'The day is not over yet, and neither is the night.'

'Oh, that one.'

'Yes, that one.'

'Well then', she said as she looked at me, 'The day is not over yet and neither is the night.' she then asked me to remind her where her bedroom was, to which I thought that was odd. 'To the right', I told her.

She nodded and then proceeded to go to my bedroom to the left. Oh no, I thought, now I am really scared, so I took a deep breath and stayed where I was.

I looked down at my journal. Do I write something about today?

<u>My Journal –Day 4 21st</u>

I met more of Zamiro's family. I still miss mine.

Will I eva get back home to Munta? I must. I gave up my secret today.

I hope it dunst cost me my life. Zamiro is here. In my home. In my heart.

What do I do now?

Chapter 29 Creedence

Morning; Wednesday 25th December: It was around 8 a.m. and thought Carlyle would be up so I used the lift to Level 11, knocked on his door and Zamiro opened it. 'Oh,' I said to her. 'You didn't get back home last night then?'

'Not quite, the boys are here already too,' she said drawing me into the living area I gave Marty and Kilby a nod as I saw them standing by the window. 'This apartment is huge sis,' Marty then said looking around, 'Two bedrooms or three?'

'Two bedrooms, three bathrooms.' Carlyle confirmed as he came out from one of the bedrooms.

'How is the bed in the spare room then Zee?', he said looking over to her trying to embarrass her, knowing full well that she had spent the night, and this morning had made the telephone calls.

'It is fine and there is a bathroom at the back of the second bedroom too. Oh, and my robe is still on the bed in there if you would like to get it for me, please. Just put it in the laundry basket.' Marty looked at her. 'Round 1 to Zee.' Kilby said drawing the same conclusion as me that Zamiro had not spent the night in Carlyle's bedroom.

I looked at Carlyle and he was confused, so Zamiro went over to him and whispered something in his ear.

I spoke first, 'So what is the plan then?' trying to draw something out of someone.

Kilby started up. 'We can't stop The Carrion. You said so yourself, so we have to get them into the shadows. How did you go with the calls Zee?'

Zamiro told us she could only get through to half of the Ground-Dwellers and that most of them did not believe that she could forecast a Carrion attack. They were still coming anyway. I knew she was disappointed and saw Carlyle move towards her for support. 'Same with us', said Marty quietly.

'So' I said, 'if we cannot stop them at least we work on herding them to exactly where we want them to go.'

'How?' said Zamiro, 'the children will be on the field. The show must go on.'

'The glass-walled sentry boxes on the roof gave me an idea.' I went on to explain we still need The Carrion to assume that the ceremony is proceeding. 'What we can do is erect larger glass-walled sentry boxes around and on the grass field within the arena. Build them big enough so that the children can move around within them and as long as those inside the boxes stay away from the doors they will be safe. The Carrion should not be able to infiltrate the boxes as the glass boxes will be too strong and too solid.'

'Good plan,' I heard Carlyle say and saw Marty and Kilby nodding in agreement.

'Bad plan.'

I then heard Zamiro say. 'You will be using the children

as bait. They will be so scared in the boxes, and if they move around too much they will use up the oxygen.'

'Not really,' I said 'Remember we will know exactly when The Carrion arrives as we can see them as they are predictable. We will know how long any Ground-Dwellers need to be encased within the glass cages too. We will know exactly where The Carrion is going to enter from as there will only be one access point through the western doors. They have to come in on the western sunlight and need the energy from the sun to operate. They will be airborne as they come in through the corridor and will be coming into an area that we can then bathe in shadow. The only risk will be how much energy they have to make it from the opening, with the sun behind them until they reach the glass boxes. The roof will be shut, the overheard lights will be off, and it will be dark in there. They cannot operate in the shadow, and we have both seen this.'

I then took a breath and looked over to Carlyle. 'Yes, good plan,' he said again and Marty and Kilby nodded in agreement again. Zamiro sat down, and I think she was pouting, so I looked over at her. I thought was beautiful even when she did that too.

'So why do we need the other Flighters?' Kilby asked me.

'In case it doesn't work as well as it should.' Carlyle said quietly to them.

Chapter 30 Marty

Dusk; Wednesday 25th December: I was already at the arena having been there since early this afternoon, and said to Zamiro looking at our handy work, 'I can't believe that we got these glass boxes built so quickly, pretty simple structure, held together with screws and even grand-fathers old Bosch drill came in handy.'

The word had got around so many of the Ground-Dwellers accepted that The Carrion was going to attack to-night, and tonight would be a golden sunset just as predicted. A team of around fifty Ground-Dwellers were involved in the construction of the arena formed their work groups and put together a procurement plan sourcing all the materials within a few hours. The boxes were at least twenty metres long and fifteen metres wide they could contain about ten people each and ten of them had been built.

Then the crowds had now started to arrive, children and parents, however many had heeded the advice of Zamiro did stay away, and although the numbers were down it was still predicted that at least three thousand people would be coming. They were aware they needed to be inside the arena before dusk, before the setting sun but as most arrived two hours early, many were getting restless.

What wasn't known, is how many of the patrons were Flighters and how many would be available to destroy The Carrion once they were trapped in the arena.

A group of Ground-Dwellers made their way over to Marty and Zamiro and one of them said, 'What now?' Others came up then too. 'I am not putting my child in your cage as bait for the Carrion.'

It was all getting a bit tense.

'Dusk in thirty minutes,' was overheard.

'Let's get this show on the road,' someone else said somewhere.

Chapter 31 Creedence

Dusk; Wednesday 25th December: 'Hi Carlo... up here,' I called down to him as he arrived on a Zoop. I was already standing on the roof next to one of the glass sentry boxes and would soon be entering the box to watch for The Carrion's arrival, but at the moment I was checking out the locking mechanism. The lock was on the inside and it appeared to be sound.

I drop-floated and landed softly beside him. 'Where is Zee?'

'Oh, she's already inside. She came with Marty earlier today as they are still trying to convince The GOD to delay the start until after dusk.'

'Good luck with that, but why is The GOD even thinking that they should be risking doing this at dusk? It is so....' searching for the right word.

'Arrogant?' he queried.

'No, I was going to say unnecessary.'

We walked over to the two newly added large steel doors and as there were now four of them across the entrance, we studied them and thought if we could secure two of each side door in place then that would reduce the gap. This will limit

171

The Carrion's ability to fly through and it might reduce their flow rate. I mentioned this to Carlyle.

'Yes. Good idea.' We found some wire, wound it through the floor wheels and attached it to the other door panel. Then tried moving the door, they were secure.

We checked that the untethered doors were free to move on either side, and they were. I then looked at Carlyle and said, 'Good luck', and with that went outside, initiated The Rush, found myself back on the roof and saw that other Flighters were now on the roof with me.

I counted at least five others, and we covered the western side as this is where The Carrion will come from, and of course they will, as they are so predictable.

Chapter 32 Carlyle

Dusk; Wednesday 25th December: I watched as Creedence floated up to the roof and gave him a mock salute. He is a good friend and I wish that I had known him sooner as it may have made our life journey as Flighters a little easier.

I stopped at the metal doors again and retried them both to make sure they would not be hindered in any way to prevent them from being shut. Everything hinged on the speed at which we could close the doors after the last Carrion had flown through and assured myself they would move easily.

I made my way back into the arena through the cement corridor and hoped we were ready. I then saw Marty remonstrating with someone a little further down the tier in front of me, and as they were getting quite animated I made my way down to them to find out what was going on.

'Tell him', Marty said to me looking at the other Ground-Dweller, but I still didn't know why the man arguing with him, and then the man looked at me.

'We can't get the door lock working properly on the inside of the last glass cage and Marty says it is important as The Carrion might see that there is no one in it and work out it is a trap, that everything is a trap. Marty wants to go in there, wants to stay in there during The Frenzy, and he could hold it. I said it was too dangerous. We don't know how strong a Carrion is, and they could just smash it open, so whoever is in there would be committing suicide.'

I looked at him. 'Marty is right. Someone needs to be in there as it is one of the first glass cages The Carrion will see and unless locked properly can get into it.'

Marty then stepped forward, 'Don't worry I will find someone to do it then' and jogged away down the tiered steps and went out onto the field.

'Great help you were', the man looked at me frustrated with the lack of assistance.

'Marty won't do it himself as it would be suicide, he will find someone else.' I assured him, otherwise, I may have just condemned my girlfriend's brother to his death.

Chapter 33 Zamiro

Dusk; Wednesday 25th December: I could see that the Ground-Dwellers were beginning to direct their children into the glass cages. We had decided that each cage would only contain five children and one adult and hoped that this would reduce the risk to all concerned. We could not however prevent the ceremony from starting at dusk, but at least we managed to alter the schedule so not everyone came onto the field simultaneously.

Each glass cage would also contain a Flighter and several Flighters had arrived earlier today to volunteer to be a part of it. They had all revealed themselves as Flighters to us which was very heroic given the circumstances. It will also be a Flighter that stands closest to the glass door of the cage, and they will most likely be the first ones to be attacked by The Carrion if the cage door is compromised.

We tested the lights, the roof, and the blinds and fully shut the large steel entrance doors, and Creedence was right, in that the whole arena would be enveloped in soft darkness once the lights were off, doors sealed, and the skylight blinds closed.

I was now standing with a group of Ground-Dwellers and

children in one of the tiers above the playing field, and we should be well away from The Carrion and should be safe here. We all hoped.

I counted the ten glassed boxes on the field, counted the seven people in each box and that made seventy people that would be immediately in danger during The Frenzy but that also meant a lot of us could be considered safe.

Seventy, out of three thousand. Good odds but still dangerous.

I looked at one of the first glass boxes again, the one that was closest to the western gap, as it would be most likely the first one to bear the brunt of the attack and could see the golden sun was beginning to shine on it through the open doors below. Its glass and position were giving me a slightly distorted view, so I looked at it again and realised there was no one in this one. I pointed it out to the woman standing next to me.

'Aya', she said introducing herself. 'I am an Emergency Responder.'

I shook her hand lightly and asked her what she could make of it. 'There is no one in that one, Oh, but wait, it looks like someone is going in there now.'

I looked again and she was correct but why only one? I thought. 'He must be a Flighter to take on a glassed cage by himself,' she said quietly. I then saw the man drop something on the grass and pick it up again, it looked like a pointed long metal stick.

'I think it is a screwdriver. I have seen them before' she then said looking down at him. 'There must be a problem with the lock.'

I nodded in agreement, then suddenly realised who the man was. 'He is not a Flighter,' I said shaking my head in surprise. 'That is my brother, Marty',

Chapter 34 Creedence

Dusk; Wednesday 25th December: I looked to the western setting golden sun but saw nothing, kept hoping I was wrong, wanted to be wrong but I wasn't, as The Carrion had arrived, and there were at least double the number that came the other night. I knew I was correct in that it had been a reconnaissance, so I climbed into the sentry box just as the others did around me.

I heard someone let out a war cry of 'Hoo-rah' as I secured myself inside, tried the lock and it held fast. The Carrion then began circling overhead and one peeled off heading straight toward one of the sentry boxes it crashed into it with such a force that it almost knocked it from the bolted attachments holding it to the roof, but the sentry box held, and the glass walls held.

We then each turned on the circuit that electrified the units we were all standing in. They had been installed as an additional safety measure just in case. The single Carrion attacked the same one again as it had circled it and crashed into it.

The sentry box held, and this time the electrical circuit over the box gave The Carrion an electric shock and it didn't seem to understand what it was. It tried to attack again and was electrically shocked again, and it flew back to the flock. I looked over to the other sentry boxes and everyone was elated, some were even raising their arms and fist-thumping in the air inside their units.

Then I saw one of the Flighters open his sentry box, he stepped out onto the roof and was giving The Carrion an almighty salute signal, with one arm across his chest and the other one thrust in the air.

I shook my head in dismay: Don't do it, please get back in, it's too early to celebrate.

He was now facing forward to the main swarm, facing west, and was still remonstrating to all of us. He was not aware that some other Carrion had circled behind him, and I could see exactly what was about to happen but was unable to do anything.

The two Carrion circled behind him and simultaneously turned their heads onto the side as they flew straight through him with their razor-sharp beaks. He was instantly split in half as his torso was severed clean off at the waist. His legs stood by themselves temporarily, then toppled over onto the roof.

The Carrion now realised that there was an opportunity to attack all the sentry boxes, so they came from everywhere. Every box on the roof was crashed into, mashed into and collided with and the number of Carrion attacking my box made it difficult for me to see out of. It was just metal and noise, crunching and screeching and it was terrifying for all of us. I could vaguely see one of the other boxes not far from me being harassed by at least ten Carrion and could just make out the person inside amongst the turmoil. The occupant had pulled her jacket over her head and was rocking back and forth in the little space. At this moment though, the glass walls were holding, but then she dropped the jacket on the ground and started thumping the walls from the inside, hoping The Carrion would move away, but it was futile.

She was now frantically moving around the sentry box banging, thumping and yelling out and I realised she was making her way around to the door side. Everything was happening so quickly, so violently, but what happened next was in slow motion, as she then hit the lock on the door, and it sprung open. The woman looked at it not realising what had just happened, but The Carrion did, as one, two, three pushed their way inside and she started screaming at them. She had nowhere to go, so folded herself back against the wall, directly opposite the open door. More Carrion came in and there was not much room left in there with her.

They took her arms, then with their talons began clambering towards her chest. I heard her screaming some more. The screaming suddenly stopped as they must have taken her head off, and then the box exploded with blood and mass as her mushed bloodied torso fell out of the door.

It was headless, armless and ghastly.

I turned myself into focus and was even more determined now to survive this onslaught, and fortunately, all the other sentry boxes held fast The Carrion were losing out. It was as if suddenly they knew the roof sentry boxes were just a decoy, just something to waste their time on and as their time is limited by the period of dusk, they suddenly stopped attacking us and moved into a tight flight circle high above us once again.

We knew that once it got dark they could not operate, at least that is what we were hoping by being up here and being so defenceless. We had simply delayed them.

They swarmed down the side of the arena, and I could see them now entering the two doors that we had deliberately left open below me, but too many tried to enter at the same time, and this slowed them down too. They were now crashing into each other, which only made them more frantic and more determined. Finally, I stepped out of my sentry box and saw the others doing the same, so I patted it softly and thanked it. There were still four of us left alive on the roof.

I wondered how it was going down below in the arena.

Chapter 35 Carlyle

Dusk; Wednesday 25th December: I heard the noise and commotion going on outside from inside the arena, and it was taking longer than I thought as The Carrion were spending too much time outside wasting their opportunity and although that was good, we then heard The Carrion coming inside. They were now swarming down the side of the arena and entered the two doors that we had deliberately left open, but this too slowed them down as many tried to enter at the same time.

They had finally entered the arena and with the golden setting sun still gleaming through behind them flew straight into the fielded area. The man standing opposite me wanted to look around the corner to see if more were coming. I shook my head and yelled out as loud as I could against the noise. I was standing on one side of the open door with another Flighter on the other side.

'It's too early…there is still more to come…just don't' but he didn't hear me, and he looked anyway. A Carrion flew into him, severed his head off and his headless body spiralled sideways into the corridor. Two other Carrion then spun around and instantly ripped him to shreds. They were still within the golden sun so there was no stopping them, and the shredded torso was flung over my side of the door. It landed very close to me and felt repulsed. I was now so very close to the two attacking Carrion, so kept very still not to antagonise them, and waited.

The Carrion flow had slowed, so I started pushing my door and moved to the designated stop on the floor. My side was now closed off, but I had to make a choice, can I risk jumping across the open space and close the other door? I knew I had to as the whole point of this was to trap them in the darkness, so counted to myself in readiness to leap the sunlight, ...one...two...three, but just as I went to make my move saw the other door moving towards me.

It was being shut, someone else knew what was going on, but I couldn't quite make them out. I realised that it was Creedence. He was puffing and short of breath, which I thought was unusual as he was fairly healthy and fit. He would have drop-floated down from the roof to be here, to help me, but that should not have exhausted him and as he had survived the onslaught. I thought perhaps he was injured.

The two Carrion near me had not noticed Creedence, not noticed the door second door closing, and although his door was almost closed now, the sunlight was still streaming in.

I turned and leaned my back against my closed door, took a breath, and when my eyes adjusted to the partial darkness could see The Carrion were still attacking the glass cages on the field, but they were not penetrating them. I could also see that the two Carrion that had attacked the dead man who was supposed to have shut his door with mine had stopped moving, stopped shredding and that they were both now in partial darkness.

There was no longer any direct sunlight to draw their energy from, so they were now just waiting there doing nothing, and the blood, skin and sinew that had covered them now collected at their feet.

I looked quickly at the scene below me and noticed at least six of the cages were already in darkness and then realised The Carrion would not be attacking those cages. There were still four cages being harassed, and The Carrion Frenzy was being concentrated on those alone.

There were at least ten Carrion at each cage, the children were screaming, the adults were screaming, but standing steadfast at each door was a single person.

A single Flighter. A single hero.

It was then I noticed that the foremost glass cage had a single person in it, one brave Flighter and this cage would be the last one to go into darkness once we had closed both doors. I was too far away to recognise him. I do not know of many other Flighters so hoped to meet with him, to thank him, if he survives.

I looked over at Creedence, he saluted me and kept pushing on his closing door but suddenly the door stopped moving.

There was still a gap, one slither of golden sunlight about a metre wide that was streaming toward the last cage not in shadow, not yet in darkness, the one containing the lone Flighter.

The Carrion were going crazy as they knew the shadows were closing in on them and were all swarming over the final glass cage The Carrion could no longer draw their energy from the sun, and most were already in shadow.

By now most had simply stopped flying, stopped moving, and most of them had just stopped and stood around on the grassy field in the enveloping blackness -looking like a flock of lost ducks. I felt hopeless for the last Flighter still in the last cage. In there all alone.

I looked over to Creedence and he looked down at the cause of the jam, it was the mangled severed head of the Flighter that was to have shut the other door. He bent down and rolled it out of the way. The door shut, and he sat down and rested against his own shut door. Instantly there was darkness, shadow, everything and everyone slowed, then everything and everyone stopped.

My eyes were still adjusting to the change of light, so I groped my way along my door and dropped down against it too. I was now sitting beside him, so leant over fumbling for his hand and eventually I found it. I said to him. 'Well done my friend.' clasping my fingers with his.

We both rested there in the small slivers of light emanating from around the sides of the now-sealed doors. The internal lights flickered on within the arena and the sight presented before us was impressive, not a single person had been injured. The Carrion had lost this battle and it was over, as they were not moving, not attacking and were simply doing nothing. I could see that it was still dusk outside as there was natural light forming a halo around the closed blinds high above us, but it did not affect The Carrion as they needed the golden setting sun behind them. The Carrion were then collected and dumped into the glass cages. As they were now docile, were easily carried. It was pitiful. It was fabulous.

I looked down at Creedence as I rose and went to help him up, but he waved me off not to, so I left him there to rest. 'I'll be back', I said to him.

'I'll be here,' he replied softly to me.

Moving down to the field I wanted to thank the single Flighter that had withstood the final Frenzy in the last cage, and as I made my way over to it Zamiro had come up the tiered steps to meet me. 'Is it over?'

'For now', I replied then I asked her if she knew the Flighter in the first cage and she told me that she did, and then said so do I and was still looking at her as she opened the door as Marty stepped out of it.

'Hiya big fella', he said as he looked at me, and smiled as Zamiro punched him softly in the shoulder and then pulled him forward to hug him.

'You…. You are not a Flighter!' I exclaimed.

'Nope, but there was no one else around', then he explained about the lock not working and having to shimmy the old screwdriver through the mechanism to hold it. He had been standing there all the time. His hand was cramped with the strain, but had chosen to ignore it as his life depended on it.

Our lives depended on it.

Meantime the other cages had been opened and by now most of the children had come out and the adults too, and several parents were filing down through the tiers and onto the field. Everyone was embracing, hugging and back-slapping but looking over to one of the other glass cages I saw that there was someone still sitting inside, next to the open door propped up against the glass wall.

I moved over to it and stepped inside to help them up, but the man then slumped to the side, slid to the ground and appeared to be dead.

'Over here', I cried out to anybody that was listening. 'I think we may have a casualty after all.'

An Emergency Responder came quickly up to me and leant over feeling for a pulse, she then indicated that there was none, so she laid the man prostrate in the glass chamber. She then went up and down his arms, legs and chest looking for any signs of an injury and looked up at me. 'There is nothing wrong with him, it looks like he just died.'

I looked down at the ER and realised it was Aya from yesterday morning. 'Hello Aya, fancy meeting you here.'

Aya looked up at me and smiled. 'I wonder what happened to him?' she said out loud looking back down at the body, and by now had rolled up his sleeves but there was no sign of injury at all. She then pointed out to me a mark on the inside of his lower arm and rolled his sleeve up his arm to make sense of it, it looked like an 'f' moving over towards his other arm. Nothing resembled the same mark, however, there were too many oval-shaped dark spots. Aya then moistened her thumb and rubbed them but the marks did not smear. 'I wonder what these are?' she said looking up to me again for guidance.

'No idea.' We then carried him out and laid him softly on the grass outside the cage, and she managed to slip on the grass.

I held down my arm to assist her rise, and as I was helping her up noticed across the way that there was a slither stream of golden light. It was behind me and was slowly getting wider. I nodded to her pointing it out, and she said that it looked like someone was opening the large entrance doors.

'It can't be opening. My friend Creedence is still there and he would not let them,' I said defiantly.

The first cage where some of The Carrion were locked up was suddenly bathed in the golden light of the widening sunbeam, and as there were only five of them, they all started moving, operating again. There was enough golden sunlight to re-generate their power source, waking them up. Then all hell broke loose inside the glass cage and the arena. I ran over to the cage yelling at everyone to get out of the way.

'Someone is opening the arena doors! Get out of the away...Get away.'

I saw Marty had noticed it too, and as he was the closest to that cage, he knew it was the same cage with the broken lock and the same one that he had spent all the time holding it closed. The only way to get it closed again and to keep it closed was to get back inside it with The Carrion. Not a choice anyone would be making.

I had to get back to the arena barn doors and get them closed behind us, to stop the sunlight, to stop them powering up and I watched Marty trying to hold the door closed, as he braced himself against it. A few of the others saw the commotion too and were trying to hold it closed along with him.

The glass door was now starting to open and close, open and close, the power of The Carrion and their momentum was forcing it back and forth. A single Carrion had managed to get its head out, and its razor-sharp beak was flaying at the opening. I saw Marty momentarily lose his footing and he fell forward just missing the flaying beak, and another Carrion managed to get its head out too.

I looked up at the widened sunlight gap and had to make a choice. If I got up there and shut the arena entrance doors it would stop the shard of light. I considered using The Rush, but it would be too slow as precious seconds would be wasted, so decided to run up the tiered steps instead.

Where is Creedence? I thought as I took the stairs three at a time. 'I'm going for the doors.' I yelled out to the group still trying to hold The Carrion at bay.

Marty turned around and waved with one hand, but he slipped again on the grass, and this time he wasn't so lucky, as one of The Carrion had managed to get its long neck out a little further, able to snake it around toward Marty and it sliced his arm off just below the elbow. He didn't notice, as he just kept pushing.

Someone noticed the blood pooling on the ground near the door making the grass slippery. 'Blood,' someone yelled out. 'Arm,' someone else yelled, having noticed the severed arm on the ground in the middle of the melee.

They all looked at each other with concern as they were also now losing the fight to keep the glass door closed. Marty then looked down and realised it was his arm. His adrenalin had kept him going, so he rolled himself away along the glass wall holding his bloodied stump.

I heard a scream behind me and was reluctant to look around in mid-stride, but fortunately, I did, as the reason for the scream was from the group holding the glass door. They had finally lost out to The Carrion. The glass door flung open, and they were pushed out of the way. The blood on the ground had made them all lose their footing.

Meantime, I had made it up the flight of stairs and kept running towards the steel doors, but still could not understand why someone would have opened them. I then saw Creedence still propped up against the door, his door, but it was my door that had been opened. I ran to the door avoiding the two docile Carrion still in the shadow being cast by Creedence's closed door.

Just as I arrived, I looked behind me once again and saw The Carrion had made their way out of the glass cage, but were not intending to hang around. They wanted to get back to wherever they came from and were coming straight at me. They were coming for the light and the golden western sun. There was still enough sunlight seeping through the gap to invoke their power.

I quickly stepped behind Creedence's closed door as it should protect me, still casting a shadow. The Carrion then flew past me and out into the western sun. I then moved back into the light and watched them go up into the sky and away into the western setting golden sun.

After that, I stepped over to Creedence and saw he was looking very pale and had a deathly pallor. He looked up at me, 'Good fight' and he closed his eyes, so I leaned down to him trying to understand what was happening.

He did not look injured, opened his eyes once and slowly spoke to me again. I noticed he'd taken his shirt off, and his hand was resting on a small leather bag, it was about a hand-width wide and had straps attached at the top.

'Here, take this. It's about The AIC. Papers, memos. I've collected them over the years.' He closed his eyes and whispered; 'Guard it with your life. Put it on...under your shirt.'

His breathing was shallower now. 'Your watch, your watch,'...tapping at my arm softly.

Why does he want to know the time?

'Tracker...Tracker,'...he then said pointing over to two docile Carrion that were sauntering in the shadows next to us as they had not been able to fly away. I realised they were not in direct sunlight and had not generated any charge as yet.

'Put your watch on its neck...put it on it.....Good fight,' he said softly.

I suddenly knew what he meant. My Phillipe Patek has a tracker in it, the trader that sold it to me told me so, and they could track it down if I lost it, he had made a point of telling me this. I undid my watch from my wrist and made my way over to The Carrion which was still waiting nearby.

I picked the larger one, not that there was much difference, and attached my watch to its neck. As the neck was much thinner than my arm I had to use the pin in the watch-band as an awl to make another hole, it worked, and it held fast. This next part was the tricky bit though, as I had to shift The Carrion to the open space, back into the sunlight. I picked up the first one, as it wasn't moving.

As I got closer to the light I sensed it knew what I was doing, and as I flung it into the sun-filled gap, it landed and stopped on the ground then took off rising into the golden setting sun. I then bent down to the next one, moved this one more slowly as it had my watch around its neck and knew I had to time this right.

The closer it got to the gap it started wriggling in my grip, so I leaned my head down just before letting it go to make sure the watch was well fastened. I thrust into the sunlight, but The Carrion suddenly snapped its head back and caught me in the face. I felt the pain instantly in my right eye and felt the blood dripping down from my face.

I then brought the two doors together, shut them and made my way back over to Creedence. Blood was dripping from my right eye, so I kept it closed, and then I noticed the arena lights had brightened up. I could see Creedence was not well. He then whispered something to me that I didn't quite catch, so I knelt beside him, it sounded like, 'Happy Birthday…Did you know it is my birthday today?' he said again softly.

I shook my head, 'No, I didn't know.'

'Today is my 40th …It's also my death day too. Read the file, the papers…' and with that he looked at me, smiled, took a large gasp of air and closed his eyes.

It suddenly dawned on me what he was talking about. Today was the day he would die. He is a Flighter, and we do not live beyond the 40th anniversary of our birth. 'The chips…where are the computer chips?' I whispered to him, still hoping he was still conscious as I knew he still had them. 'Are they still safe?'

His eyes fluttered as he was barely conscious, but he managed to say: 'My place, apartment, the blue sea…look for the blue sea.' He then held up his forearms to me. 'You will need to cut these out…my wrist chips…to get into my apartment.…

I am dying…. will die here …...now.' He took one last breath, looked up at me and smiled. 'Thanks for helping, and for being my friend.'

Then he died.

I waited there hoping that I was wrong. I wanted him to wake up, but he didn't, he wouldn't, and it was then I called out for help. I then looked at him, and the leather bag. 'The files, Creedence. I can't read…'

Chapter 36 Aya

Evening; Wednesday 25th December: I noticed another person was remaining in one of the other glass cages and his posture looked very similar to the one that Carlyle and I had just removed from the glass cage. As Carlyle had moved away I was making my way over there too when I heard someone yell out 'I'm going for the doors' and looked up and saw it was Carlyle. He was scaling the tiered stairs three at a time. Doesn't he ever stop? a sensitive guy who also wants to be a hero, my kind of guy I thought.

I called over to one of the other ERs that was also down on the grass with us, and as he came over I told him about the other victim I had found just before. We entered the cage, and he checked the man, checked for his pulse, and then looked up at me. 'Yep, he is dead,' he concurred flippantly.

'Check his arms can you though', I asked him as he was still squatting down next to the assumed victim and looking up at me, then pulling up the right sleeve asked, 'What am I looking for?'

'That', as I pointed to the mark on the inside of his lower arm resembling an 'f' I moved in beside him and raised the sleeve of the other arm there were the same marks as the other man, the two oval-shaped dark spots. 'What are they?'

'I don't know yet…but we are striking two for two and the moment' It was then I looked around the arena and noticed the glass cages had someone left in them.

The bodies were slumped against the inside walls. As I made my way towards the next one, all hell broke loose as The Carrion had broken out from one of the glass cages, the one at the front, the one that I had just noticed myself that was now bathed in golden light, and this was the sunlight that was coming from the direction that Carlyle was now running up and into. I then saw someone roll away from the door that the group of them were trying to restrain, it was the cage with the five remaining Carrion.

The man was holding his arm, half an arm anyway and it was a bloodied arm and then the rest of the group all fell away as the resistance on the door gave way too. The Carrion had exploded from the open door flying straight in the direction of the golden stream of light, the same direction that Carlyle was running.

I ran over to the bleeding man, his arm was severed at the elbow and was going into shock, so peeled off my shirt and tore it in half. He looked at me and went to move away, so told him sternly to keep still and when he looked at me again he said: 'I think it's my arm…I think they got me…they got me,' and with that, he slumped to the ground.

My ER training kicked in, so I kept slapping him lightly on the cheek to keep him awake, and I saw the sunlight coming through the gap had suddenly been closed off. We were momentarily in lesser light once again and the internal arena lights got brighter. Meantime, I had managed to keep the man awake and he looked to me for confirmation, 'It's my arm ...I think it is over there...on the ground.'

I looked over and saw a woman had picked up the severed arm and was bringing it over to me. 'I think this is his', she said with a trembling voice and the man looked at her; 'Heya sis...it looks like you just joined the army...with my armie.'

'Marty, what did do that for?'

I heard her say Marty as I tied off his arm in a mock tourniquet. Ok, so it's Marty then. Now I had a name. 'Now Marty, you have to stay awake. We have to get you to an ER base,' and with that, I heralded the ER crew to come over and deliver him to the closest ER station. Stat. I then held out my hand to the woman. 'I'm Aya, we meet again.'

'Zamiro.' she replied. 'And that was my brother Marty. He was the one in the first cage by himself holding off The Carrion.'

'Brave,' I acknowledged back to her.

I then heard someone calling out for help and it was coming from the cement corridor, the one that The Carrion had just flown through, and this was the same one where I had seen Carlyle running to just before. The person calling out came to the front platform and I saw it was Carlyle and I was relieved. I left Marty to the ER crew and made my way towards him. The dead can wait and hope that I didn't have to keep Carlyle waiting.

He saw me and called out, 'Over here.' I made my way along the corridor and looked towards him, and I saw another body slumped against the closed door.

'What happened?' I enquired squatting down next to the deceased man.

'He just died.'

I looked up at Carlyle and could see he was upset, 'And he was my friend.' I stood up next to him, moved in closer and we held each other momentarily. I then noticed that his right eye was bloodied as he was keeping it closed. It appeared that it had been split across the eyelid. 'Your eye, it looks bad.'

'I know, but I am not worried about that now as I have another eye,' he said stoically to me. I could like this guy I thought, as I looked down at the man.

'Creedence...his name is Creedence,' Carlyle said to me.

'Ok, Creedence. What did you do to yourself?'

On a hunch I rolled up his arm and saw the same marking, so I pointed this out to Carlyle. '*f*'

'Do you know what this is?' and then I asked him to roll up the other sleeve where there were the same two oval-shaped dark spots that I had seen on the others. 'And these?'

He shook his head to deny it, and I trusted he didn't know.

I rose closer to him this time and wanting to acknowledge my feelings in all the tenseness of everything leaned in and kissed him on the lips, but he did not reciprocate and was taken aback. 'Sorry...sorry. I just ...it was ...just.' I looked at him as he then lightly pressed his index finger onto my lips.

'My eye. Would you mind looking at that instead?' he said quietly to me whilst removing his finger slowly.

'Sure, let me have a look at that instead.'

I led him back to the platform at the end of the corridor as there was better light back here and looking at his eye could see the bleeding had now partially slowed.

'Can you open it?'

'No.'

'OK, keep it closed. I will lead you down to the grassy area. There will be medical kits. I can flush it out with saline and we will see from there.'

I held his hand as we made our way down and over to the kit guiding him to sit on a step so I could work on him. I carefully flushed his eye and was determined to keep my focus but being so close to him again. He was certainly intriguing.

The woman, that I had met before then came then over towards us, Zam or Zee...something, trying to recall her name, but I knew it was her brother Marty that I had just sent off to the ER Medical Centre.

I found myself staring into the eyes of Carlyle sitting so close to me again, and as I was working on him it was becoming quite intoxicating. Maybe that was just the stress of the events tonight and I was so tempted to kiss him again, to hold him again, to say everything was going to be all right, and his eye should be OK.

I will give him a patch to wear for a couple of days, maybe a week or two and I would have to keep an eye on him I thought chuckling to myself. I saw the woman again in my peripheral vision. Why was she hanging around us? Did she know Carlyle?

'Marty lost his arm', she suddenly blurted out. I don't know if it was directed to me or Carlyle, but I already suspected it couldn't be saved.

I finished up by placing a gauze pad over the eye and

wrapping a bandage around his head for added protection from infection and stood back a little to admire my handy work. By now the woman stepped in closer to us, and I was hoping that she had decided it was all taking too long and to move away, but she hadn't. 'What happened up there?' she asked him. 'And who opened the doors, and where is Creedence?'

So she knew Creedence, I thought. Does she know Carlyle too?

I looked at Carlyle, my Carlyle for a sign of recognition but there was none. Then she said to him. 'And where's your watch?'

He shrugged his shoulders, then stood up gingerly lightly patting the bandage around his head. 'Good job,' he said looking at me, then looked at her and together they moved away.

Right, I thought, that is that. Goodbye Carlyle, but I hope to see you again soon.

Chapter 37 Zamiro

Dusk; Wednesday 25th December*:* I could see that Marty had seen the commotion in the glass cage as The Carrion were now going crazy and I could see why as there was a golden beam of sunlight shining straight onto it. Someone must have re-opened the doors, and I watched as a group of Ground-Dwellers moved over towards the glass chamber encasing The Carrion. The five remaining Carrion were now trying to get out, whilst Marty and the group were desperately trying to keep the door shut. Suddenly saw that he had moved to the side grabbing at his arm and there was now blood spooling on the ground and the glass box. The Carrion were winning.

I then heard someone calling out, 'The doors', and it sounded like Carlyle, and it was, as I watched him scale the tiered stairs three at a time.

The glass cage door was then opened by The Carrion, they had won.

Not The Frenzy again, no not now, not in here I thought, turning away in horror.

I then felt a phantom pain on the side of my face of my memories, my scar still so raw. I willed myself to look back and saw that The Carrion was not invoking a Frenzy as they just wanted to get outside. I was relieved but realised they were heading straight towards the corridor that Carlyle had run towards moments before.

Would I lose him too?

I then looked back at Marty as he was being attended to by an ER. She was slapping his face to keep him from slipping into a coma, and then I saw his arm on the ground so picked it up carefully wrapped it in my jacket brought it over to them.

Aya nodded as I gave it to her, and think I told her it was his arm and I left her there working on Marty as I moved away. I then watched Marty leave in a Medical Shuttle that had been driven onto the grass through one of the entrance doors on the eastern side. I doubted they would be able to save his arm. It would make it interesting scanning left and right chips, buying and selling for him but thought it would be the least of concern as he will not be able to work at the AIC anymore, and Kilby will have to find another partner.

I looked over and could see that Aya was now moving between the other glass cages intrigued by something and she was now calling another ER agent into the glass chambers with her, and I watched as they kept raising the sleeves of the Flighters that were remaining in them.

All the while I noticed that The Flighters kept very still, and I felt they were still alive for some reason, then I saw the golden light beam shut off as someone had managed to close the door, and after some time saw the internal lights come on throughout the arena again. Someone must have opened the doors but why?

I then heard someone calling out for help and it was coming from the cement corridor, the one that The Carrion had just flown through and was the same one where I had seen Carlyle running to minutes before. The person calling out then came to the front platform. It was Carlyle, so I was relieved, and I watched as Aya ran up the tiers. She met him on the platform at the front, and they both disappeared into the half-darkened chasm.

A little time later Aya and Carlyle came down the stairs and she was holding his hand. It appeared he was not able to walk properly, was he injured? I kept moving closer to them and she had managed to sit him down on a step, but was leaning in very close to him, almost too close or was I imagining it?

I eventually decided she was close enough, so I blurted out: 'Marty has lost his arm,' to interrupt whatever I was imagining of her and my Carlyle. I could now see that Aya was almost finished with Carlyle's bandage, so I asked him who opened the doors, and where was Creedence, and then saw Aya look at Carlyle.

I also noticed he had lost his watch so ask him where that was too.

He said nothing.

We then moved away leaving Aya standing there, and he was guiding me upwards to the corridor where he had just come down from, but this time was holding his hand tightly as we made our way back up the steps again.

'Creedence is dead up there,' he said pointing up towards the corridor as we rose through the tiers.

'How?'

'He just died,' he said looking at me. 'The Carrion did not get him. He was not injured. He just died.'

We made our way back up to Creedence in the corridor and he was still propped up against the door. He looked so peaceful, and Carlyle was now staring down at him and I felt he wanted to ask me something.

'What?' I said.

'Do you have anything that can …. cut open his arms?'

'Why?'

'I need his wrist chips.'

'What…Why?'

'To get into his apartment', he said looking at me, and as I trusted him knew he would not be doing this if he could avoid it, I handed him the pointy screwdriver that I had taken from Marty just before he went off to the ER base.

'Will this do?'

He looked at it, rolled it in his hand, and felt the double-sided flat ends. 'Maybe.' He then bent down to the cement floor of the corridor and began scraping it back and forth twirling it as he did so. 'I need a bevelled edge; it needs to be sharper. I need to hone it for a sharper edge.'

This went on for a couple of minutes and then he moved over to Creedence. 'Be at peace my dear, dear friend,' and he began gouging into his forearms with the modified tool. The right-hand side chip popped out easily but the left one took a little longer, then eventually it yielded. Carlyle then asked me to tear some gauze from his head bandage which I did, so then he carefully folded them into the swathe that I had given him and put it in his pocket.

'What now?' I asked.

'Now, we go back to the field and see if anyone needs us here. Then we go home...to my home...Will you come and stay with me tonight?' then he paused, 'You will have your room.'

'Sure.'

As I looked at him, a small group of Ground-Dwellers walked past me, down the corridor carrying large hammers in their hands. I had seen these implements before at my Grandfather's place. I think they are called sledgehammers.

Chapter 38 Aya

Evening; Wednesday 25th December: I saw Carlyle and Zamiro coming down the tiers again and he had the pointy screwdriver in his hand and wondered what he had just done with it up there so then they came over to me as I was standing in a group of Ground-Dwellers asking them about the marks on the forearms of The Flighters but most of them looked at me shaking their heads in denial. I then looked at Carlyle and Zamiro and asked them. 'Do you two know anything about the marks on their forearms?' directing them to look at the deceased Flighters.

I felt Zamiro was thinking carefully about her response: 'Maybe my grandparents have said something about the common markings.'

'Come with me you two.' I beckoned them to follow me knowing the deceased Flighters had been removed from the glass chambers and had been lined up alongside each other. It was still a gruesome sight. They were all dead but why?

I walked up to another one of the ER team and surveyed them in the line, then went along each body raising the sleeves until all the marks were showing, every one of the deceased Flighters had the same markings. I walked around the bodies, stopped and then said to Carlyle and Zamiro. 'Tell me what you see?'

Zamiro said back to me, 'Death.'

'Yes, but what else can you see apart from that?'

Carlyle said, 'The markings look the same, in different places, but the same.'

I squatted down and pressed the 'f' on the arm of the first body and winced, they were dead, but felt I was still desecrating them. I then moved to the next and pushed my thumb into the two oval-shaped dark spots there too. 'Do you know what else is the same?' I said looking up at Carlyle. 'Their ages', I said knowingly, 'How old is this one you reckon? Go on, have a guess?'

'About forty', Zamiro said and then looked to the next one, 'And she is about the same age, over there too.'

Carlyle then looked at me. 'Creedence turned forty today. He told me it was his Birthday…. Then he said it was his death day too.'

'Yes, and I suspect they are all having their birthday today too, they all chose today to die. They volunteered to die today, and if needed to kill as many Carrion as they could. Today, on their death day.'

Zamiro looked at me. 'Flighters are heroes.'

I nodded in agreement 'That they are too,' and I looked at Carlyle, but he didn't say anything. I clasped my hands together 'I've got it!' I then moved some of the Flighters closer together so that their arms were almost touching, and this meant that the 'f' and every one of the two oval-shaped dark spots now lined up, and I looked at Carlyle and Zamiro. 'Now read it as an 'F', and the black spots read them not as two ovals but the letter 'O'.'

I don't think Zamiro understood what I was getting at, so I looked at Carlyle and thought he knew. 'FOO' he said softly looking down at them. 'They are all FOO – Freedom of Others, FOO-Flighters. They had lived anonymously, but all died today as heroes.' He then looked at me but said to Zamiro. 'Ask Dave and Courtney next time you see them what The FOO do for The Forced.'

I looked at him, 'So, how do you know about the FOO and The Forced?'

I guessed Zamiro thought the same thing as she was looking at him too but instead, they ignored me and moved quietly away.

'We are going home now.' I overheard Carlyle say to Zamiro.

'We', I then thought. Now that is disappointing.

Chapter 39 Kilby

Dusk; Wednesday 25th December: I was late, and will not make it in time, as I am trying to get to the arena before dusk, and before The Carrion. I was supposed to be there to help build glass-walled cages, damn these Zoops as I gave it up dropping it onto the ground, it had run out of charge. They do this if they do not get enough sunlight or overnight recharge.

It is expected that if you ride it you find a way to re-charge it but sometimes it doesn't work out that way, so I then started running. It was getting closer to dusk and as it was a bright day there was no doubt The Carrion would come just as Creedence had predicted.

I came around the street corner and was almost there but so was The Carrion. They were already here but fortunately, they were high up above circling the roof of the arena. I was safe at least for the time being.

I then stopped and knew I was still too far away for them to see me at least that was what I hoped, so took a quick read of my surroundings looking for places I could go, to enter and be inside and be safe, then I saw the commotion up on the roof of the arena.

The Carrion were going crazy I could see why, as there were glass-walled sentry boxes at various intervals around the roof. But that wasn't the crazy part as I could see that there were people in them, and I recognised the person in the box closest up above me as it was Creedence. 'Why?'

I then saw movement up on the roof over to my right, could just make out that someone had just stepped out of their sentry box and was gesturing aggressively to the circling Carrion, then watched as some of The Carrion moved around behind him and realised he was not looking in that direction as they swung down behind him and flew straight through him. I turned away. There was more noise up there now and I saw another box explode in a burst of blood, just how many people are up there. Why? Why??

I then realised it could be a stalling tactic and that The Carrion was falling for it and maybe they would be there for too long and it would get too dark for them to continue but they suddenly stopped and began circling again. Then they flew down beside the arena walls into the open gaping doors, still all within the light, the golden setting sun, as it maintained the energy for them to fly down.

What is going on now? I thought as The Carrion were all rushing to get inside, and they had now made it inside the arena, through the open doors. I saw Creedence step out of his sentry cage and he drop-floated down to the ground, so walked up to him to say hello, but he left me quickly as he began running towards the sunlit gap, and was following The Carrion inside.

He had so much courage as I could see that he had now entered through the gap and immediately turned to the left as the right-hand side door was already closed and then the left one started moving, but it abruptly stopped. I saw him lean down pulling something from the ground rails by the bottom of the door, it looked like a red ball of some kind but on a second look, I knew it was a severed head. Then the doors shut, which I assumed was to make it go dark inside and realised why as The Carrion would not operate in the dark. Creedence had mentioned this the other day. It was all a trap and I hoped all the people inside were ready.

I waited outside for what seemed ages. I had no intention of joining them in there, but then I saw the doors opening, one side anyway, and a single man stepped out. Just one man. Where is everyone else?

He looked over to me, then looked behind him as he must have known he had left the door ajar. As he ran past me noticed he had a uniform on. I think it was a Represents uniform. I managed to read his name on the label stitched to his breast, it looked like 'Haw' and he saw me looking at it so pulled his arm across his chest to shield it from me. He turned his shoulder to prevent me from reading it again and kept running.

I knew he hadn't shut the door behind him, but no one else was coming out so thought I should go over there and close it, but where was The Carrion? I kept waiting, and then I heard more noises from inside that sounded like The Carrion noise and I realised the partially opened door must have cast the western sunlight into the arena. I saw the first Carrion come out tumbling backward, and whilst I was watching them I looked for a niche of shadow somewhere close behind me.

One, two, three, four...five...The Carrion flew upwards into the setting sun.

I had made it into the shadowed niche and watched for more but there were none, and thought it might now be safe. I then saw another one come out, but this one looked like it had been thrown out by persons unknown, and then I saw another Carrion land on the ground outside the door. This Carrion though had managed to snap its head back and had made contact with whoever was thrusting it out into the sunlight.

I could see that this contact was right in their face, into their right side, and most likely the eye, as I saw the person react by moving their hand to their face. As they took flight over me, I saw the second Carrion had a ring around its neck. It looked like a watch, a timepiece, and wondered what that was all about.

Whoever it was then stepped into the light to watch The Carrion fly away.

I then realised that the man in the light was Carlyle. He then turned, drew the two doors together and re-entered the arena. The doors were now closed, and the arena was sealed from within once again. I decided to make my way around to the eastern side of the arena. I should be safe as long as I keep out of the western light but did not know if more Carrion would be exiting the arena.

I took a roundabout way to get there and eventually saw the next entrance gates. They had started to open as an ER shuttle was making its way slowly outwards. There must be casualties. The van was going slow enough for me to look in, so I made a casual glance through the rear windows and saw that it was Marty. He was holding his arm or what was left of it, a bloodied stump, wrapped in a shirt. I went forward and banged on the side door of the driver. 'He is my brother...let me in.' They stopped and I climbed in the back.

Marty looked at me 'You made it then?... Look what I did', he said raising his half-arm to show me. 'I don't think I will make it to work tomorrow.' And with that comment, he leaned back onto the gurney, closed his eyes and the ER officer placed a plastic moulded mask over his nose and mouth.

'I gave him something for the pain, Nitrous Oxide gas. It might make him a bit sick, but the ER station will monitor him closely.'

I looked over to him. 'Not Helium, you don't use that instead?'

He shook his head. 'No. Where did you hear that?'

I looked down at Marty. 'Just around. I thought that Helium is what the ER uses as it is much quicker.'

He responded quietly. 'Not at all, I think all The Flighters have concentrated Helium in them, but Nitrous Oxide is the gas of our choice. They are even putting it into Sheesha's to get a quick rush. Some are now even adding in Helium, calling it Hell of a Nite. We are picking them up under the influence of the gasses. Some of them wake up, and some die. I guess that is what they do for excitement. I wish they should fight The Carrion instead.'

Then the ER crewman started to fill me in on the battle within the arena as we drove slowly away towards the nearest ER station. He went on and on about the effects of Helium and how The Flighters are using it to save themselves and not others from The Carrion and The Frenzy.

Spare me the minutia I thought: What is this all about?

He finally finished with, 'Your brother was the only one hurt apart from The Flighters. They all died, and they were all FOO as it turned out. Who knew?'

I then thought: 'Well I did.' I then had a second thought: 'All the Flighters died...Did that include Creedence and Carlyle?

Chapter 40 Carlyle

Morning, Thursday 26th December: I rose from the bed, put on my robe moved toward the window facing the sea and the morning was beautiful. I looked down to the futon behind me as Zamiro was still entwined in the sheets, still asleep, and she looked beautiful too.

I saw myself in the reflection of the glass window and felt Aya had done a good job as I softly patted the patch over my eye, although the head bandage had caused the helmet to be a little tight on the ride home last night on the Zoop. I felt good and wondered if I would gain my sight back, she said I would, but she had also kissed me last night too and what did that mean?

I then heard Zamiro waking behind me and turned to watch her as she stretched out, the sheet had moved down a little from her chest, so she pulled it up for modesty. I like that about her. I love that about her.

'What a day, what a night,' she commented, and I knew that she was not referring to us though. We had been both physically and mentally exhausted, had both showered before climbing into bed and she used the second bathroom. I told her that Marty had not removed the robe from that room as she had instructed him to do earlier as it was still on the bed. I still didn't understand what was meant regarding the family banter with the bedroom and robe.

As it was later in the morning, I said 'Watch, what is the time,' forgetting I no longer had it on. Zamiro had noticed. 'Did you lose it?.... What happened to it?' she asked sitting up and propping herself with the pillows behind her back.

'No, actually I gave it away,' I stared out to the blue sea in front of me. The blue sea? The blue sea? Now what had Creedence meant by that? I turned around to explain to her about the watch and waited whilst she donned her robe and came over to me.

'Who did you give your watch to?'

'Not who to, but what to', I replied to her as she raised herself to me, and softly kissed my lips. 'Morning,' she then said after extracting her lips from mine.

I smiled at her, 'The Carrion,' then I explained about Creedence's idea and the tracking mechanism within the watch. 'I gave it up so we can find out where they go. It can't be far from The Frenzy, as the sunlight would be falling whilst they are flying back to wherever they come from.' I went on to explain how I managed to get it onto its neck, and she then asked me about my eye, so I told her about that too, she then rose up and softly kissed the bandage.

'Breakfast then?' she asked me and then said 'and then shopping for clothes. I keep I keep coming back here with you, but don't have a change of clothes. Do you think, I could you know, have my cupboard and drawers?'

I smiled at her again, as if I would give her my whole world if it was mine to give. I left her there and went off to shower and dress myself. After we showered met back in the kitchen and I managed to find her some of my clothes that she could wear instead of re-dressing in yesterday's attire. She makes baggy look pretty.

We then caught the lift downstairs, found breakfast, and the clothing boutiques, and returned to the apartment around noon. The telephone was ringing so Zamiro went over to it, answered the call, and told me it was Kilby.

'Why? Who said that?' she then held the handle out from her ear and looked over towards me: 'So, the ER told you that they were all dead. They told you that all The Flighters were dead, and you want to know if Creedence and Carlyle were dead too as none of the Flighters survived. Let me call you back Kilby as I have to ask Carlyle something. OK, I will see you in about thirty minutes then.' She hung up the telephone, looked back at me, and crossed her arms over her chest. I felt she was annoyed with me.

'So you need to tell me something?' she said looking sternly at me.

'Yes, I am a Flighter', I said quietly, and to that, she looked away, so I went to her, and she softly slapped down my out-stretched hand.

'Why didn't you tell me?'

I hung my head. 'I don't know. I couldn't. I didn't know how to and it would be dangerous for you to know. I am so sorry.'

She looked at me and shook her head. I didn't know what she was going to do and thought I had lost her again, so went to move to her again, but this time pirouetted slowly and smiled back at me. I was confused.

'I knew it, damn you...you saved me that day as you lifted me, carried me to safety. You saved my life from The Carrion. I knew it.'

I looked at her and was still confused. 'You know Ground-Dwellers and Flighters should not get acquainted as they say it is dangerous for both of them.'

Zamiro smiled again. 'OK, Carlyle, why don't we see just how dangerous it is? I am not going anywhere and will not leave you now either.' And with that, she moved towards me, and we kissed again, but when we finally broke apart she added, 'I do know of a Special Stones Jeweller around here that is just waiting to have us back.'

I looked at her. Is she referring to a fingerband? She wants a fingerband. I might be up for that...I think....just maybe?

She looked at me and grinned. 'Yes, as he will be able to track your lost Phillip Patek.'

Very funny I thought.

We couldn't think of anything to do whilst waiting for Kilby, so I looked down at my journal on the kitchen bench, called Zamiro over and re-read the entries. I tried to correct the spelling errors, then I agreed to leave the syntax to her, so we worked on it together.

Zamiro commented she would move away if I wanted to enter something private or personal for the 4th day. I crossed out and re-wrote every error, and then decided to write about day 5. Yesterday.

My Journal –Day 5 22nd

My life has changed so much now. I have frends agan for the first time.

I am in love. I think it is love. I feel that Zamiro's family is becoming my family.

I miss my own family even more now.

How can I pay them homage? I must get back to the farm in Munta.

Will it stell be ther?

Will Zamiro come with me if I go there?

Chapter 41 Kilby

Noon; Thursday 26th December: I had left Marty in the Medical Centre earlier this morning as he would be safe there though there was no attempt to re-attach his arm and realised he would not be able to work with me for some time on the AIC assembly line, if ever at all.

I drove myself to the first checkpoint at the AIC after leaving him as I was interested to know if I would be let in as a single team member, and although scanned my wrist chip and passed at the first panel I could not go any further. The only indication that I could not penetrate the next area was it would not let me through although there was no sign, no symbol, nothing. I turned around and headed back home to my Berg. I decided to take an alternate route coming back so I could go to see Carlyle instead. I knew that Creedence and Carlyle lived in the same apartment in Evoh and wanted to know if they had both survived The Carrion.

I had been informed by the ER that they were all killed, that all The Flighters had been killed, and that was all I could find out as Marty was still not conscious. Nobody was saying anything apart from that it was almost a complete disaster. I even mentioned to the ER crew that I had seen someone, a man, maybe a Represent, leaving the door ajar at the arena and this caused The Carrion to re-waken inside the arena.

They ignored me. Either they didn't know, or would not.

I was curious beyond frustration. Were Creedence and Carlyle dead?

I needed to make a telephone call to his apartment, so remembered the location of a Ground-Dweller that would accommodate my request, so I went there and called, and I was surprised that Zamiro answered. I considered she may be at the apartment looking for solace in the death of Carlyle. When I mentioned that I was told he was dead, I was even more surprised when she told me she would be calling me back after saying: 'Let me call you back as I have to ask Carlyle something.'

He was still alive.

I told her I was on my way to Evoh and would be there in about thirty minutes, so I dropped the shuttle off and swiped my wrist on the door panel to enter the foyer area. I made my way over to the lifts but as I swiped, I saw a man lurking in the shadows by the side of the building, just beyond the side alley. I wondered what he was doing there, and what is more I thought I recognised him…. but from where?

The elevator doors opened as I approached so entered and pushed the button for the 11th floor, but it would not light up so wondered if I should take the stairs. A woman came up to me whilst I was in my quandary. 'Where are you trying to go?' she said.

I noticed she was dressed in an ER uniform. '11th floor.'

'Me too,' she replied and looked over at me as she pushed the button for 11.

I looked back at her. 'Do you live here? I don't, so I could not use the elevator. I can only get into the foyer. Just the common spaces.'

'I don't live here, but I am ER and have access to all the floors. It is part of The GOD Rescue Authority, but I cannot enter the apartments without further authorisation.'

The elevator chimed as we came to a stop on the 11th floor and we alighted. She was looking around as I made my way towards 1103, Carlyle's apartment and she began to follow me. '1103. Do you know him too?' she asked me.

I noticed that she had a nameplate on the chest of her shirt as her jacket was agape, and this was previously covering the name badge. 'Aya' it read as we came to the door together.

I knocked on it and called out: 'Yo...Zee, it's me.'

Carlyle opened the door, looked at me, and then at Aya. 'Hello, Aya. What are you doing here?'

I looked over at Aya, and meantime Zamiro had come to the door as well. 'Hi Kilby, how is Marty?' She then said 'Oh, Hello Aya'

Aya was standing next to me I saw that she had raised her hand to her face and stared at us all thoughtfully whilst caressing her chin. 'So, Kilby, Carlyle and Zamiro. You all know each other, and Marty is the name of the G-D that I had sent off to the ER station last night. He had lost his arm to The Carrion. How do you know him then?'

Zamiro spoke first. 'Marty and Kilby are my brothers, and Carlyle well, he is my boyfriend.'

To that, I heard Aya say almost disapprovingly, 'Oh, I guessed so.'

Carlyle then brought us into the apartment, and Aya

finally introduced herself to me. 'I was there yesterday, saw it all, we almost lost to them and this guy over here, well I think he may have saved us. He was one of the heroes and your brother was another. The only other casualties were The FOO.' She looked specifically at me after the FOO comment, but I didn't react and didn't think I should.

Zamiro looked at me and I said to her. 'It's OK sis she has worked it out. The FOO have tattoos, maybe self-inflicted, *'foo'* reads on their forearms in a tattoo.' I thought Carlyle instinctively pulled his sleeves down over his forearms, but maybe I imagined it.

'So how is your eye?' Aya said over to Carlyle moving towards him, 'The bandage looks good, would you like me to take a look?'

'No. Too soon.'

'So, you are alive then?' I said to Carlyle and moved towards him.

He put out his hand to shake mine, but I was not having that, so grabbed him in a bear hug and told him not to scare me like that and as he stepped back out of the hold told me about Creedence. He beckoned to move away from the others and told me that the computer chips were somewhere in Creedence's apartment.

We knew we needed to find them soon as there was limited time to access them before the locks closed down. He also told me he has Creedence's wrist chips. He then leaned closer and whispered: 'The AIC would already have been notified or know that Creedence died, so they will automatically shut the chips down.'

'Let's go right now then,' I said to him, and he nodded.

'Apartment 503 is down below'.

Aya and Zee wanted to know what was happening, so I looked over at Carlyle and told him this could get dangerous for all of us. He agreed and told them to stay in there, but I got the impression that they did not want to do that. I also got a feeling that something was going on between them, something to do with Carlyle.

Zamiro then said to Carlyle, 'Do you know about the Blue Sea then? Just what did Creedence mean?' I looked at her, 'What is that about?'

'He told us to go to his apartment, and look for the Blue Sea.'

Aya wanted to know what was going on too, so Carlyle explained to her, but I was not impressed as I did not know that he knew Aya so well. She then explained how she had met him. 'We met at Munna Cliffs. Oh, and by the way I used to work at the AIC, on the computer chip line. Before I became ER.'

I was surprised about that as I had never known anyone else who worked there apart from Marty, nor had never known anyone to admit it either. I would keep that in mind as she might be useful I might be able to keep her to myself if only I could get her back in. How can I make it work?

We decided to all go down to the apartment and arrived at the door of 503. Carlyle said he would miss Creedence I said I would too, he then removed the folded gauze swathe from his pocket and separated the two chips and they were still bloodied.

I went to ask him how he got them, but Zee must have

known what I was thinking as she put her hand lightly onto my shoulder, and simply said, 'Later Kilby.'

He waved the first one over the lock, but nothing happened, so he gave it to me and then held the second one over the lock but again nothing happened. This was not going to work, so we all just stood there Aya then asked for one of the chips.

Carlyle gave it to her, and she produced a little spray vial from under her jacket. 'Saline' she said giving it a small wisp whilst holding it in her hand. Some of the blood then came off, so wiping it dry on her sleeve, held it to the lock again, and this time it clicked open, and we all moved cautiously inside.

It was the same configuration as Carlyle's, except there was an extra room off to the side of the bedroom corridor, but not a third bedroom as it was too small, more likely just for storage. The apartment was otherwise tidy, so we started looking around, going through drawers but they seemed not to contain many items and it was as if he had only just moved in. Maybe he had.

'Nothing here,' came from Aya.

'Here either,' this came from Zee.

After about fifteen minutes we assembled again in the middle of the living room, and were all looking out to the sea, to the blue sea.

'Just what did he say exactly? Word for word,' Aya said to Carlyle.

He thought about it, 'Exactly word for word, he said to me. My place, the apartment, look for the blue sea, then he died right there in front of me.'

We all looked around once again but there was nothing else, nothing but the blue sea out of the window in front of us.

'OK,' Zamiro said 'Let's go through again as we must be missing something.'

Aya then said, 'Try this with four eyes, not two this time. Kilby come with me, and we will go this way.'

We headed toward the bedrooms. Aya and I went into the first room, to the storeroom, and apart from a few cardboard boxes there was nothing much in there. I went over to them as they were three piled on each other. I pulled the boxes from the wall, and as they were empty came forward easily, so I looked behind them.

'Found it', I called out looking down at a crescent-shaped item before me, 'I think,' clarifying my first statement. It wasn't the blue sea we were looking for at all and I looked down at it. It was a blue 'C' The letter 'C' was blue, painted sea blue. It was indeed a Blue C. I lifted it from the back of the boxes and carried it to the dining area.

It was not heavy, maybe made of paper so laid it down on the table and turned it over. It was sealed at the back but the paper was soft, so I probed my finger into the back of the C and it tore, so then wriggled my finger through the tear and made a wider gap and felt something was in there.

It was a small cardboard square and managed to extract it placing it on the table.

It too was sealed. 'Anyone have a small knife?' and with that, Aya pulled a small knife from her breast jacket, very resourceful I thought, and I am starting to like her. I carefully slit the sides of the cardboard, fanned the square open and seven pristine computer chips present themselves to us.

'What now?' I said as we all peered down at them.

'Nothing more now as we have found them,' Carlyle said then added: 'I am still exhausted from yesterday, so let's meet up here again tomorrow at my place. I suspect this apartment will be shut off soon and we won't be able to get in without raising suspicion. I am going upstairs for rest and will take the chips with me."

Aya looked surprised and said 'It is too dangerous for you to do that alone. What if you get caught with them?'

He looked at her, 'I will get away somehow,' and with that, both Zee and I looked at each other realising Aya does not yet know Carlyle is a Flighter.

Carlyle then looked at the computer chips, folded them back into the cardboard but they would not quite close properly, so Aya looked at him reached inside her jacket pocket on the left side this time, and pulled out a small tube and held it up.

'Here use this, we call it Supa glue,' then she proceeded to squeeze the tube studiously to smear the liquid lightly along the edges of the cardboard square. 'We use this to hold minor wounds together as a quick fix.'

Once it was sealed Carlyle slipped it carefully into his pocket.

I looked over at Aya again. 'Lunch?' and was surprised when she said.

'Why not.'

We then both left the apartment, caught the elevator downstairs, and just as we were exiting the building I saw the same man lurking around the outside again so I asked her if she knew him, but she said no.

We had a late lunch, and I rode back with her on the back of a Zoop, dropping her off at the Central Shuttle terminus to go back to Munna Cliffs. I noticed that the terminus premises were looking a little untidy as there was more litter around.

'What happened to the cleaner?' I said out loud just as Aya was stepping onto the shuttle. She admitted she didn't know that either so I then asked her when she would be returning.

She stopped mid-step and mentioned that her ER partner had just been killed in the recent Carrion Frenzy at Munna Cliffs and she was able to relocate if she chose to. She was considering coming back to Edi-Aleda anyway as she used to live in the Central Berg. I quickly mentioned Creedence's apartment.

'A bit early don't you think?' adding 'But it does look like he never actually lived here so maybe he was just moving in?'

'Maybe.' I then thought about my ulterior motive as she might be able to replace Marty at the AIC, and that meant I may be able to keep my job, just maybe.

I waited for her to leave then went up to the Hologram guide and asked the question about the cleaner being missing. *Thank you for your concern however our loyal employee Creedence is no longer with us.* It paused momentarily and then added: *'He is dead.'*

A smiling headshot of the cleaner then appeared on the screen in front of me, 'Oh', I thought looking at the image, then I recognised it was our Creedence. I was still thinking about him as I made my way home to Yelnu. I stepped off the Zoop leaving it by the stoop, and went inside.

It was now dark, and The Carrion had not come tonight.

Everyone wanted to know everything, so I told them but left out the part about the stolen computer chips, and The Blue C.

Chapter 42 Carlyle

Evening; Thursday 26th December: I was exhausted. Zamiro had come back up with me to my apartment and as Aya and Kilby had already left together and gone to late lunch, I entered the apartment and Zamiro followed me in. We made lunch from my reserves in the cooler then rested and it was about 4 o'clock when we both stirred again, from our separate rooms. I commented that it was at least a couple of hours until The Carrion would arrive, and hoped they would not come, then realised that she had not been at the ELC today.

'Not teaching today?'

'No, like Kilby I am on repat leave too. I called in and told them that I needed a couple of non-work days to recuperate.'

'What a crap way to spend it then.'

'Not really. Now if can only work out how we can defeat them.' I agreed and then said; 'Now if only we can work out how to defeat them.' as I was deep in thought. 'That is what I just said,' she said looking back at me. 'Great minds think alike,' and I nodded again, so we sat and waited for The Carrion together. It was nice, it felt safe and just for a brief moment I felt loved.

We waited and waited, but they did not come even though it was a golden sunset and a beautiful end of the day, so as we watched the sunset set I wondered why. I was thinking about The Carrion that we had herded into the glass chambers yesterday. 'Do you know what they did with The Carrion at the arena?' I asked Zamiro.

'I hope they smashed them all into a million pieces,' and she continued, 'When we were leaving did you notice some Ground-Dwellers go past us carrying large rectangle metal blocks on the end of handles back into the arena? I think they might be called sledgehammers as Grandfather Dave has one in his home. They are very heavy as I once tried to pick them up. They used them to break up the cement roads, so can only imagine what they would do to some metal boxes of nothing like The Carrion. I would have loved to have hung around and watched.'

I looked at her having nothing to say to that comment.

'It is late, so let's have dinner and I will get you to have a look at my journals if that's ok.' I went on to tell her I hadn't recorded anything in the journal for a couple of days and she said that was fine and there were no rules, no timeframes, no judgements so she agreed to look at them with me.

We made some changes and had some laughs, well she did, but I didn't and as it was about 9 p.m. she said she would retire. I told her I wanted to stay up a little longer to complete another entry in my journal that I would show her later.

My Journal – Day 9 26th
So much has happened in the last few days. So much death.

The Flighters. The FOO. I lost my best friend.
The Carrion almost beat us. We have a plan to beat
them. Will it work?
I have given up my secret. Marty & Kilby know. Dave
and Courtney know. Zamiro knows.
They accept me anywy. I wantoo make a diferents. I will
make a diferents.
We all will make this work. We must make this work.
We will defeat them. We must defeat them.
I want to spend the rest of my life with Zamiro.
How eva long that wil be?

I saw that she went to the bedroom, my bedroom again
this time, and I was still nervous about this, still nervous
about us then heard her showering, so waited a little and then
joined her in my boudoir. 'I want to see Marty tomorrow,
will you come with me?' she asked whilst looking at me across
the futon as she pulled the sheet back climbing in. I was now
dressed in my swimming trunks, and she was dressed in a
nightshirt that was purchased during our shopping venture
earlier, and even though it was too big for her still looked
beautiful in it. I nodded and added: 'Let's go to the arena as
well to see what happened to The Carrion. Would they still
be in the glass cages you think?'

She nodded. 'Sure, but maybe they are all destroyed by
now too.' I rested back on the bed, and was thinking about
Zamiro and that she was so close to me tonight. I wanted to
say something profound to her, but I fell asleep too quickly.

Chapter 43 Aya

Morning, Friday 26th December: It felt so right about what I was about to do, so I went into my supervisor's office and told her I needed some time to sort things out as had just lost my work partner Axa and had witnessed the slaughter of my colleagues.

The Carrion had won that fight, but I wanted to go to war.

I told her I was leaving Munna Cliffs, going back to Edi-Aleda as I had met someone and wanted to know what it would feel like to feel again. I have seen too much death and think she understood. I took a deep breath, boarded the Shuttle to Edi-Adela with my two packed bags and headed into the unknown.

I left Munna Cliffs behind me in the rear window, and as I had arrived early at the Central Berg, alighted the shuttle, dropped my cases on the ground and stood there. I was alone, no one knew me and had nowhere to go.

I went over to the Hologram guide, but it looked like it was not even operating as yet, so asked it a random question about a shuttle and it started buffering which was to me a little amusing, it then said something that sounded like 'He is dead.'

I wondered who so I asked it, then a headshot appeared in front of me that I immediately recognised as Creedence and thought to myself that it was a sign.

I knew exactly what to do now.

I went over to the local ER base, waved my way in and was told by one of the Supervisors that my ER pass would continue to work indefinitely, to access all areas. I found what I was looking for, and made a telephone call which was then answered quickly.

'Hello, this is Kilby.'

We made a little small talk and then I finally told him to meet me at the ER station where Marty had been taken on Wednesday night. I made some other decisions on the way. I would move into Creedence's apartment even if it didn't suit me straight away, but at least it was something.

It was somewhere that I already knew I would be safe.

I would take Marty's job on the assembly line, but it might be difficult working back there given my previous working history at The AIC. I would have to work closely with Kilby. He was nice enough, but there are the feelings I have for Carlyle to deal with too. I met Kilby outside the ER station and filled him with my plans and he seemed to be pleased for me, but also seemed to be pleased for himself too, and I wondered what that meant for us. I was then formally introduced to Marty, and we talked about The Carrion. I was sorry that I could not save his arm but assured him his own life was more important and he seemed to be happy with that. I then told him about my plans, that I was to move into Creedence's apartment and my working with Kilby at the AIC.

I think I saw Kilby do a little fist pump which I took

that he was happy with everything that I was doing. Then Carlyle turned up with Zamiro. Oh Carlyle just who are you? I thought.

I then told them how I met Carlyle, about The Water Carrion, The Carrion, about losing my ER partner, losing my ER friends, about Howard and Bernie and all that kept them quiet for a while, however I got the feeling they were not telling me everything, keeping something from me.

Maybe I've been in an ER too long.

Marty made really bad jokes about losing his arm, and we told him about yesterday and finding the computer chips, the loss of Creedence and I was about to say about the time I got lost at the AIC and that I'd found another area I had never been in before. Marty then suddenly became suspicious of the surroundings and did a whirly thing with his finger that I think meant no more speaking, so we then decided to move on, move elsewhere. It was suggested to go to the Central Berg library, as there is a bunker there.

We were off to make plans to save the world, at least our world anyway.

Chapter 44 Marty

Noon; Friday 27th December: I woke, where am I? Looking around realised that I was still in the Emergency Centre, in a bed, still in a recovery booth shrouded by a blue curtain and at the foot of my bed were Kilby and a woman. I think she is an ER nurse and remember her from the arena yesterday.

I tried to say 'Hi' but it sounded like: 'Hrrupth.'

'This is Aya,' I heard Kilby say to me, so raised my hand to salute her but nothing happened, I looked for my hand, but it wasn't there neither was my forearm and I remembered that a Carrion took it from me. Kilby came around to the side of my bed, looked at me and asked how I was doing, then asked if I knew what happened.

The woman, Aya, stayed where she was though. I told him that The Carrion had taken my arm and I looked at Aya as she said she had tried to save me, put me in an ER shuttle and brought me here.

'Today is Thursday right?' I asked them.

'No, Friday', she said.

I looked at her. 'You were brought here Wednesday and

today is Friday. You have been here nearly three days. I looked at Kilby. 'Three days?'

'Yep,' he replied then went on to explain how he had seen the ER shuttle coming out of the arena, that he had looked in and realised it was me. He had ridden in the shuttle with me to the ER centre, and Zamiro had given Aya his arm.

'It was not possible to save your arm, so they saved you instead.'

'And The Carrion?' I asked.

'Well, some of the Ground-Dwellers got to take their revenge on them. Do remember the heavy-headed hammers that grandfather keeps in his work shed? Let's just imagine the damage those things do in a confined space to little boxes of soft metal. There's nothing left.'

I smiled. 'I remember seeing some get away after I let the door go. Did some get away?' Both Aya and Kilby nodded at me. 'About five or so.'

'We also lost about seven Flighters but as it turned out they were FOO; they all chose to die protecting us. Aya worked out that Wednesday was their common death day. They had all decided to spend their last day protecting us from The Carrion. They were heroes, every one of them.'

I looked at Kilby, 'Creedence and Carlyle too?'

I wanted to say something, but realised Aya doesn't yet know Carlyle is a Flighter. 'Creedence didn't make it, but Carlyle did.' I hoped Aya didn't get the connection between them both being Flighters and that Carlyle did not die as he is much younger than the others.

During the pause, Carlyle and Zamiro had arrived. They came up to the end of the bed and nodded a hello to me and

Aya. I saw that Carlyle had an eye patch over one eye and assumed it was from The Carrion.

Aya then addressed our group: 'I have decided to take a temporary leave of absence from being an ER. I keep my full entitlements which include access to all areas pass. I have also decided to move back down to Edi-Aleda and into Creedence's apartment at Evoh. It looks like he never actually lived there.'

We all looked at her and thought I saw Kilby give a little fist pump. 'And,' she then continued, 'then I am going to go back to work on the assembly line at the AIC with Kilby.' I looked over at him and he shrugged his shoulders.

'We checked it out this morning bro. The AIC will not allow you back to work at all as you don't have the use of both hands. Aya is an ER, and Aya has worked there before so has access to other areas at The AIC facility as an ER, and Aya will be living in Evoh too.' He was almost hyperventilating with all the news.

'OK I get it, I get it, but what am I going to do? I might still be handy around the home though as I still have one left, maybe I could open a second-hand shop?' I claimed flippantly but think they got my bad pun though. They all groaned, and then suddenly Carlyle said to Aya: 'What did you just say about access all areas?'

'My ER pass. We can wave our pass at the panels and go through sealed doors into areas that the public cannot get into. It's part of the GOD Rescue Authority.'

'Why?'

'Because it means that you can go deeper into the sanctity of The AIC building, and you might find something else in there. This might be where they manufacture them, The Carrion, or be where they return to after The Frenzy. The site is too large to only make the chips. Something else happens in there.'

'The chips,' I said remembering that they were with Creedence, and he is now dead. I called Kilby over closer and quietly mentioned them to him.

'They all know Marty, they know just about everything,' then he explained about the Blue C and the Blue Sea, but it didn't make sense to me, but at least the chips were located and were all safely hidden away.

We then looked around at each other realising the opportunity we had, and then Kilby looked at Carlyle raising the issue of the stolen computer chips.

'What can they be used for?' he asked.

'According to Creedence we have a window of about twelve hours to wipe and re-set and that might be enough to get another person through the checkpoint gates with you so we might be able to hide in a larger shuttle and get in that way.' Aya began to say she had heard about a time when.... 'Not here, not here.' I then raised my other hand and twirled around my index finger as Kilby had done many times to me before, which I still find so infuriating. 'These walls have ears.'

They all nodded in agreement with me. 'Where to then?' I heard Zee say.

'Go to the bunker...the library ...That's fine off you all go leave me here, all alone...by myself and you guys go off and save the world without me.'

Zamiro leaned over and kissed my cheek softly, and then

Aya did so too on the other cheek. 'We don't need another dead hero,' Zamiro said looking down at me and they gave me a wave, and all walked out together. I assumed they were heading for the library to plot the plan to save the world, at least our world anyway.

Chapter 45 Carlyle

Evening; Friday 27th December: We had left Marty at the ER station and he seemed to be in good spirits, even saying a bad joke about losing his arm. I had to get Zamiro to explain it to me, but I still didn't understand it. We left together and went to the library, and went through the same corridors. Kilby explained about the chance meeting with Creedence, and the safety of the bunker.

Things were starting to gather momentum, but as we rounded the aisle to the bunker the large steel door was closed, shut tight, even though Kilby had assured us it was kept open 9 – 9, so we all stopped. He started looking around for someone to talk to about it, but didn't expect anything from anyone though, then we heard someone coming behind us. We had nowhere to go.

I nodded to Zamiro and Kilby to try and leave as I believed Aya and I could most likely handle ourselves if needed. The voices came up to us and acknowledged our little group. 'You can't go in there any more ladies and gentlemen as the AIC has closed it off.' We tried not to react to the news, but what does that mean we all thought? Is the AIC onto us?

We then decided to leave and went out to dinner together

and found an intimate place near the markets to try to put a plan together. What we came up with was outrageous, and we knew we had to get into the inner sanctum of The AIC.

We are going to use subterfuge - deciding that I would hide in the shuttle whilst Aya and Kilby go through the checkpoint, and would also have to somehow manipulate the view that the cameras have on the shuttle. Then, as Kilby goes around the back of the shuttle to change sides as part of the checkpoint process, I would climb out and use my pass. I would then go around the back and he would climb out of the back of the shuttle and use his pass. This would go on until we got some form of reaction.

We would be dressed the same, same shirt, same trousers, same shoes and same cap and perhaps the checkpoint would let us through. It might work but perhaps it won't. It was a stupid plan, and it just might fool The AIC.

We hadn't realised it was getting so late as there were no longer many people around, and it was nearly dusk the sky was golden, albeit a little cloudy, it still might be dangerous to be outside as The Carrion might come. I told them to wait inside as it was about the time for The Carrion.

Aya looked at me raising herself from her seat, 'Let me go too' but I said no. I was right as it was cloudy tonight, but there was still enough golden setting sun to invoke The Carrion. I could not see enough from where I was and needed to get higher, needed to see further. I needed to use The Rush.

I looked around and there was no one in the immediate vicinity so dropped my hands to my sides, and felt the sensation take me. The Rush. I began to float upwards making it high enough to get to the roof of the highest building within a couple of minutes had had a much clearer line of sight, so watched and waited.

The Carrion did not come tonight.

It was well past dusk, and I saw the others down below me existing from the eatery we had spent the last hour in. We were safe tonight. I went to drop-float and saw someone looking up at me. I could barely make him out, but he was looking directly at me and I suddenly recognised him. It was Hawke, The Represent.

He made a hand signal as he looked up at me whilst smiling broadly. He slid his flat hand across his throat as he kept watching me. I think it meant a kill sign, a sign of death, and assumed he had seen me float. He now knew I was a Flighter, and I was terrified.

I decided to move anyway, so I made the climb back down to the ground via some stairs. I didn't use a drop-float and was exiting the building, but dreaded coming into the open as he would be there waiting for me. I took a deep breath and stepped out onto the street.

I noticed Aya, Zamiro and Kilby were standing across the street from me in a semi-circle, and there seemed to be a fourth person with them. I moved closer and realised it was Hawke. I will lose everything now. He saw me and made a move to try to evade them. What was about to happen I thought?

Aya made a second move to block him from getting through and he then yelled at me, 'I know! I know!' I watched as Aya was trying to drop him to the ground. She folded her leg through his stance, and he reacted by moving to one side, but she was too fast.

She had already predicted his move, and his fall ended with a grunt. She then rolled him over face down, bent his arm behind his back and splayed his fingers out on his wrist.

He was now writhing in pain, but she held him there anyway.

Zamiro then came over to me and I asked her what was going on, and she told me that Kilby had recognised him from the arena and he realised it was Hawke that had opened the steel arena door. When he saw him looking up at me he also knew it was Hawke lurking around Evoh the other day. He recognised the uniform, recognised the man was a Represent, as he was still wearing the same uniform, and recognised him from the night of the arena.

I took a breath. It was Hawke who almost killed everybody, and he had awoken The Carrion in the last glass chamber. I walked over to him and looked down at him. He appeared to be resigned to his predicament.

'Why?' I said looking at him.

'I wanted to kill them,' he replied almost spitting out the response.

Aya looked down at him and held him tighter, said: 'We all hate The Carrion.'

Hawke looked up at her, 'Not The Carrion you dumb woman! The Flighters, I wanted to kill The Flighters. I knew they would be FOO. It would have been the greatest thing. I would have been famous. No one had ever done so many of them at the same time.'

Aya then kicked him in the back, and then Kilby kicked him too, and he winced in pain.

I didn't react as I thought it was sad. I thought it was pathetic. I looked over to Zamiro and she was crying.

A group of Ground-Dwellers then came out of one of the other buildings and Zamiro waved at them, wiping her tears away. She knew them from her ELC as some were the parents of the children that she was teaching, and also mentioned that some of their children were actually there on the day, on the night, and were almost killed.

They came over to find out what the commotion had been all about and saw The Represent on the ground. 'What is up Miss Zamiro?' one of them said so she explained who he was, and what was going on. Another of the Ground-Dwellers moved towards us, then another three stepped up.

'This guy,' one of them said.

Zamiro nodded, 'Yes.'

The man continued: 'So, he opened the door, let the sunlight in and The Carrion reacted, one took your brother's arm...put everyone in danger? And why did he do that?'

She then told the Ground-Dweller group about his intention to kill all The Flighters and thought I heard her tell them I was a Flighter too. She then told them that I was a hero and also told them I was her boyfriend but had also made sure that Aya was out of earshot when revealing all of this to them.

I didn't say anything, I didn't move, I couldn't. I didn't know to be proud or to be afraid.

They looked at Hawke and asked Aya to politely let him up, so he began to rise and one of the Ground-Dwellers then said: 'I think we need to persuade him to forget about your boyfriend over there,' nodding over to me.

'Oh ...I don't think so.' Hawke said, having risen from the

ground and trying to stand tall, 'And I know where you live Carlyle.'

I felt threatened by him, and I was threatened by him.

One of the Ground-Dwellers stepped further forward. 'I think we may have to persuade him to forget don't you?' The man grinned. 'Hi Hawke, please let me introduce the persuader.' He began to heft a sledgehammer from his left hand to his right hand.

I thought the group must have just come from the arena, so Zamiro asked him, and he nodded in confirmation. 'Oops,' he then said dropping the heavy rectangle metal head of the tool onto one of Hawke's boots, onto his foot.

Hawke looked back at him in pain, and then an expression of fear came across his face.

The group proceeded to frog-march him to the corner of the building. I overheard one of them say something about wanting to have a quiet word with him, something about Ground-Dweller justice, and to find out where he lives.

We watched Hawke go off with the Ground-dwellers and Zamiro then told all of us that she thought it was time to go home. Aya and Kilby left together, as they mentioned they were going back to see Marty, and then to Creedence's apartment at Evoh.

I looked at Zamiro, 'Shall we look at the arena then?' She said no, as it was too late now, so we jumped on a Zoop and this time she let me drive. I took her home to her place at Yelnu.

I went home alone and was comforted that Hawke would not be bothering me tonight, and perhaps not at all as my new Ground-Dwellers friends would take care of that for me.

Maybe forever too.

Chapter 46 Aya

Evening; Friday 27th December: I went over to Zamiro, tried to get from her what had just transpired and why Carlyle was looking a little nervous, and noticed he was a lot quieter than usual, but she would not elaborate so I left it alone. I did hand her the Phillipe Patek instructions book though, as it had been recovered from Bernie's clothing at the scene of The Carrion attack at Munna Cliffs on Saturday and was not required to be kept by the ER.

Kilby and I left the others at the Central Berg and took a duo shuttle back to the ER station to see Marty. I was feeling a sense of momentum, everything seemed to be coming together and we could fight The Carrion, we could fight the AIC, but could we win?

We needed to believe.

Marty was not looking well, but he was still asleep which was good. The loss of his arm was taking its toll on him, and I knew the ER were doing the best they could. I hate The Carrion.

Kilby asked if he would now take me home to Evoh, and I realised then that I am officially on leave from my position with the ER and am now officially living here in Edi-Aleda.

Am I frightened or ready for the next challenge? I have seen things I don't want to remember and know things I don't want to forget.

Carlyle had already explained to me the routine of gaining ownership of the apartment and expected that he was also correct in that Creedence's ownership would have already been defaulted within twenty-four hours of his death and I wanted Kilby to stay with me.

Although the exercise of gaining access to the apartment went as suspected, I was mildly surprised when Kilby wanted to have joint access, so we both registered as tenants as he told me it was for my safety reasons.

I thought that would work as I could keep an eye on what Zamiro and Carlyle get up to, but the comment about my safety was a bit dubious given that he had seen me take down Hawke, a man almost twice my size. I didn't question it though. I did feel a little safer, and a little less alone for one of the first times in my life.

We both went into Apartment 503 and moved Creedence's possessions into the small storage room. We then cleared out the drawers and cupboards, and it was still surprising that Creedence had so few items of clothing and other belongings.

It was now getting late and so I thought about asking Kilby to stay tonight, 'for safety reasons' I justified it to myself, so I did, and he agreed. He told me he would sleep in the second bedroom. I offered him the storeroom instead, he looked at me and laughed.

We both did, and it felt good.

Chapter 47 Kilby

Morning; Saturday 28th December: I woke. It was early, it was just sunrise, so I looked out of my bedroom window and saw the sea. I sat up in bed. Where am I? I then realised I was in Aya's apartment at Evoh, or was it still Creedence's? Then I realised that it was partially mine too as I had registered as a joint tenant, but don't quite understand why Aya had let me as yet.

My comment about her safety was a bit lame, as I think she can handle herself better than I ever could in a confrontation. She had hammered Hawke and he went down like…a…..sack of …. I then heard the shower running in the room next door, and knowing the two bedrooms and bathrooms have a similar footprint, I rose, de-clothed and climbed into my shower room.

I could get used to this I thought as I don't have to share it with any others even though our home in Yelnu Berg has four bathrooms. I still have to share it with Marty. I wondered if I could share this place with Aya. I will have to wait and see, but also wondered if she would cope with my cooking, and then I wondered if I could cope with my cooking. I had managed to collect some of Marty's spare clothes from the ER station as are roughly the same size as Mata had taken several extra clothing items in for him and was unsure when he would be well enough to go back home.

He won't miss them, and probably he won't even notice.

Today we will attempt to re-enter the AIC facility as we had talked about this on the way home last night and it should work. The AIC are expecting a team of two, and as she is ER should have immediate clearance, so we sat together eating breakfast and discussing our plan.

I do like her as she is frank, reliable and resourceful so I called up a duo Zoop and we caught the lifts to the ground. I explained to her about the 'Zoops having gears' which she understood and acknowledged our need for secrecy.

We had also brought with us two of the blank computer chips just in case and she had secreted them somewhere on her person but said that in the interest of my safety, she would not tell me.

We were now on our way, and this could be the day that everything changed for everyone. Aya and I arrived at the first checkpoint at the AIC, and we had been seriously considering the consequences of our next actions and understood what we were about to do was dangerous, it might get us killed and it might get everyone we know killed too.

I had asked Aya if she thought that, and she had said absolutely, but she certainly hoped not. I stepped out of the shuttle nodded to the camera, swiped my personnel pass across the black panel and climbed back in. Just follow the process and act normally. It was now Aya's turn. I had to prompt her to move, she then looked over to me and leaned into me and thought she was about to say something but she placed her hands lightly on the side of my face, and kissed me.

'Here we go,' she said stepping out of the shuttle.

I told her to follow the process, the camera first, then the panel and she followed my instructions although the camera scan was easy as we would not see any reaction from it anyway. The card scan was next, so she tried, and nothing happened, then looked at me as I had suggested she try the blank re-set chip next. I saw that she was thinking about it but shook her head sideways very subtly and reached into the inside of her shirt between the V-neck and her chest.

I assumed that she had secreted the chips in there, but she then brought out a small card pass that I had not seen before. She scanned it, the red light registered it and the gate opened so she climbed back in the shuttle and showed it to me.

I looked over at it, it was a cut-down version of my current card but a much older version and there was a picture on it that was a younger version of her, and she looked so vulnerable, so demure but the name on it though was not Aya. It was her picture but not her name, as it read 'Priscilla-Rose'

I was confused. Could she be a Represent? I thought about it so asked her what it was and told me it was the original pass that she had previously reported lost when she worked at The AIC facility years before. She had subsequently found it, but as it had been replaced, when she left The AIC she had only returned the newer replacement card. They had never asked for the original, and this meant we did not have to use the re-set chips, well not yet anyway.

I could tell that she wanted to explain to me about the

name discrepancy but said 'Tonight, at home,' quietly and I would have to trust her. I will trust her.

We passed through the next two checkpoints without further incident and arrived at the designated carpark but as we climbed out she said to me the next test will be the big test. We then entered the building, and it was all too easy. I wanted to know why, so I asked her, but she didn't respond. We went through the routine of entering through the internal doors and then out to the assembly line.

'Nothing has changed' she said quietly to me. I reminded her of single-word sentences only, and she nodded, 'I remember', two words this time though.

We then parted, and Aya moved over towards her station the session was uneventful, we saw no one else and no one else saw us.

The shift was now over, and I went to my house at Yelnu to collect some belongings. As my parents were not home I did not get to say goodbye, I did not get to thank them for everything. I was finally moving out, and thought it felt good, felt independent, felt adult, so I headed to my new home at Evoh.

Chapter 48 Zamiro

Noon; Saturday 28th December: I had asked Carlyle to collect me from my house at noon so we could see if the Phillipe Patek watch could be tracked, and we will then need to go back to the trader that he had purchased it from in the Central Berg. I was reluctant to go to the watch trader in Evoh as he might get other ideas about us as a couple.

I was waiting for him outside by the stoop, the sun was high in the sky, another beautiful day I thought, too nice to do what we are about to do, and it will be dangerous too as what we are about to instigate the tracking of The Carrion.

Am I ready for it? Are we ready for it?

I hoped so and knew that with Carlyle by my side knew we were ready, we had to be, it was time, and time to make a difference. He arrived in a duo shuttle and looked comfortable in it, so I assumed he must have been practicing driving. I climbed in beside him and as it wasn't far to the Central Berg from Yelnu Berg, the ride took about fifteen minutes.

We alighted and the shuttle was quickly commandeered by another couple wanting to go back from where we had come from. I recognised them from my ELC. They wondered why I was not teaching today so I told them about Marty, told them about The Carrion at the arena, and they then understood.

Carlyle then directed me to the Watch Trader, and we entered the premises. Trader looked up at us and smiled. 'Welcome. Do you want a finger-band? You two look so much in love, I would know as I see others like you every day. We have just taken in new stock, and you will like them. We also have others on special today too.'

I looked at Carlyle and asked him whether he had set this up, and he shrugged his shoulders looking over to me. I smiled. 'No, I am sorry. This is my brother, Marty,'

Carlyle then looked at me wondering what I was doing.

'Only kidding, this is my friend Carlyle. He has lost his Phillipe Patek that you sold him the other day. Saturday the 20th.'

The trader looked at him, 'Lost it already?'

'So can you locate it? I asked.

'It depends on whether it was stolen or how you lost it. Do you know when and where it went missing then?'

This is the tricky part I thought, as once we squeeze the toothpaste out of the tube there will be no putting it back, Carlyle and I had gone over this to get our story straight, or at least try and keep it logical. We decided the truth was our best ally.

'You mentioned The AIC, and it is their system that tracks it. Is that right?' Carlyle asked him. Here we go I thought, all or nothing.

'Yes, that is the case but it is much simpler than that.' He explained he registers it as 'lost' on their system and it all happens pretty quickly from there. The AIC will either accept the trace as legitimate or something else. He didn't clarify what something else meant, and I hoped it was not something else, so I felt for Carlyle's hand against my side. I found it, entwined my fingers into his and whilst my hands were sweating a little, his were not.

'Do you still have the book? The instructions book? I need it to start the trace on the Phillipe Patek, the watch.'

Carlyle looked at him and suddenly looked so dejected. 'No, I do not. The Carrion killed him, The Water Carrion. Bernie, last Saturday. He just wanted to go for a swim, then The Frenzy, Munna Cliffs, last Sunday. Howard. The Carrion killed everyone.'

The trader looked at him; 'I'm so sorry'.

I looked at Carlyle and thought he was about to cry, but the patch over his right eye would make it difficult. I then realised what he, and what they we talking about. I had it, the instructions book. Aya had given it to me last night before she left with Kilby. 'Is this it?' Carlyle looked at me and didn't understand, then he did and simply said to me. 'Aya,'

I nodded, and he smiled.

The trader took the book from me, opened to the last page, rose from his desk and moved over to another terminal. This one was attached with wires to a box with a glass screen. I had seen them before, but not for a long time, and turned it on.

The screen blinked and 'AIC' was now emblazoned across it. I looked over to Carlyle and he was as stoic as ever, the best game face you would ever see. I thought I must teach him Poker, the playing card game that the boys, Fata and Grandfather Dave always wanted to teach me.

'OK,' the trader said with his hands poised over a keyboard containing several letters and numbers. I had not had a keyboard in years. I recalled the last one I had seen was at the library before the AIC destroyed the building. The AIC again. I thought this could either be as simple, as the trader has implied, or it would be a disaster and I hoped the earlier.

Carlyle then told him about The Carrion attack at the arena the other night, the trader already knew about it and knew of the loss of the Flighters and that they were FOO too. He was now getting quieter and quieter with his questions and responses, then I think he realised what we were about to ask him to do. He looked up at us. 'The Carrion took your watch, so you want me to track The Carrion?'

We both nodded.

'Oh boy,' was his only comment as he then explained what he was about to do may not work. The AIC had provided this tracking system to him only recently, and it had taken him a long time to obtain the authority and trust of the AIC to give him his type of access.

It was all very new, and The AIC had only just finalised the upgrade of their communication system. The AIC were rebuilding a network, their network and not many other traders knew about it and not many other people knew it was being built without the knowledge of The GOD. He then stood up, flexed his fingers and moved past us over to the front door.

I looked at Carlyle as it appeared that it was over before it began, had we failed so soon? But then the man stopped just before the door, turned around and faced us. 'The Carrion you say. Just how did you manage to get one to eat your watch?'

Carlyle then told him about his friend Creedence, having enough courage to do all that he did just before he died on his death day, then the putting the watch on The Carrion's neck. He then pointed to his right eye. 'They did this to me', he told him.

The man turned back away from us, looked towards the door, moved towards it again and stopped at the lock, then he locked it and turned back around. 'My name is Brosnan by the way. This could be dangerous for you both and me too, so I am now going to lunch.'

We both looked at him stunned.

He then smiled, 'But before I do though I might just have to give my new trainee a lesson on how to lodge and follow the tracking of a lost Phillipe Patek. They are very expensive watches you know.'

He then came over to me and directed me to sit down on the chair in front of the keyboard and glass-boxed screen. Brosnan then explained to me about entering the details from the back of the instructions book into the database.

I followed his lead and an option came up immediately regarding lost or stolen, so I chose lost and pushed the enter button. It then wanted to know what time and where, so entered that data too and we waited. The screen then went black, and I looked up at the trader. 'Wait, it is thinking.'

Carlyle had not spoken much but chose his next words carefully. 'Why does a machine have to think? It's just a machine. What you see is what you get. It only knows what it knows. It cannot learn.'

'This one does as it is part of The AIC as it generates its responses, its questions and answers them itself. The AIC never stops learning.'

The screen blinked back on, as did a flashing dot, but it wasn't very clear and didn't show much at all. I was waiting for further instructions from Brosnan, he looked at it and said this is where the tracking started from. He then leaned over me, pushed another button and we watched the dot moving across the screen. It was still hard to follow as it was just a black screen with a red flashing dot.

'This is the old analogue system that we were using before to track the lost watches but now they have upgraded to a digital image. It has taken them years to develop the upgrade and I didn't know that they were capable, but they are, and it is scaring me. Just what are they planning next?'

He then looked at us and told us he would need a moment to think about what he was about to do, 'You know the Carrion killed my wife and my children. It was years ago but will never forget it, I thought I could.'

He went quiet again, 'And that is why I run this place as it still brings me hope when people purchase finger bands and jewellery from me. They say love lasts forever. Did you know The AIC blew their plane out of the sky, and that was also the last time, the last day that the planes were last in the sky? The AIC took over that day, and became too powerful.'

Carlyle looked at him. 'At the airport?'

'Yes'

'It will be seven years ago next Wednesday, the 1st.'

I looked over at Carlyle, and Brosnan looked at Carlyle too then said to him; 'How do you know?'

'I was there, my family, my girlfriend too. I was fifteen summers. I was here to get my wrist chips. We had all come over from Munta Berg. I was the only survivor.'

I looked at Carlyle as he had never mentioned anything about this.

Brosnan nodded at him, 'I didn't know there were any survivors in the plane or the airport.'

'No, I was lucky. I was on the ground waving to my parents as they were flying back home. Back to Munta.'

Brosnan considered this momentarily and then told me to push another button on the keyboard, this time pointing to it and then to another. 'You need to use three fingers, here, here and here,' then added, 'I don't want to do it in case they track it back to me, as I could lose everything to The AIC.'

I pushed them as instructed, and the screen went black again, then it opened up in colour and showed everything, we could now see The Carrion in flight and it was now a delayed tracking view of their departure from Ed-Aleda, from the arena on that day. I looked up at him and he nodded at me.

We were now watching them, The Carrion, where they were going and as it was an overhead view Brosnan explained it was from an AIC satellite high above us, high in the sky up in space.

I asked him how long The AIC have had this technology, and he detailed the AIC's recent improvements with their satellites whilst The AIC seemed to be permitting the installation of the wires and cables for the telephone networks within Edi-Aleda, it had been working on its agenda. The AIC now controlled their satellites, the self-installation of satellites and a wireless network. I wondered what they were doing it all for.

Meantime Carlyle was still focused on the computer screen and watching The Carrion as they swooped down and landed on a large flat metal boat that resembled a very old flat garbage scow. It was about five metres by ten metres but as there were two platforms joined together, it formed a rectangle roughly ten metres by twenty metres, it was untethered and simply floating in the middle of the sea.

As the overhead visual was from high above, we could just make out the beaches of Edi-Aleda on one side of the screen. Carlyle pointed out that the other side of the screen looked like the farming village of Munta where he had been raised. He could remember them from long ago, and that the subdivision of the Munta farming allotments was very distinctive in both colour and shape. 'I have never seen them from a view like this though.'

I looked up at Carlyle, as we had been so engrossed in looking at the screen, we hadn't noticed that Brosnan had gone back into another room and was eating his lunch by himself.

We stayed there watching the screen but could not quite make out the individual Carrion as the view was so far away. Brosnan came back over to us, then watched it whilst munching on his lunch, leaned over me and pushed down on another button. It then zoomed the view, so he released his finger that stopped the view just above a group of about ten Carrion. We could see that they were still able to move around, even though the sun was now much lower in the sky.

'That your watch?' he then asked Carlyle.

He nodded in confirmation, and Brosnan then walked away again. 'There will be more to see than just the Carrion that has your watch, so don't lose the view.'

He was right, as not long after we saw a larger rounded-nosed boat enter the view from the middle of the scene, and it eventually anchored against the flat scow so we watched to see if anyone boarded on the other boat, but nothing happened. Then the scow started moving as it had now attached itself to the other boat but there were not any ropes that I could see, perhaps magnetically then? I wondered.

I scanned back on the vision to get a view from a higher perspective and watched it push the scow around in a half circle as it headed off towards the side of the screen again and assumed that it would move out of sight, but it didn't as then the screen refreshed itself and we were able to follow it towards a destination. It was now slowly cruising perpendicular to the coast of Edi-Aleda, started to reduce the angle towards the land and the screen refreshed itself once again and we had a line of sight to the actual land. It was a vision of rectangles and blocks, and I realised it was an establishment, man-made, well at least AIC-made I thought, and looked again at Carlyle as he appeared to be deep in thought.

He then took a pencil and a pad of paper from under the desk where we were, drew two lines on it and then the angle of the angle of direction where the scow was heading.

'I know where it is going, I have been there once and you would have to, it's where the AIC assemble the computer chips and is where you get them on the celebration that is your Installation Day. It is the AIC precinct. Marty and Kilby work there, and I assume that Kilby is there today with Aya.'

I looked at him and knew he was right, but the memories of my wrist chip installation day would be very different from his. My own was distressing, and I have almost managed to forget the day, and hope I never have to go back there either. Ever.

Brosnan then came over and asked us if we had seen enough, which we agreed and we knew where we had to go next. ' You are not supposed to be on The AIC tracking system for more than ten minutes at a time, so I hope that nothing comes of it. Maybe they didn't notice.'

I certainly hoped he was wrong.

We left the store and could not thank Brosnan enough for everything he had done and everything we had seen. We wished him to keep safe and hoped he would be and then went back to Evoh.

Carlyle had mentioned that he had not been keeping up to date with his journal entries, but I said it didn't matter as we were making our memories, together.

We watched the golden sun setting out on the balcony waiting for The Carrion but they didn't come again. This time though we knew where they were and knew where they went, but just what were we going to do about them?

Chapter 49 Hawke

Morning; Monday 29th December: I am home alone. It was early, and my feet, back and ribs still ache from the Ground-Dwellers dropping the head of the sledgehammer onto me. I know I have to resign myself not to harass Carlyle. I know he is a Flighter but for my safety, I will leave him alone. It must be nice to have friends like that.

I felt a vibration at my hip. This was the new implement of communication that The GOD had introduced to The Represents. It was a small square radio box that only vibrated, though did nothing else. It meant however that I was required to contact someone at The GOD, someone anonymous and they would direct me to a job. Something anonymous. I called them on my telephone.

This was another perk of being a Represent, apart from being licenced to kill. The recorded voice directed me to meet another Represent at a place in the Central Berg. It was somewhere near the markets, and I was intrigued as I had never been requested to work with another. I always work alone, so rode a Zoop into the Central Berg and made my way to the destination. As I got closer could see another Represent was waiting at the front of a Special Stone Jeweller store, and although he was in the same uniform as me. I didn't know him, but he acknowledged me as I walked over to him.

'Columbus,' he stated his name to me holding out his hand, so I shook it. I was still limping from the injuries sustained from last night and had noticed, so told him I had fallen down some stairs whilst chasing a Flighter. He appeared to believe me.

I took a breath. 'What's in here? I didn't know we had both been directed to the same site.'

'Your recorded instructions told you to come here too?' he enquired. I nodded and told him the metallic voice had mentioned a jewellery store in Central Berg. I looked at him, and he confirmed that we seemed to be in the correct place.

We both went in and I noticed Columbus had locked the door behind us. He then moved towards the overhead camera inside the store and aimed a small fob that he held in his hand towards the camera. The fob clicked, so I assumed he had been able to turn the camera off. This was even more intriguing to me as I don't have one of those fobs either.

'Can I help you?' the man in the store asked us. I saw he was alone as he raised himself from a chair behind the counter. 'Are you with The AIC?'

I looked at him suspiciously and wondered why he would have even mentioned that straight away. 'What made you ask that?' Columbus asked him without hesitation. 'I was on the... I was tracking a lost Phillipe Patek yesterday. I probably spent too much time logged on. I was eating my lunch and forgot about it, so thought you might be from The AIC.'

I looked at him and assured him I was a Represent, from

The GOD and I just wanted to have a look, 'Nothing more, nothing less' I assured him.

I looked at Columbus for confirmation, but he was not looking at me or the man as he was looking at the computer unit on the desk. It had a screen and a keyboard. I had not seen one of these before. Columbus took over the conversation.

'You were authorised to use it for tracking only, and you were allocated specific instructions and timeframes for this. My records show that you logged in for over thirty minutes. You would've located the lost watch after about five.'

The trader nodded again and apologised profusely for his oversight. I still didn't understand why Columbus was concentrating on this breach of The AIC policy, then he walked over to him and placed his hand on the man's shoulder. I still had no idea what was going on.

He then persuaded the man to come outside with him, almost forcefully leading him back out through the front door. He seemed to be directing him to peer into his storefront window, and by now he had his hand tight on the nape of the man's neck. What happened next horrified me, but was also so exhilarating. To the left of my peripheral vision, I saw a driverless, large AIC Laundry shuttle bus coming down the street behind me.

I then watched as Columbus tightened his grip on the man's neck, spun him around and just as the laundry shuttle neared us, he propelled the man forward into the front of the vehicle and under the shuttle. It drove over the top of the man and spat him out from the rear, killing him instantly.

I had just witnessed the very thing that I have been unable to affect myself. The Push. I looked at Columbus he simply said to me, or no one in particular: 'Now that was clumsy of him, he didn't see the shuttle coming and what a shame he is now dead.'

Columbus then indicated that we were to go back inside the store. I followed him in as instructed and noticed that a crowd had gathered around the dead man. I knew that the ER would be here soon too. He headed straight back to the screen and the keyboard on the desk, turned it on and I still didn't even know what it was. 'It was tracking The Carrion,' he said.

'How do you know that?'

'A Phillipe Patek timepiece has a tracking locator on it, so someone, somehow and I don't know how must have been able to get The Carrion to swallow the watch or something like that. I don't know yet,' and with that, he pulled up the last picture vision on the screen. 'Huh,' he then said. 'I know where that is. It is where The Carrion goes after The Frenzy.'

I looked at the screen and recognised it as well. It was an overhead picture of the AIC warehouse facility at Ravilob, the one where you get your wrist chips installed. I looked over to him. He leaned closer to the screen. 'Let's see whose watch it was, perhaps they were here too when it was being shown.'

He played the screen backwards as we watched and it showed everything, but in reverse, the boat that collected the flat scow of the group of Carrion, The Carrion flying backwards, then flying through Edi-Aleda, backwards from the arena and then the vision suddenly stopped.

'Nothing else on there, still don't know how they did it,

perhaps The Carrion simply ate someone's arm or hand and that is what happened.'

I then asked him if he knew how The Carrion managed to stay still on the flat-topped barge/boat whilst in transit and the sea.

'It's a flat giant magnet that holds them in place as The Carrion are made of metal and gold.' He told me that the flat top was a solar panel for The Carrion, with enough charge to keep them active, but not enough to invoke another Frenzy. The AIC controlled all of it from their facility. He had heard about it but didn't realise it was so close to Edi-Aleda.

'How do you know all this?'

'It's part of becoming a modern Represent. I have only been training for about a week, and this is my first assignment.'

'And your first kill too. The Push.' looking at him directly.

He said nothing, then moved back to the camera and faced it once again, then pressed his fob a couple of times and as he walked back to the monitor, he told me he would now be able to work out who came into the store about the same time as the access was granted for the tracking of the watch. This too came up on the screen in front of us. 'OK, it's a man and a woman, let's see what they do.'

I looked at the couple and thought I knew them but was so engrossed in how much this Represent knew about all of this that, didn't take much notice. He is well-trained. We then watched the overview of the jewellery shop; it showed the woman sitting down in front of the screen. The man stood next to her, and our now-dead trader stood a little behind them both. They all had their backs on us, then the trader moved away.

'No sound?' I asked Columbus, and he was about to reply when the view suddenly changed as it went to black.

'Mmm, he has turned the store cameras off, he must have gone back into the little room back there,' Columbus informed me pointing over behind him with his head, then his fingers were poised over the keyboard once again. 'But I can fix that though.' He pushed a few buttons on the keyboard and the screen woke up again, this time it was a front view of the woman's face and we could see both of them clearly on the screen in front of us. 'There is a camera built in the top of this unit'.

I looked at her on the screen, 'I know them,' and with that, the soreness in my feet suddenly flared up and my sides were now aching again too.

'Me too,' Columbus nodded, 'That is Zamiro, and I know where she lives. Not sure about him though, I have not met him yet, but I will soon.'

I nodded again. 'I know where he lives too, so maybe we will pay him a visit.'

Columbus shook his head, 'No. Let The AIC handle him, and handle her too.'

I didn't know what he meant with that statement.

He then turned off the screen and indicated that we were to leave. As we made our way outside I saw the ER had arrived at the site and they were asking for witnesses but no one said anything, and no one seemed to care. A man has just been run over by a shuttle, by a machine and the shuttle could just not stop in time.

End of story, end of the man, end of life.

I overheard one of the ER saying that The GOD should be

doing more to make the laundry shuttles able to stop quicker, but no one seemed to notice that comment either, and no one seemed to notice that two Represents had just exited the jewellery store from where the dead man had from come although his name 'Brosnan' and the name of his business was emblazed on his shirt.

I looked down at him and felt saddened by it all.

Chapter 50 Kilby

Morning, Monday 29th December: I am still suspicious as to how Aya and I had made it so easily through all The AIC checkpoints, and onto the assembly line. Something was not quite right. I felt it, we both felt it. We had spent most of the night trying to understand what we could do and what we should do. We decided to meet with Carlyle and hoped that he would be awake this early too and I wondered if Zamiro was staying with him tonight, as it was too early for her to go to work.

We left our apartment and rode the lift to level 11, I knocked on Carlyle's door and Zamiro answered, so she had spent the night and not that it was any of my business, but it was, as I was her older brother.

I trusted Carlyle as he had saved her life and suspect that he would save mine if he had to, as he is a Flighter and knows now that Flighters will save others if they can. They welcomed us both in, so we sat down in the lounge area and looked toward the morning light. I was first to break the silence, 'At The AIC facility yesterday we both went through without any disruptions.'

'We found out something too,' then Zamiro said to us.

'The Carrion, they fly out into the sea after The Frenzy and then land onto the flatboat and are towed up to the AIC where you work.' I looked at her, 'What?'

Carlyle then explained about the watch being attached a Carrion's neck, that it was Creedence's idea and then being able to track it via the Special Stones Jewellery trader in Central Berg, and seeing it all on a screen, learning it all and now knowing where they go.

Aya suddenly interrupted him, 'Yesterday, you were there? A watch jeweller was killed yesterday. He fell in front of a shuttle, but others believed he was pushed. The ER is looking for a man and woman, and they are considered suspects.'

I looked over at Aya, then to Zee and Carlyle, What was going on? I thought. Then they explained about the meeting they had with the jeweller, but that was the day before, on Sunday not Monday. Aya considered this and mentioned that she would have to make a report to the ER to remove them as suspects. Although they were there, but not involved, it would be a delicate conversation with her ER superiors given what she now knows about The AIC and The Carrion.

I looked at her, 'But you are not with the ER anymore as we have the job together at the AIC.'

'I am still able to do both' she clarified, 'The AIC work is only a couple of hours a day. I can assist with the nights at the ER, so it's all about balancing priorities.'

I was a bit disappointed when she said that as I was hoping that I would become one of her priorities, maybe her main one but maybe not by the sounds of it now.

'Oh no,' Carlyle went on to say quieter this time, 'I would say that we got him killed, but we didn't kill him.'

I looked at him and he then explained that they had seen The Carrion on the Phillipe Patek tracking screen, they had seen where they go, and I was astonished.

'What exactly do we do now then?'

After talking about plans again, we decided that we needed help. The FOO, the Ground-Dwellers and maybe we could wrangle some amnimates into causing a distraction.

We need a plan and need it fast.

Aya and I decided it was time to go to work, so we left Carlyle and Zee and made our way downstairs and outside, located a duo Zoop, headed off to the AIC and she asked on the way if I thought it would be an easy today as yesterday. I replied I don't know; I just don't know.

We had an uneventful trip and an even more uneventful entrance through the checkpoints back into the assembly line area, and as we have been constantly talking about what we need to do I am no longer afraid of the AIC but we must do something to prevent The Carrion attacks as we know now where, but don't know how.

We were currently having our scheduled break and suddenly heard a blaring siren from within our holding room and looked at each other not knowing what it was. Aya then confirmed that it was an Emergency Response siren and not a siren of The Flush. Was there an incident within the AIC plant? We both then wondered what it was, and what we needed to do.

It had never occurred before in the three years that I have been working here with Marty, so we agreed it would be in our own best interest to venture from our enclosure. The exit door, which was usually locked, was now unlocked, so we stepped out and looked around.

I told her that I knew of only six others who worked on the assembly line. There were only two other staff around somewhere and she nodded in confirmation then her demeanour suddenly changed as I could see that she was now in ER mode, and it was inspiring to see.

I wanted to be a part of it, and I knew I was about to be, so she indicated I needed to follow her lead. I knew instantly it was the right thing to do.

We ran down the corridor and as this would be taking us back into the assembly line area, we re-entered the large room and saw that the assembly line had now stopped, this was the first thing I noticed, the second thing was that there was not another team within the immediate vicinity, so we ventured cautiously through the area but there was nothing, yet siren continued to wail. We then went back through the door that led to the holding rooms and this time I pointed Aya to another door off to our right as it was open and could see that it led into another corridor, so we went through.

As we made our way along the noise from the siren was dissipating but there was another noise emanating through the din that sounded like another conveyor belt assembly system. What would else would the AIC be manufacturing here?

I kept that thought in mid-jog as we ran towards the source of the noise, and then I slowed down as the noise became louder, almost intolerable.

Aya looked at me and then yelled over the din. 'I think this is where the siren is emanating from.' I stopped and put my arm out to prevent her from moving any further in the corridor as I could now see it opened out into a much larger space.

The door at the end was open, and I assumed it went out into the open sea, as I could taste a slight salty breeze from my left. Aya and I stepped cautiously out into the space, and there was a large cement channel before us, it was about five metres across, but it was empty. To our right was a large steel door that opened upwards onto a large roll, but it was currently closed, and to our left, we could see the sea in the distance.

There were two large square steel doors at the end of the channel to our left and I could see the channel then flows to the sea, the doors must keep the sea out when closed and allow the water in the channel to flow into when full so the doors must open into the sea. I mentioned to her that this may be how they get The Carrion to float in and out as they must fill the cement channel and open the doors to allow the scow to float through.

'Behind the roller door,' she pointed over to it, 'I bet we would find The Carrion in there behind the roller door and would say they are made in there too.'

I shuddered with that thought.

Aya then saw a shape up by the wall, by the sea doors, and it seemed to be moving albeit slowly, so we made our way up there together and there was no movement from the steel roller door behind us. I thought we would be safe at least for the moment, as it was not yet dusk, but there was a cloudless sky.

We approached the shape carefully. I realised it was a

man and he looked at us, but we could not tell if he was relieved or disappointed. I tried to talk to him over the siren, the noise. He then yelled at us that we could turn it off by pressing the red button under the sign that read: "Emergency Use Only". I did, and the siren stopped.

I then realised why he was not moving as his leg was pinned between one of the steel sea doors and the cement wall of the channel. He did not look well at all as his leg was skewed at a very interesting angle and it looked very painful.

'How long have you been out here,' I yelled at him, then realised that the siren was no longer wailing, 'sorry,' apologising to him in a softer tone.

'Long enough to die.'

Aya then surmised the situation, 'How did you get yourself into that?'

He explained normally climbs down the ladder, and he nodded toward the cement channel, then pointed to the ladder on the other side, but today he decided to run across the top of the two opening sea doors instead. He didn't even make it off the cement without falling into the sea door gap. 'I am Mitchell, and do the maintenance here at The AIC plant.'

I noticed there was a large canvas bag next to him that was partially opened, and there were tools strewn across the cement platform all around him, including a hammer, saw, large ceramic knife, large wrench and a smaller metal box of sprockets. He must have realised what I was looking at as he explained that the bag was still in reach when he fell and became trapped. He had spent about twenty minutes throwing various implements at the Emergency Button until he managed to strike it and turn it on.

'So can you move?' Aya asked him.

'No, and I hope The Carrion doesn't come out as the sea doors will open crushing my leg even more. Just leave me to die,' he said to us dismissively.

'Not a chance,' Aya came back at him with, 'I can save you but probably not your leg. There is an ER kit back in the corridor area that should contain enough gauze and medical supplies. We should be able to use that.'

I then pointed out to him that she was ER.

'My lucky day,' he said quietly and added 'and no one will see you save me.' He then told us that there were no cameras here in this area, unlike the assembly line, and that is why he had resigned himself to die, as no one would see him and no one would save him. 'The AIC don't want anyone to see where The Carrion comes and goes from or where The Carrion is stored at night or during the day, and did you know the AIC are paranoid?' he elaborated with a stifled laugh.

'Fancy that, a machine being paranoid of people trying to kill it, when it makes The Carrion right here to kill people.'

I looked over to Aya, and she looked even more determined to save him if that was even possible, then she asked me to go back to the corridor and retrieve the ER kit. Then she looked at me. 'I need to knock him out, so you may not want to watch.'

I didn't know what she meant by that comment, so I ran towards the open doors to locate the ER kit. I turned back to them and saw her punching him hard in the head. His head snapped back with the force of her fist. I turned back around and made it into the hall. After stopping for a breath, I decided to look back again as it was compelling. She hit him again but this time as his head hit the side of the concrete. His head then lolled, and he was now out cold.

She then looked up and saw me watching. 'Hurry,' she yelled to me.

I found the kit and returned it to her quickly, so she opened it and knew exactly what she needed as withdrew a container of antiseptic, then proceeded to gather the nearby knife and splash it to cover it in the liquid. She looked at me again and then at Mitchell. 'Here goes, let's hope that this ceramic serrated knife will do the job quickly,'

Fortunately, the knife was very sharp and mostly unused, so bit easily into his trousers and then into his leg. 'That is the easy bit,' she muttered then the blood came, so she continued with urgent fervour and the serrated knife coped easily with the cut. It was clean and quick, but she struck bone as the cut was being made just above the knee joint. I was in awe of her.

'Get ready to move him, here under his arms,' she said, wiping her bloodied forearm across her forehead. I stood behind him and saw he was still out cold.

'Now' she said, and we separated him from the sea door. I dragged him backwards towards the grass behind us, and he was now bleeding profusely.

'Tourniquet' she said out loud, then she wrapped the bloody stump up neatly and placed her hands inside and around the leg stump to make sure it was clean cut. It was.

'Let's go, right now,' she then said.

I hadn't noticed anything else that was going on during the intense experience, but Aya had as she looked at me and said, 'The roller door is moving upwards'. She then grabbed Mitchell's legs just as we heard another siren, 'The Flush' she pointed out to me, so we looked around for somewhere to hide, the three of us and Mitchell, still unconscious, still dead weight.

We saw a grassy knoll and it was closer to the end of the building. I thought we might make it, but she shook her head. 'No, we have to get back inside, back into the corridor'.

I lent down and collected some of the tools that had been strewn around, placing them in Mitch's canvas bag of tools, heaved it over one shoulder and saw it was emblazoned AIC MAINTENANCE on both sides, so I hefted Mitchell's torso higher into my arms and we started to run. Aya had meantime turned around and had her back to me, so we ran as best we could carrying his dead weight and just managed to get back into the corridor shutting the door behind us as we caught our breath and just as I shut the door, I noticed the roller door was fully open.

I realised the AIC used The Flush to fill the cement channel, using the then flooded channel to float the scow to the sea. The Carrion leave from here.

Everything happens from here.

I had to look myself and gently opened the door with the smallest of cracks and peered out. I was right as there was a floating flat scow full of at least fifty of The Carrion. They were not moving, just standing idle, waiting, not taking flight, simply waiting.

I quietly shut the door and said to Aya that there would be a strike tonight and this meant The Frenzy. I leant my back against the wall inside the corridor resigning myself to the fact there is nothing I can do to prevent it. Nothing we can do.

When I opened the door again saw that the large roller door to my right was now closed as they only use sufficient water in the channel to get the height to float the boat into the sea. I looked to my left and noticed the water level was now at the height of the sea beyond the doors.

The two doors, where we had just rescued Mitchell from were now starting to open and the sea was flowing in to meet the water in the channel, but suddenly the doors stopped moving and so did the floating boat containing The Carrion.

The Carrion boat softly nudged into the unopened sea doors but as they were jammed half open the float was now stuck fast and the sea doors were stuck too. Nothing was moving.

'Look at that,' pointed The Carrion closest to me as I could see a watch, a timepiece. It was clasped around its neck.

Aya nodded, 'Carlyle's?'

It was not long after that I then saw something odd, and mystifying, as a saw, wrench, hammer and other metallic objects that I had left uncollected on the cement platform were all starting to shake and tremble. I pointed that out to Aya when suddenly the tools took flight and slammed into the side of the metallic tray on which The Carrion was standing. 'It has to be magnetic, the platform, and that explains how they stay on during the tow in and out of the sea.'

We then watched as the black round tug boat moved towards the sea doors, did a full U-turn, reversed back to the doors, slamming into them and the doors shut with the force of the collision. The scow began to move again with the rippled waves made by the force of the tug boat. The sea doors also started moving again and this time they re-opened and I could see from where I was there was now something floating in the water as it had been jettisoned from the doors. It was Mitchell's severed leg.

'At least this had delayed them maybe about half an hour, maybe longer' Aya said quietly then adding 'and they won't make it far tonight, maybe just to the Edi-Adela beach.'

I looked at her suddenly remembering that Zamiro mentioned there was to be a sports function on the beach tonight, and hopefully it starts after dusk. Mitchell began to wake up. We knew would have to work fast to save his life, and he pointed to his canvas kit bag, then told us about a little fob within the inner sleeves that would control a metal gurney.

I found it, threw the canvas kit bag onto it and we used a gurney to make our way through the corridors and back out to the carpark with him on board. All the doors were still open and everything was quiet. It made me feel uneasy and we both agreed The Carrion would have killed him there and then if we had left him there. Most likely us too.

We then lay the semi-conscious Mitchell into the back seat of the shuttle, and I stuffed the canvas bag in the small trunk space in the rear. We returned to the AIC facility without any further delay and took him to the nearest ER station. I knew he would survive as Aya had saved his life.

Maybe I had helped a little too.

Chapter 51 Zamiro

Dusk; Monday 29th December: As there hadn't been any Carrion for days everything was good in Edi-Aleda I had decided to treat my students to a day at the beach tonight after their lessons, and although it took a little planning it was otherwise fairly easy.

I let Kilby know too, and he said that they would try and join us too if he could, as he lives so close now however there was still a timing risk as we couldn't get away until after all the exams the students had been sitting were completed.

We eventually arrived about thirty minutes before dusk, but I knew Carlyle, my guardian angel would be watching over us though from his citadel on the 11th floor, Apartment 1103.

The shuttle dropped us as close as possible to the beach, so we alighted and gathered together on the warm sand. I had arranged for nets to be strung on poles across the sand in little rectangle-boxed areas for the ball games. I was trying to keep everything in control and Marty had also decided to join us as it was his first day out of the hospital. There were about fifteen children and five adults, all Ground-Dwellers. We were managing to get some organised games together, but as it was getting closer to dusk. I was becoming anxious and looked skyward for The Carrion. I then looked up at the apartment behind me and could just make out a person on the balcony.

It would be Carlyle which made me feel a little more assured, and he was waving. It was now a little later, and I thought The Carrion would not become. I tried to convince myself as it was getting too late for them. I heard a squeal, thought it was a scream, and quickly looked around but was just some of the children running in and out of the water, however, it was then I noticed The Carrion.

They were in the sky above the children, and although the sun was much lower, they were still heading straight for us within the golden setting sun. I was so wrong, felt so stupid, and so disappointed in myself.

They were much lower tonight.

Then I realised that Carlyle was probably not waving as he was trying to get my attention and quickly looked up to see if he was still up there. I then saw him running towards me. He must have drop-floated down and that was a very risky move in broad daylight, but I was very thankful.

We quickly corralled the children together as there would not be much time and looked around for options. The water? Could we dive in and keep our heads under the water for the duration? I doubted that. I then heard a noise behind me. It sounded like a loud soft squelching on the sand, an engine labouring, and I looked up and saw it was Marty. He was driving the shuttle bus towards us.

He was managing to control it with his one arm and his stump, but it stopped well short in the soft sand but just close enough for us to quickly climb in. The Carrion had arrived and had somehow realised that there was no one on the beach, at least I hoped there was no one.

They circled above us and in an ever-decreasing whirlwind, started slamming into the side of the shuttle, onto the roof, and the back of the shuttle. We hoped we were safe inside and they would be able to get inside. They suddenly stopped for some reason and were just standing altogether on the roof of the shuttle. All we could hear was the scraping in their talons along the metal, so I spent my time trying to placate the children. How much longer? How much longer?

Most of the children had their hands over their ears and eyes firmly shut by now, so I looked over to Carlyle, then to Marty and they were watching everything too. The Carrion was still not moving, and I could now understand why as the shuttle was facing the water, towards the sea, facing the western setting sun and it was getting too late for them. The sun was now setting and we would be safe.

Carlyle yelled out above the cries and the screams of the children that it was almost over, it was almost sunset, and The Carrion would go. So we just had to wait a little longer. The Carrion suddenly flew away, so we disembarked the shuttle. I moved out onto the sand and once again as the children gathered around me and the parents too. I was so horrified that I had almost caused a disaster and would have never forgiven myself.

I don't think I can even consider how I could explain to the other parents what I had just done so collapsed on the ground and cried. That was not the worst of it though, as they saw there were casualties. I saw the dismembered bodies of two

Ground-Dwellers down at the water's edge. They must have been oblivious to The Carrion and had been slaughtered. There was so much blood and gore, and the incoming waves were now bleaching the sand with red.

Carlyle and Marty made sure the children could not see this by directing them back off the beach. I picked myself up off the sand walked up to the scene and the massacre, and looked down at the bloodied torsos. I could just make out two different hands, two separate hands were still clasped together. Whoever they were, and I will need to know, must have died just as they lived, together, and by now as the parents and children had left and I could feel their hatred, and my shame.

What was I thinking?

Carlyle came up to me and looked down at the bloodied remnants. 'I think I know them,' he said to me quietly, 'They moved into my apartment complex recently. Live on the same floor as Creedence, sorry I mean Aya, I mean Aya and Kilby. I know them, I mean I knew them.'

I vowed to myself I must fix this.

We must fix this, and it must stop now.

Chapter 52 Carlyle

Evening, Monday 29th December: I tried to console Zamiro as best as I could as we went back to our apartment but I could see she was in so much pain. I tried to convince her it was not her fault, it was The Carrion, it was the AIC but don't think she believed me.

Aya and Kilby had meantime arrived back at the apartment complex, so we joined them in their apartment. Marty, Zamiro and I then explained about this afternoon's events.

Then they told us about their experience and together we were coming up with a plan for The Carrion, and Marty had said that he wanted to help too. I hoped my plan was simple and decided that I would go tomorrow with Aya and Kilby to the AIC and would take the place of Mitchell in the Maintenance Office.

We wouldn't need the other plan that we had come up with the other day. This one was simpler, and made sense, but would it make sense to AIC? Would it work? Hopefully, the AIC would not have been able to replace Mitchell so quickly as long as the work was completed to an expected standard. I was able to convince the others that I had sufficient knowledge about general maintenance.

They seemed to accept that.

Our next objective was to make a distraction, something that the AIC would deem innocent enough not to raise suspicion and Kilby suggested the Emergency System again.

That should work I thought, and it would also get me out to the cement channel, but we still had to sink the scow though, stop it from floating, fill the channel with water and drown The Carrion. Would all that work?

It had too.

Aya explained how Axa had used a surge of electrical power to kill the Water Carrion at Munna Falls, and that it would need to be supercharged this time as there would be at least two trays of The Carrion, maybe 100. Would that be all of them though?

The next challenge was how to sink the scow, but how can we stop The Carrion from flying, would they try and move as they would be held to the scow by the strong magnets? Could it be as simple as that? If the Emergency System could not be manipulated, which would then implement the opening of all the internal doors, we could maybe utilise the re-set computer chips if needed.

As Kilby had extracted them from the blue C earlier placing them on the kitchen bench we agreed to take two each, and I placed my two in my pocket. The next part of the plan was to prevent the tug boat from trying to enter the cement channel and Aya believed that as long as the AIC believed that everything was happening normally, nothing would be worrying the AIC sea walls. There must be nothing out of the ordinary. We needed the weather to be in our favour, but tomorrow was expected to be cloudy with a chance of light rain, and we had become aware that there was to be a change to the weather pattern later this week.

We knew The Carrion would not venture out in the rain, so we also needed an incentive for The Carrion to invade the city. Fata has informed us that The GOD, in its infinite wisdom, had decided to hold another event at the arena tomorrow night. It would be bigger than the event of the 25th of December and would be the day that The GOD announced to the AIC that Ground-Dwellers would no longer fear The Carrion.

We decided it must be tomorrow.

It was now or never.

Chapter 54 Marty

Evening Monday 29th December: I had spent a lot of my time thinking whilst recuperating, and had countless visits from Fata, Mata, Dave & Courtney. They told me they know a lot of Ground-Dwellers who want to help, so I'd come up with a plan and needed to tell all of them right now, right here, right now.

Would it work? Would they listen?

I needed them to know what I knew. 'Carlyle, Aya, Kilby & Zee, I need to tell you all what I have found out in the last four days lying here at the ER station and just need you all to listen, please. Dave & Courtney know the neighbours that operate the farm directly next door to the AIC facility at the seashore, and there is an adjoining fence that might be able to give us access. Every day farmers take a boat of Amnimates to the markets at Edi-Aleda, and any unsold beasts are returned by boat to their farm.

We often see the black AIC tug boat moored just outside the sea wall of the AIC facility, and sometimes they have seen The Carrion being towed out to sea, but have never had enough courage to act on this information. In isolation, it does not mean anything, but if we can commandeer their boat, we could maybe crash it into the AIC tug boat and disable it. It wouldn't be able to tow the scow filled with The Carrion.'

I now had their attention, so kept going with my plan and further explained how

I researched the AIC facility with the assistance of other Ground-Dwellers and ex-workers at the AIC. I have discovered that this is where all the clothing and washing from the Bergs in Edi-Aleda is laundered and they use Borax to facilitate the cleaning.

Aya suddenly spoke up. 'Borax is also a flux.'

We all looked at her, so she continued. 'A flux can reduce the melting point of metals, the temperature that metals liquefy. It means that should we be able to trap The Carrion in Borax and get some heat to them it could melt the gold off them, and they will be destroyed.'

I nodded, and then I said, 'There is more,' so I kept going as I had their full attention now. 'Ethanol is the basic compound in hand sanitiser, and this is also stored at the AIC facility. They use it to manufacture the solvents that we all use to keep the germs at bay, and there are rooms for the stuff kept in containers. We could use that as the accelerant, the incendiary agent to increase the heat.'

I took a breath gathering my thoughts knowing the next part is where it gets harder. 'We know The Carrion then comes out from behind the large roller door and floats on the scow out to the sea wall waiting for the water level to rise so the tug can take control. We can trap them there, in the cement channel before they get out to the sea. Then introduce the Borax, then get the Ethanol into the cement channel, and somehow ignite it.'

'With what?' this time it was Kilby.

'I don't know yet,' I said quietly.

'We need a charge and spark.' Aya said 'We could use the Emergency Button tower; it has a bank of lights on it. If we can pull it down and have it drop into the water whilst still full of electrical charge that would work.' We nodded.

This was getting somewhere, and this time Carlyle spoke. 'A pulley system. I have seen it work before when we needed to take down an old windmill on the farm. We used a triangular set of ropes. You make notched cuttings in the structure pylons and as you pull on it will topple to the ground folding at the weakened struts.'

He then pulled out a piece of paper and began drawing lines on it and I tried to work out what he was doing. 'I've got it here,' he said then showed us on the paper. It was elaborate and fanciful and involved using the momentum from the boat which we would be using to collide with the Carrion Tug. Someone would need to bring a rope from the collision boat across the water, through the fence of the AIC neighbour, and wrap around the Emergency Tower, and as the boat moved towards the Carrion Tug the rope would go taut and pull down the tower.

'Simple, outrageously simple' Kilby said. 'Let's sleep on it and make it happen.'

'When?' Zamiro asked, 'It can't be tomorrow, I can't help out tomorrow as I will be at the ELC teaching.' Carlyle looked at her and said, 'Tomorrow it is then, as I don't want you there.' She punched him in the arm, but he looked at her solemnly. 'You're serious!' This time we all answered, 'Yes.'

We all left the apartment without further comment, much to Zamiro's dismay.

Chapter 55 Carlyle

Morning Tuesday 30th December: I watched Zamiro leave for the ELC on a single Zoop from the ground floor foyer, then turned and rode the lift up to Level 5 where Kilby and Aya were waiting for me so we all moved out to the balcony and looking to the sky wondered if it would rain today as the morning sky was a pale red colour.

'Red sky in the morning sailors warning,' Aya stated, then added, 'And it is going to rain today, maybe not soon, but later and I would guess that means cloud, so no consistent sunshine, and no Carrion this evening.'

I looked at her and so did Kilby. 'So not today but what now then?' I enquired to them both.

'Test run today. Do our recon, and see if everything is where we think it is. Let's make sure everything works, make sure we can get through the checkpoints. How it all works, what we know, what we don't know and what we need to know.'

Aya then said. 'So we go anyway?'

'Yep,' they both replied. We then made our way downstairs and climbed into the same shuttle that Kilby and Aya had brought home last night. It was large enough to take us all to The AIC. We each had a small pack with us containing supplies which I placed on the seat next to me. Aya drove and it didn't take us long to get to the AIC however I thought that the time dragged on as we didn't make much conversation. Aya had her game face on, at least that is what Kilby told me.

I didn't understand what he meant by that though, and it wasn't long before we came to the first checkpoint. Aya slowed the shuttle to a gentle stop, and now it gets interesting I thought.

Kilby stepped out first whilst Aya and I remained in the shuttle as instructed. She leant back to me from the driver's chair and whispered what the procedure was all about. It needed to be meticulously followed. Kilby walked up to the camera for the facial recognition process, held out his personnel pass against a black panel, then his left wrist chip and it was all very methodical. He then climbed back into the shuttle and Aya stepped out to go through her routine, and everything was good so far, but we did suspect there would not be an issue here anyway.

Now it was my turn. I climbed out of my seat and went up to the camera, but nothing happened, swiped my left wrist and again nothing happened so I stood there and then looked back at them. They were both facing forward. So that is a game face I thought, as both of them had the same blank expression whilst looking back to me through the shuttle windscreen.

I wondered what to do next and realised that I had forgotten the black panel personnel pass, and we had discussed that the best option was to use one of the re-set chips. Maybe that would work.

I was reaching for the one in my pants pocket and saw something glinting in the morning sun coming towards us, it was high in the sky and was coming towards us rather quickly.

The objects separated into three different objects, and I finally recognised what they were as they came closer. It was three AIC drones. We had been caught by The AIC, and by now Aya and Kilby had both seen them, so they climbed out of the shuttle and looked at me.

'Play it cool,' Kilby said quietly to me.

Aya also responded with, 'But unless these drones now have microphones on them they won't be able to communicate with us. They normally only have a camera.'

The three drones had now arrived and immediately began hovering over us so I looked up to them. All this was my fault I thought and was all too fanciful.

I then held up my wrists at them hoping for a reaction, and one of them instantly hovered up higher into the air as if I had annoyed it. It was nothing of the sort as it soon drifted down to join the other two, so then I made a movement closer towards the shuttle and all three this time raised themselves.

It was a stalemate.

The plan was coming apart, and I had just jeopardised everything with my naivety. Meantime Aya had moved around to the back of the shuttle as there was little space there for storage. It is not big enough for a person as I had alluded to in my previous plan, so I kept watching her. She then opened the rear hatch and removed a canvas kit bag. It was emblazoned AIC MAINTAINENCE and she nodded to me. 'Here take this hold it up and show it to them.'

I did and the three drones then swopped downwards at me as I held the bag up in the air. I also kept my head bowed as the three drones hovered over me momentarily, over the bag, and then they flew upwards and waited, so we waited too. Then we heard the best sound ever as the checkpoint gate clicked, and the drones flew away.

We were in.

'What just happened? I mean I know what just happened, but how did you know?' Kilby said looking at Aya.

'I didn't. I remembered seeing the kit bag last night when we stopped but didn't think anything more of it as we should not have had it. I saw it there last night when I went out to make sure the shuttle that we had driven home was still there so we could then take it again today, and on a hunch, it might work as there is an AIC tracker in everything. Perhaps if they scanned the bag, they would assume that it was Mitchell's, and maybe they would assume it was still Mitchell with us this morning. Maybe it would work.'

'Well it did work,' I said to her and moved towards her to hug her as a simple handshake just would not be appropriate in this situation I thought. She gracefully accepted it, and Kilby joined in, so we all held each other, and hopefully, there was not a camera somewhere watching us. We passed through the next two checkpoints without any further fuss as each time I simply held up the AIC MAINTAINENCE bag to the camera and the black pass panel instead of my wrist chips.

We eventually parked the shuttle and moved through the entry area. It was here that I left Kilby and Aya as they made their way towards the assembly line and as Kilby had told me where to go. I went through the corridors making my way towards the cement channel. I didn't have to hesitate as I had the canvas AIC bag held it up and scanned at each entrance door.

It was so simple and was a deficiency of the security AIC facility, and I realised it likely gave me access to all areas. The closer I made my way to the cement channel, the more confident I felt that the plan would work. I headed for the nearest door. The first couple of rooms were empty, but the third one was more interesting as Aya was right, they did store Ethanol on site. It took a couple of minutes for my eye to become used to the minimal light. I realised it was an immense space and could see the flat trolleys that would be able to be used to move the containers to the cement channel. I walked up to a trolley noticing that there were not any controls on it as it was simply a flat tray with four wheels.

I looked around for anything that would initiate the control of the trays but there was nothing. The room was devoid of everything apart from the trays and the containers, but I did see there were raised lines on the floor so assumed that it was all automatic and strictly controlled. I went over to one of the containers, and it was clearly labelled ETHANOL CAUTION FLAMMABLE DO NOT MOVE WITHOUT PROPER AUTHORISATION and wondered whose authority I would need to move them. Why the warnings? Who reads them?

I looked around for inspiration, but it was not forthcoming and had no idea what to do next. I left the space and moved back out into the corridor to explore the next rooms but again there were more empty rooms.

I also knew I was getting closer to the cement channel, to the large roller door that Kilby had mentioned, to The Carrion and the sea. I took one last leap of faith and opened the next door, but as I did fumbled over The AIC canvas bag and it dropped to the floor. The zipper across the top split open and the contents spilled out. I picked it the empty bag and noticed it was much lighter. Aya had mentioned a saw, wrench, hammer and some other metallic objects had been magnetically attached to The Carrion scow when they rescued Mitchell. This left a couple of smaller items including a few spanners, a smaller saw and a box of ratcheted sprockets.

I stopped, collected them and started putting them all back into the bag, then I peered inside and noticed a small pocket on each side of the inside. In the pocket, on one side there was a small grey foam block, so I extracted it.

It was split in the middle, so I pulled the two sides apart and it contained a fob with a single button. I wondered what would happen if I pushed it, so I did, but it did nothing although the red light had blinked and shone on the top of the fob, but nothing more. I then heard some noise from somewhere behind me, it was from one of the rooms that I had already been in, and think it was from the room where the Ethanol was stored.

The door then opened out into the corridor, and not having realised they were two-way doors, out from the room came a roller tray but there was nothing on it, so I watched as it followed the tracks embedded in and along the floor. I wondered if the fob controlled the tray, so I pushed the button on the fob and the tray stopped. No way I thought, so pushed it again and it started moving towards me again - problem now solved. I wanted to find Aya and Kilby, wanted to tell everyone about my plan.

I buoyantly moved through into the next area and was almost at the end of the corridor where the area opened up to the sea. The large roller door is off to the right and the Emergency Light Tower is off to the left. I stepped through into the space. No more options. I then heard the roller door moving, it was opening but there was not any water in the channel though, so stepped back into the corridor for safety.

There was nowhere to hide.

But then the door stopped, and I waited there to see what would happen next, but nothing did. I wondered if it was the canvas bag that was making it open. I stood where I was and began swinging the bag out into the space and the door moved again, so I pulled it back and the door then stopped.

Neither Aya nor Kilby had mentioned this, so it was likely that Mitchell and his bag were needed to operate the door, but this did not make sense, and then it did, however, he hadn't mentioned this to them when they saved his life.

I realised that AIC still needed human intervention to ultimately oversee everything, to make it work, to make sure it all worked, so wondered how far I could go in through the roller door.

As a precaution decided it would be better if Aya or Kilby was with me, so I went in the other direction to check out the Tower Light. It was made of metal as we suspected and looked up to the light tower to see if we could get it down and if it would fall directly into the channel. It appeared to be malleable enough, so I pulled out the ceramic saw from the bag, made a small cut into the strut and it went into it easily. I kept cutting into it and made a slender slit across the front. I then went to the back of the tower and could see that other power wires were external too.

We would still need the strength of the pulley system to bring it to the ground and into the channel, and I was disappointed with that as we will still have to involve then others, the farmers from next door and Marty's plan with the boat and The Carrion tug. I decided to make my way back to Aya and Kilby but did not know how long I had spent down there not having yet retrieved my watch, so went directly back to their holding room, and fortunately, they were still there.

Aya asked. 'We finished a shift about fifteen minutes ago and have about thirty minutes before we have to get back to the assembly line, so what can we do?'

I explained to them that I had located the Ethanol containers, about the mobile trolleys, being able to use them to move them, but I hadn't yet found the Borax, and I hadn't yet found The Carrion.

Aya said that when she was here years ago the whole place was much smaller then, and the original chip assembly line was behind the roller door area, now it is nearer the front of the complex.

'We better go into the new area then ASAP.' Kilby said.

We agreed, so I left the holding room used the canvas bag and went quickly through the corridors back to the cement channel area and the roller door again.

It raised as I approached, but this time it went all the way up. We had no option other than to continue our quest, so we cautiously stepped in together and Aya was right, as this was where The Carrion are stored, and it was The Carrion that was the first thing that we saw.

It was eerie and uncomfortable, they were motionless, they were evil and there were about a hundred of them standing on the flat metallic platform that I had seen from the Jewellers AIC screen. The second thing we noticed was the smell, as this was the laundry too as it was the acrid hot smell of laundered clothes and linen that infiltrated our nostrils. We also located the Borax.

'What is the plan from here,' I whispered to Kilby 'And where is the AIC in all of this?'

He shrugged his shoulders, so we made our way over to the platform containing The Carrion. It was a simple flat tray on top of hollow metal boxes. Each of the boxes had a plug about halfway on each of them. Kilby leaned down and pulled on it as there was a round ring on each that enabled the plug to be unsealed and decided to immediately unseal all the plugs.

We then climbed onto the platform and into the channel bay as every plug was now opened this was too easy and I realised that if the first pontoon was filled with water it would flood the next one, and if we got weight onto the front and hold the platform below the water line the platform it would flood. But where do we get the weight from and how do we avoid The Carrion whilst we are doing it?

As we completed that task, Kilby looked at me and Aya, and then nodded towards the old assembly line that she mentioned before, the Borax was stockpiled on the old assembly line and the old line led back into the channel as they must bring the laundry in or take it out by sea.

I was relieved as the Borax was already on the assembly line so we could simply open the containers and drop them directly into the channel. Our next challenge though was to initiate The Flush, sink the platform, pull the electrified tower down into the channel crash the tug boat and destroy The Carrion.

Easy.

'Times up,' Aya said and began running back through the corridor with Kilby following close behind, but I was a little slower though as I was already running a little low on adrenalin myself, but nothing else happened at the AIC today. I had made myself busy pretending to tinker with whatever I could and accessing all areas had its benefits as I could stay in the vicinity of the assembly line with Aya and Kilby until their shift finished for the day.

We then left together in the shuttle, and I made sure that I had the canvas AIC MAINTAINCE bag with me. I held it to my chest most of the way back but just as we made our way through the last checkpoint the heavens opened, it was now raining and did not abate until we were almost home in Evoh. We knew there would not be an invasion from The Carrion and also wondered if the event was still on at the Arena tonight, but perhaps it was too wet after all.

We hoped anyway.

Chapter 56 Zamiro

Evening; 30th December: Marty and I were standing out on the balcony of Carlyle's apartment and had been watching the rain as it had been teeming down for hours, but in the distance though we could see that the clouds were beginning to break up, and that it should be a fine day tomorrow. Carlyle, Kilby and Aya were yet to arrive home, but we expected them very soon, and it will be interesting to hear how everything went today at the AIC facility and the plan.

Will it work?

Marty told me about his day. 'I was speaking to Fata about the Arena event. Did you hear it was postponed tonight as they had left the roof open during the rain storm and could not get closed quickly enough? This caused the ground to be too wet but they were even bringing in large heated fans to get it dry.

The event is definitely on tomorrow night though as they are expecting fine weather all day tomorrow and a golden sunset at dusk.' So The Carrion will come then instead, I thought.

Marty also said that he had located the farmers that live next door to the AIC at the Central market earlier today and was introduced to him by his grandfather. They are a man and his daughter. He believed the man is of late thirty summers and the girl is around seventeen summers, and thinks their names are Myles and Khat.

He didn't become acquainted with them though, to protect them from the repercussions of tomorrow's plan, but they did confirm that the boat would be available tomorrow around noon. They will ensure that some Amnimates will not be sold at the market to disguise the intent of having to return with an animal-laden boat back to their property.

He was still unsure that they would allow him to pilot the boat but he will deal with that tomorrow. 'I met with them, and they genuinely seemed committed to what I was going to do, what we are trying to do, but what they didn't understand was how I was going to manage to swim ashore carrying the thick marine rope that was going to be used for the pulley system and told me that I would end up swimming in circles with my one arm and I might even drown.'

He then asked me if I had any ideas. I didn't and just as we were contemplating that issue, saw the apartment door open behind me and the three amigos came in so I nodded to Kilby and Aya, went up to Carlyle and gave him a welcome home kiss, and he seemed to like that.

He also seemed to be worried and a little more aloof than usual, but I hoped that he was simply just focused, then noticed was carrying a canvas kitbag that had AIC MAINTAINENCE on it, which he dropped gingerly on the floor.

Aya started talking first and mentioned that they had called into the ER station to visit Mitchell this afternoon. He was doing fine and was thankful we had saved his life. He was very interested Carlyle had so easily taken his place. She also mentioned that his life partner, Dana, also worked at the AIC. I wondered what that meant for us.

Marty listened intently as we all did, as we knew of no one else that worked there and when they had asked Mitchell what shift she was on, he said was not on the assembly line as she worked in the AIC Control Room, this meant she was the other person that Kilby had mentioned at the AIC.

It might have also been that Dana had sent the drones, rather than The AIC itself, we may never know. She also may have recognised Kilby and Aya from when they saved him from The Carrion, and when Aya had asked him if she would help us if we needed her, he had nodded that she would.

I didn't know what she could do from in there, but he told us to keep her in mind if we decided to destroy the whole facility and we had to assure him that we were there only for The Carrion, he was thankful for and wished us the best of luck. We eventually decided to sit down for our meal as they had also collected food on the way home, and we opened a bottle of wine or two, but Carlyle refused to partake, and I understood why.

'Here's to courage,' Kilby said as he raised his glass, so we chinked our glasses together, and then it got serious. I looked over to Marty as he ran through his schedule for tomorrow, but he didn't mention the concern that Myles and Khat had raised regarding whether he would be able to complete the swim from the boat carrying the marine rope.

Aya went through what they had discovered at the AIC, where everything was, and what they would be able to achieve, and I noticed Carlyle was now very quiet and noncommittal. Aya then stopped momentarily and then Carlyle finally spoke. 'If it all goes to plan we might all be heroes, if it doesn't we all might be dead,' and that comment closed down the conversations very quickly. He went on to say that if Creedence was still alive it would only be the two of them putting it all together, and he then looked across to all of us.

'I have not lived a very social life, and have missed so much since losing my own family. I consider now that you are all my family and knowing how important family is to all of you, this is getting all too much.'

Aya interjected, 'I get it, Carlyle, I do, but we have to do this, we have an opportunity to make a difference tomorrow, not just to us but to everyone that lives here in Edi-Aleda, here in every Berg, here in every part of our world and we don't even know that The Carrion exists outside of Edi-Adela. If they do and we bring them down tomorrow it will affect everything, as The AIC will have to yield to us not the other way round. It is our time; it is our turn.'

Great speech, I thought and think that the others concurred. 'Great speech,' I heard someone say looked around and it was Carlyle. He was nodding in agreement.

'Tomorrow it is then,' Kilby said as he stood up from his chair, and held out his right hand with flat palm down into the middle of our group, so we all followed suit.

Aya placed her hand on top of his, and I followed with mine, then Marty, but Carlyle just stood there and I assumed that he had never seen this before, so I took his hand in my left one and raised his hand to the top of the pile of hands. He complied, so we lowered our hand pile and then raised it upwards.

'Hoorah,' Marty exclaimed loudly.

I tried to convince myself that tomorrow it is, and I won't be there. I am needed at the ELC. I believed I could make a difference there instead, but I wasn't convinced.

Chapter 57 Marty

Noon; Wednesday 31ˢᵗ December: I located Myles and Khat at the market and was getting more anxious now. It was all starting to happen so made my way over to them and they nodded in recognition. They were herding the unsold Amnimates into a shuttle truck for the short journey back to the boat harbour just north of Evoh and had loosely explained to me what they needed to do to get the beasts onto the boat and back to the farm. It all seemed to make sense.

I was able to help them as best I could due to my one-arm situation, but as the Amnimates are so docile and easily lead, I could manoeuvre them around as I needed, as we needed.

We arrived at the boat harbour and loaded the beasts onto the boat which was much larger than I thought, and Myles then explained that it could ferry up to fifty at a time but only five Amnimates were going back to the farm today, quietly mentioning to me that is all that he is prepared to sacrifice should it all go wrong. I didn't take much comfort in that. I untied the ropes around the bow and stern bollards, threw the ropes on board and even doing that action was clumsy with my one arm. I began to understand what they had meant about my need to swim with ropes, but it had to work. I jumped aboard.

I had never actually driven a boat before and assumed it would be a quick lesson. Myles called me to the wheelhouse and started showing me how it all worked, the throttle, the depth gauge, the right and left, aft and stern, port and starboard.

I looked at him 'I don't need to know how to drive it, I just need to know how to crash it into the Carrion Tug.'

He smiled. 'We didn't think you were serious. You are going to have to line the bow up with the tug, gather enough speed, maintain a straight line and then just as you are near enough collide with the Carrion tug, jump off with the rope, swim to shore and carry the marine rope with you. All with one arm, and meantime, you just want us to stand by and watch?'

I had to admit I was feeling a bit green with the rolling boat movement and was hoping that the boat trip would not be too long, but he was right. It was an impossible task, and even in my uncomfortable state I still managed to wonder how the others were doing: Aya, Kilby and Carlyle.

I suddenly felt the need to rush towards the side of the boat as my early lunch had just become burley. I wiped my mouth with my sleeve and looked at Khat as she was laughing. 'And about in fifty minutes, the real fun begins,' she said shaking her head.

I knew what she meant.

Chapter 58 Carlyle

Late afternoon; Wednesday 31ˢᵗ December: All was good so far, and the checkpoint procedures were uneventful again today, as we maintained the same method as yesterday. I had taken the AIC toolkit home with me last night just to make sure everything went as planned, and it was almost too easy as we made our way up to the entrance doors. I went to say something to Kilby, but he twirled his finger around at me. 'Sshh. The walls have ears,'

I didn't understand what he had meant, however, Aya had meantime moved towards me, quickly hugged me, and whispered that nothing more needed to be said now, she then gave me a light kiss on the cheek and said quietly.

'See you on the other side.'

I left them there to make their way to the assembly line. Aya had previously explained that the wrist chips installations are in a completely different part of the AIC facility, and that is why we are not seeing any other people. She also explained that they have even changed the access roads to accommodate and control the flow of the Ground-Dwellers. I also mentioned they had even built a few more buildings since her time about five years and was surprised that her original AIC pass still allowed her access. I considered it might also have something to do with her being an ER as well, as her ER pass still gives her access to all areas.

She mentioned that it was a coincidence, but I didn't think so as I didn't believe in coincidences, especially when it involves The AIC. I again moved quickly through the corridors holding up the AIC tool bag to each scanner. I went to the Ethanol storeroom, loaded the containers on the gurneys, retrieved the fob controller from the toolkit bag and headed through the corridor toward the cement channel.

We had been relying on the simplicity of the plan and it seemed to be working as I was able to relocate at least twenty trays to the cement channels, so then I began pouring the liquid into the empty bay. I realised there would not be enough to even cover the bottom of the area so decided to shift my focus to the front sea wall area as this is an area of the source of the ignition but realised even that wasn't going to work as I needed something to contain the liquid, a large metal box or something.

I looked around, but the only thing I could come up with was the pontoons that were under The Carrion platforms. We had already pulled the plugs out from them yesterday, but I would need something to syphon the liquid from one container to the other, and fortunately, I had seen black plastic tubing in the space behind the roller door. Could I risk it? I had to and ran back to the door with the AIC kit bag. The door opened and I moved in but was immediately met by The Carrion sitting idle on the metal platforms. I set to work and jumped down into the channel, linking the black plastic tubing to each of the unsealed pontoons, enabling gravity to transfer the liquid.

The Ethanol began decanting into the empty bases. It was working, but then I noticed that the plastic tubing was not compatible with the Ethanol, the tubing was melting, and it was reacting with the solvent-based liquid. I soon realised there might be enough of everything to make this work.

The channel was not yet full of water, so the platform still didn't move, but the weight of the pontoons, having now been filled with Ethanol, would hold the platforms under the level of the water. Soon The Carrion would be low enough to be immersed in the water/ethanol solution.

Now, for the Borax. I was starting to get tired and needed to rest, but there was still so much to do. I took a deep breath climbed up from the channel and sat down on the platform containing The Carrion.

I looked at the docile ugly instruments of death and then realised the nearest one had something around its neck, it was my watch, my Phillipe Patek. I extracted it and put it back on my wrist. It was still working and I wondered if it was still being tracked by the AIC. I assumed so but left it secured on my wrist anyway.

Suddenly, I heard noises coming from the corridor, maybe there was someone else here, but where could I hide? Kilby had mentioned three other teams, but perhaps someone had seen me after all. I heard two voices I knew, and then I heard two more, and another two. I didn't recognise them. Six people had arrived at the end of the corridor, which left two working the assembly line. All good.

There were now eight people, nine including me, to

achieve what we needed to do, and I suddenly wondered if they were all coming to help out, but didn't know if they were allies or enemies or under the direction of the AIC.

Aya waved at me, but I still didn't react, and then they came towards me. 'We have brought reinforcements,' Kilby said to me with a large grin. 'Give me the fob, and I'll get more Ethanol from the storeroom.'

I handed it to him, and along with Aya and two of the others went back through the corridor with the empty trolley trailing behind them.

'What I do to help?' Another one said holding out his arm to assist me climb from The Carrion scow onto the platform. 'They call me Ziggy,' he said introducing himself, and as he pulled me over to the cement path.

I noticed we had swapped places.

He then went to the front on the first Carrion platform, leant down over the front where there was a large black flat switch that I hadn't noticed before, pushed it in and moved towards the first Carrion. 'Oops,' he said kicking it off the Carrion scow, then he kicked the second and the third into the cement channel below. Soon others joined him once there was enough space. 'He has turned off the magnet,' one of the others said so I asked him how he knew where the switch was.

'That is cos I built it. The Carrion Tug controls the magnetism of the scow. This button and it switches it in and off so they can fly or be transported when they need to,' then he continued with a much sterner tone. 'And they paid me lots, and gave me a job here and then well, they killed a boy and his girlfriend didn't they?'

We all stopped and looked at him.

'They had only just moved into together. They were so happy.'

'When?' I asked him not noticing what he was doing with The Carrion, but not too tired to listen to his plight, as it was so emotional.

'Last night at the beach, Evoh, that is where they lived in their new apartment, he was my only boy.'

I looked at him full well knowing what had happened last night as I was there, but I don't know if I can ever tell Zamiro.

Meantime, the three of them had climbed onto the platform and were pushing, pulling, and throwing The Carrion into the empty cement channel below. Ziggy then jumped from the now empty Carrion tray and back to the platform where I was and began to sing - it sounded like: 'Raindrops keep falling on my head.'

We were all watching him now as he was moving further into the roller door bay and stopped when he found what he was looking for. It was a large round red wheel, so he started turning it and water started flowing from outside somewhere.

It was The Flush, and picked up The Carrion that were strewn across the bottom of the channel and they started floating on the water, colliding together but there was not quite enough water and Ethanol mix to reach the sea wall beyond. There was no siren this time though.

'What's next?' he asked. 'The Borax' and I nodded to him, explaining the rest of the plan.

He grinned. 'That will work, it will melt off the gold and

they will not be able to fly or move and will get clogged up with the Borax and Ethanol. Great plan.'

We began to remove the lids from the containers of Borax, and the granules spilled easily into the channel. Once the containers became empty we threw them into the channel too. Ziggy jumped up onto the assembly line and began rolling the containers to the others at the front and spacing the remaining containers a little farther apart. It appeared that none were missing at all from the initial supply.

Clever I thought, and the channel was becoming clogged with a combination of the empty Borax containers, empty Ethanol drums and the docile Carrion. Then the powder started to react with the Ethanol, and some of The Carrion were affected by the slurry. It was all working quite well.

I noticed, however, that some of The Carrion were still managing to get to their feet and some were even trying to take flight, but fortunately, they were still mostly in shadow. The sun would be getting lower soon and this concerned me.

I mentioned that Marty had not yet arrived to help us take down the Emergency Tower, and explained to them this would be the catalyst to ignite the Borax, and the Ethanol. This was the last piece of the plan.

Meantime Kilby and Aya had returned with another load of Ethanol, so we started opening these and emptying them into the drain. Kilby realised what we had been doing with The Carrion and yelled out: 'What's going on? Why are The Carrion off the scow? How can we keep them away from the sun? No, no. no.'

I then also realised our predicament, and what had

happened as I should have been paying more attention, but it was too late to do anything else.

The plan was going awry.

Ziggy looked at him and I assumed he went to explain, but all he could get out was, 'Oops.' I told them that I had partially filled the scow pontoons with Ethanol so we could decant from them and get more into the channel. Aya then threw me a small hatchet axe. 'I saw this in the corridor. It was in an ER box. I didn't know if it would come in handy.'

I took it and began smashing into the bottom of the pontoons and fortunately, as the metal was thin, the Ethanol flowed from them too.

'Thanks, Carlyle.' Ziggy said to me.

'Lucky,' Kilby said helping me out of the cement channel. I looked at the axe and pointed to the Emergency Tower.

Kilby nodded and took the axe from me and he began to run towards the tower, and Aya called out to him as he passed her. 'Don't use it on the tower, the axe head is metal. You can't use it to hit the tower. It has electricity running through the back of it and up to the lights.' I wondered if Kilby had heard her above all noise from The Carrion, Ethanol and Borax.

Chapter 59 Marty

Dusk; Wednesday 31ˢᵗ December: I was slowly getting my sea legs, but even now there was a long way to go, and it was still slow going. Myles had also explained that years ago these types of boats operated on petroleum-based diesel engines and were now solar-charged charged stored with batteries on board. Then he said something about the torque having affected the draught, I wasn't listening as I was focused on my part of the plan.

Khat then came up to me and said that we were almost at the point of no return, so she handed me the marine rope which I lifted onto my shoulder. Although it was rolled into a circle it was heavy, almost too heavy. I hefted it up a little and looked down into the moving seawater, and over to the land.

We were now getting closer to their farm, getting closer to the AIC facility and getting closer to the Carrion Tug. I then dropped the rope back onto the deck, moved towards the wheelhouse to talk to Myles, and felt the boat slowing down.

Myles looked at me as I entered the small wheelhouse box. 'Nearly ready?'

'Yep' I replied, nope I thought, and went back to the deck

where Khat was waiting, and she said something that I didn't quite comprehend.

'You know it's not going to work don't you?' I looked at her, 'It has to,' I said solemnly. Myles had then slowed the boat to almost a stop and we rested on the gentle swell of the sea. I again hefted the marine rope onto my shoulder. It was a difficult maneuver with one arm, and by now the boat had stopped still. I looked at the water, then at the land and realised it was about a hundred-metre swim.

'It does get shallow quickly though at low tide though,' Myles then added; 'but we are not at low tide.'

I then decided to leap into the seawater as there was no going back from here. We had agreed that they were to drive the boat straight towards the Carrion Tug and I would make the swim. I saw them both looking at me as they knew that I was being indecisive.

Myles stepped up to me and then pulled the marine rope off my shoulder. 'You know I have been thinking, maybe if you drive the boat, with your one arm it might be better, and it would be easier to explain how a one-armed man lost control of the boat and crashed it into the Carrion Tug now wouldn't it?'

I looked at him and then at Khat, 'But that means you will have to make the swim instead.' To that he replied, 'Not exactly.'

I looked at him again thinking to myself, so this is where the plan ends.

'We will both get the rope to the fence.' Khat then said as I looked at her.

'We are both Flighters,' she said defiantly. I didn't know

what to do. Whether to hug them both, whether to yell out loud or whether to panic, as this now meant that I did have to drive the boat and crash it into the Carrion Tug, by myself I then considered all the options and realised the last one was the best, so they took the marine rope from the deck and moved to the side of the boat.

I watched as they secured one end tightly to one of the cleats on the boat and I knew there was plenty of rope to make the gap across the sea, to the land, and beyond to the tower.

They then both dropped their hands to their sides, clenched their fists and held their heads high. The Rush, was amazing as I had never seen it so close or at all and realised that there wasn't a higher level for them to float to, to aim for, and was about to say that but then they floated parallel out over the water as they were able to do a multi-directional float, and was even more amazing to watch.

Flighters are heroes, I will always be in awe of them as I watched them take off.

I realised that soon they would be landing on the fore-shore, right next to The AIC fence and it had taken no time at all, and I would have still been floundering in the water. I could then see them passing the rope to someone through the fence and it would need to be tied around the Emergency Tower now.

We were almost there, and the plan was still working. Still standing watching it all when suddenly realised I still had a job to do. I rushed back to the wheelhouse and threw the throttle upwards to initiate the speed. I still needed to make the collision, and I could see the Carrion Tug starting to make a turn. It needed to face the stern into the sea wall to collect the Carrion scow, so I willed my boat to go faster and think it listened to me, as the boat was picking up speed. I could now hear the Amnimates bleating around me - they must have sensed something different was happening.

I was getting closer to the Tug and lined it up as best I could, but as the Tug was making its turn it was becoming a smaller target. I had been hoping to hit it side-on as this would be the best opportunity to disable it and I was getting closer now, but the tug was turning, and it was a race to a collision. It was now directly facing me so I would only be able to make a passing bunt.

Would it be enough? It has to be and was determined to make it. I took one last line up and made a small adjustment to the wheel as I was only about one hundred and fifty metres to the Tug now. It was getting very close, and my thoughts went to the Amnimates and hoped I wouldn't sink this boat.

A hundred metres now, seventy metres, but suddenly realised that the last adjustment to the wheel had put me out of alignment altogether. 'Aaarghh' I yelled out in frustration and pulled at the wheel again, this time however I went the wrong way and had now completely missed the Carrion Tug. I looked behind me just as the marine rope began to get taut.

Chapter 60 Kilby

Dusk; Wednesday 31ˢᵗ December: I watched the boat out at sea as it was now almost still, and it was close enough for me to see that Marty and the two others were discussing something. I then saw something that astounded me and all of us here whilst we were watching and waiting for them at the AIC.

The two Ground-Dwellers that lived on the farm next door actually took the rope from Marty and stepped to the side of their boat themselves instead, then they appeared to slowly jump off the edge of the boat, almost in slow motion.

I thought the girl would be too small to take the weight of the rope, and the man may be too old, and the plan was changing again. But they didn't go into the water instead they both began to fly/float towards us horizontally over the seawater. It was impressive and I knew then they were both Flighters.

'Flighters,' said Carlyle standing next to me stating the obvious, 'and she already knows how to multi-directional too. So young, yet so good at it.'

I then moved towards the fence where we were to rendez-vous and they were there in little time at all, so they passed the rope through the fence and around the solid pylon that we would be using as the fulcrum for the pulley system. I saw that Marty had started the boat moving again but thought the direction was skewed.

I calculated he would miss the Tug altogether, although hoped it wouldn't.

Regardless, I continued to pull the rope hand over hand through the gap in the fence as quickly as I could although my hands were hurting from the rope burning. The man and the girl then moved quickly away, not using The Rush this time, so I threw a mock salute at them as they left me alone, and then I felt less pressure on the weight of the rope behind me.

Aya and Ziggy had now joined in pulling the rope through, so gathering a coil I made my way to the cement channel. It was filling fast now with the water, the borax, the ethanol slurry and The Carrion, so I quickly made my way down the ladder and up the other on the other side, tied the rope around the Emergency Tower and cleated it off at the joining ends.

The rope was getting tighter, and The Carrion were all starting to move around a bit more in the drain as the sun was lower in the sky now. I feared that the lower golden sun could awaken The Carrion. It could invoke a Frenzy right here, right now, but I hoped not.

We all hoped not.

I looked out to Marty and the boat and looked up and could see where Carlyle had made previously his notch cut. It was too low I thought as it needed the height of the rope to be pulling above the middle. It has to be above the centre of gravity to make the tower break, so I pulled on the rope, and it was still malleable enough for me to raise it higher up the pole.

Would it be high enough? I didn't think so.

I could see the water in the drain getting higher, and the Ethanol and Borax slurry was having the desired effect on The Carrion, but we still needed to ignite it so then chose to use the axe instead along with a ladder. I had left them by the pole just in case, maybe it was fortuitous. I picked it up and hefted it in my hand and could hear Aya yelling something behind me, but didn't catch what she said.

The rope was now getting tighter so I looked out towards Marty's boat and saw that he had missed the Tug boat altogether, and The Carrion Tug was heading directly to the sea wall to the doors. It was now backing towards the doors and would be able to open them and release The Carrion.

I had to make a decision, so I threw the ladder against the tower, quickly scaled it and lined up where I needed to sever the pole. I realised it would be well above head height, well above where the rope was now and managed to drag the rope higher up the pole. It was well above the middle of the pole, so I would have to cut just below the rope.

Aya was screaming at me now, and some of The Carrion were trying to take flight as the golden sunset was blazing directly into the cement drain. It would not be long before they could take flight.

This would be a difficult cut, so I swung the axe around me for a test and expected to have only one chance at this. Carlyle was yelling at me now too and I hoped they were compelling me to do this, so I waved back to them dismissively. I swung the axe and it bit into the pole and saw the light tower shudder above me. The lights remained on as electricity was still going to them.

I looked down into the mire behind me and at The Carrion. It was unsettling as they were re-generating and starting to move around. I swung the small axe again, and this time the lights above me flickered.

One more time, one more time…..

The severed slice in the tower was exactly where it needed to be as the tower was now starting to yield to the strain of the rope. I thought of Marty as I took one last swing, and I realised by missing the Tug, he had made it easier for me as the rope pull would be even tighter.

I made good contact however the electrically charged Emergency Tower bit back this time as I fully penetrated the pole. The metal head of the axe hit the electrical cable powering the lights and the tower then began to bend above me but this was the last thing I saw. I blacked out and fell backwards from the ladder into the cement channel behind me. The toppled tower followed me, and when the powered tower hit the water it exploded in a shower of sparks. This was the catalyst needed to ignite the Ethanol.

Chapter 61 Aya

Dusk; Wednesday 31ˢᵗ December: I realised that Kilby had taken the small axe, and the ladder and left them next to the Emergency Light Tower. I wondered if he intended to use it as Plan B but hoped not as the axe head was metal and the pole had the electrical wires running up the back of it, and through its hollow middle.

I hoped that he was not going to try and cut it down himself as the rope pulley system should work. Ziggy and I were now pulling the marine rope through the fence, and Kilby gave a mock salute to the farmers as they moved away.

They went back home and I knew they were Flighters too. Kilby had grabbed a coil of rope, clambered down and up the ladders in the cement drain, and tied it off. I could see that it was set too low on the pole and would need to be moved and was trying to tell him that but could also see The Carrion were waking up in the direct sunlight too. He seemed to realise this and raised the rope to the pole as there was enough slack in the rope to raise it higher. I then watched him gather the ladder and the axe.

He was going to Plan B.

He again raised the height of the rope. I tried to warn him

over the noise of the water flushing and The Carrion that the axe head was metallic, but don't think he heard me. I then heard Carlyle yelling out to him now too, so we made our way as close as we could to the edge of the cement drain.

I think he heard us that time, but he waived us off, and we watched him make three more attempts to sever the pole and it was starting to yield. We all watched with elation as the toppled tower fell into the water, and then it exploded in a shower of sparks and ignited the Ethanol. A plume of gas and water escaped from the drain, ignited, and then the exothermic cloud flowed back into the roller door area and took out everything else.

It melted the gold from The Carrion, and they all were destroyed.

We had all managed to step back from the drain just as the tower was falling and we were lucky that the water/ borax/ ethanol level was not high enough to breach the top of the drain platforms as the cloud only flew upwards and then along the drain instead.

We were all safe, we were all saved, we were all elated, and the remnants of The Carrion now began to float on top of the slurry. There was nothing much left of them, just molten metal lumps and not much else.

Meantime, the Carrion Tug had reached the sea wall doors and as it began to open the water containing the now destroyed Carrion began to float out to sea. We could see that Marty had managed to turn his boat around and was coming towards us as well. I then realised that I had not seen where Kilby had ended up, and having assumed that he had fallen from the ladder, I hoped he had landed safely somewhere over on the other side. We did not see anything after the light tower hit the water, then exploded and ignited the Ethanol, so we all started calling out for him.

Marty had berthed the boat, tied it up to the Carrion Tug, climbed off the boat and stepped up to us all and were all holding up our hands, clasping them together and there was also a lot of hugging.

'Where's Kilby?' he said, and we all looked around again.

Carlyle then saw him first and pointed down into the drain. Kilby was dead.

The remnants of his body were entwined in the collapsed tower. There was not much left of him either, as the heat from the cataclysmic cloud had taken its toll on everything.

'What have I done?' I then heard Carlyle say.

Meantime, Marty had come up to us, his face wide with a smile. 'All The Carrion were in there weren't they?'

I turned to look at him but couldn't hide the sadness in my face.

'What?' he said triumphantly, 'They are all destroyed aren't they?'

I then heard Carlyle say softly to him. 'I'm so sorry Marty, I'm so sorry, it's all my fault. I shouldn't have let you get involved. I shouldn't have let any of you get involved with this.'

Marty looked at him, 'With what?' spreading his arms out across the scene of the carnage up and along the drain. 'The Carrion had been obliterated into blobs of molten metal and there was nothing else left apart from a few shards of their triangular beaks and a few talons.' Then his expression changed as he could see directly into the cement channel below us, and at the collapsed tower.

I began to sense that he knew too.

'Oh Kilby, Kilby, no!' he exclaimed loudly having just now noticed his brother lying dead in the drain with the remnants of The Carrion, then he moved towards the ladder to make his way down.

I had to hold him back. Carlyle and Ziggy were now helping me too.

'Let me go, let me go,' he yelled in frustration trying to shake us off, 'I have to get down there, let me go' and he was now starting to sob, and heavier sobs came between each gasp of breath. He then stopped moving and sat to the ground holding his head in his hands. 'Oh Kilby,' he finally said much softer this time laying backwards onto the platform. He covered his eyes with his hand and his half arm.

I looked over to Carlyle. 'We had better call the ER,' he nodded and said aloud, 'Watch. Call the Emergency Response,' and I instantly heard a metallic voice answer him. 'They have responded and will attend within twenty-three minutes.' He held up his arm showing me that he had retrieved his Phillipe Patek watch from the neck of The Carrion. Ziggy interrupted us.

'How do we explain all of this to the ER and The AIC?'

I realised I had no idea.

Then we heard voices calling from behind us as I turned realised it was Myles and Khat as they must have come back. 'Over here, over here,' they called out beckoning us towards them. 'Come to the fence, we need to move the rope.'

There was not much of the rope left either as the section in the drain had also been disintegrated, but there was still the burnt end by the drain and the remainder snaked across the grassy knoll behind us. They started to pull it back through the fence had now coiled the remnants of the rope on their side, and were now moving along the fence towards their boat.

I then saw Carlyle walk up to them and they all started talking. There was a lot of nodding going on and I wondered what that all meant.

I started to move towards them and realised that I had a right to be here as I was ER, so I stopped and looked at Carlyle, Ziggy and the others. Three of the other AIC workers were already making their way back into the corridor, most likely going back to their holding rooms, and perhaps they would be able to claim that they had been there all the time, completely oblivious to what had happened out here.

'There are no cameras here so The AIC would not have seen any of this,' I called out to them.

Marty had now raised himself from the platform and was walking parallel along the fence line to them towards their boat as well. I watched Myles and Khat invoke The Rush and gently float over the fence, and then he joined him on their boat. It was soon un-tethered, and they began to motor away with Marty on board.

'Just us to get make up the story then?' I heard Ziggy say.

The ER arrived within the determined time and I recognised some of them from the ER stations in the local Ravilob Berg, but there were two other men with them. I knew one of them as it was Hawke, The second man I did not know, but he seemed to know Carlyle.

'Hello Carlyle. Just what have you been up to?' he said looking around at the decimated Carrion lying in the cement channel, and at the collapsed tower lying with them. Then he saw the remnants of the body. 'Who is that then? Is that Kilby down there? Well, that is interesting.'

I saw Hawke shrug and look at him.

Meantime the ER had made the area safe by disconnecting the electricity at the mains outlet, and they noticed the dead man in the channel. Carlyle looked at Hawke, nodded a recognition, and then looked over to the second man.

The man grinned at him. 'I see Zamiro is not with you today, but Hawke and I, well, we had a good look at her the other day when you two were tracking your watch on The AIC viewer at the jewellers. I see you found your watch and by the way. I don't think she is going to be happy when I tell her you have killed her brother.'

I was horrified as I realised that these two men were Represents.

Carlyle simply nodded, and they both grabbed him. He was determined to break free, and I didn't know what to do. He managed to weave from out of their grasp and started backing away from them. He had nowhere to go but did manage to get about ten metres away from them, back towards the roller door. He then stopped, dropped his arms to his side, clenched his fists and raised his head. I realised what was going on. He is a Flighter, and I never knew.

He then began to float slowly upwards and two Represents were just too slow as there was just enough gap between them. He made it safely up to the roof of the building and perched himself there. I looked up to him.

'Coward,' I heard the second Represent say looking up to

him. 'Fight or Flight. When does a Flighter ever stay and fight? You are all cowards.'

Hawke and the man came towards me. 'So what is your story then?'

I noticed Ziggy had managed to escape during the melee, and I was all alone.

Chapter 62 Carlyle

Dusk; Wednesday 31ˢᵗ December: I was standing with Aya and Ziggy when the ER Team arrived and we were still trying to work out a story, something believable, but were not having much luck when I noticed two other men came in with the ER. One was Hawke, the other I didn't know but he seemed to know me though.

He then stated that he had watched the same vision we had at the jewellers when Zamiro and I tracked The Carrion. They then grabbed me, so I fought a little, managed to escape and was backing towards the roller door area when I saw Ziggy move around us and make his way back through the corridor. That left Aya and me alone here. I had no choice, so invoked The Rush and floated up to safety on the roof of the building behind me.

'Coward', I heard the second man call out to me as I rose then he mentioned something about Fight or Flight and watched them turn their focus to Aya. She was being backed towards the open drain, and they were now on either side of her. I had no doubt they would push her in. I decided to fight. I drop-floated down from the roof and there was just enough height to control the fall and directed myself into the back of the second man. We toppled into the drain. I had landed on top of him, and he tried to get up and turn to fight me, but his left leg had been caught on one of the triangular beaks of one of The Carrion.

Although it was a deep cut and was bleeding profusely, he managed to stand face me. Hawke and Aya just stood there watching, along with two other ERs. I have never been in a fight and had no idea what to do. He feigned a lunge at me and laughed as I reacted, so he moved a little closer feigned another lunge and laughed at me again. 'Well... a Flighter that fights. That's something I thought I would never see.'

He then threw a punch at me and it connected. I fell to the floor of the cement drain. It was sloppy and slippery, and I probably couldn't move from here, so he hobbled towards me and kicked out with his good leg and that too connected. I still had no idea what to do, and he was laughing louder now.

'Do you know who I am Carlyle?'

I shook my head. 'No.'

'Well, my name is Columbus. Remember that, and I once thought that your girlfriend's sister, Tristesse was going to be good for me. I knew how to treat her too. She told me that she didn't like being slapped when she was out of line, but I told her it was all part of my training to be the best Represent I could. It looks like I will have my choice of both sisters when I return to Yelnu. I'll tell them what you have been up to. Killing their brother and all.'

He then stopped talking and leaned down to me. I thought he might say something else, but he just straightened up as his bleeding leg was giving him grief.

I was trying to cover my head as I instinctively knew my

body might be able to take the hits. Something told me to protect my head. He kicked me again, and again, and again. I thought I heard someone call out; 'Stop, that's enough' from somewhere up above me, and opened my eye.

It was Hawke and he was holding one of the ER's Tasers and it was pointed at us.

Columbus turned to him. 'What, Why? This is our job to kill Flighters.'

'Maybe,' Hawke said. 'But you already killed the guy at the jewellers in the Central Berg.'

'Practice,' Columbus said dismissively.

'Brosnan, his name was Brosnan and he helped us do all this,' I said quietly, although I think Hawke heard me.

'I knew him too.' Hawke then said. 'I had met his family. It was years ago. His wife had already died. He was all alone, just working for love. He had lost his family and his job helped him cope.' And with that comment, the Taser he was holding went off, and the barbs hit Columbus, one in his chest and the other on his face.

Columbus blurted out something unintelligible and collapsed to the floor of the drain. His body was convulsed with the charge, but as he fell there was a sharp piece of undamaged Carrion beak in the way, and it split his head open upon impact.

I lay back exhausted, and Hawke climbed down the ladder and he helped me out of the drain. 'I guess I just quit being a Represent. It involves just too much killing. Life is just too precious.' He said to me.

Chapter 63 Zamiro

Morning Thursday 1ˢᵗ January: I was home waiting for them, and when Carlyle finally arrived he told me everything. The Carrion, The boat, The AIC, Myles and Khat, Kilby, Marty, Columbus and Hawke... everything. I didn't know whether to be elated or to cry and we didn't get much sleep last night.

I left Carlyle lying in bed as I heard a knocking on the apartment door, opened it, and it was Marty and Aya. I could see that they had been crying too, so hugged them both as they entered.

'I couldn't go home last night Zee, just couldn't. Not yet. I stayed on the farm with Myles and Khat. Did you know he is a Flighter?'

I nodded, 'Yes, Carlyle told me.'

'Well, he is almost of forty summers, next week. It will be his 40ᵗʰ and that will leave Khat to run the farm by herself. Her mother died last year, and she was a Flighter too.'

I wondered where this was going.

'Well, they offered me a job, a one-armed, no experienced, non-boater, landlubber like me. They offered me a job. I can pilot the boat on market days and help out around the farm. I can also use the boat to go fishing or other stuff.'

'OK', I thought that's great, but why are you telling me all this today, so early I noticed Aya was keeping silent.

'That is why I am here,' he then said softly.

'I am going to be taking Carlyle away this morning, to safety. It's the best for all of us as The AIC will come looking for him.'

I looked at him and then at Aya. 'What?' I said loudly, and with that remark saw Carlyle standing at the bedroom door behind me. He had two bags packed.

'I have to do this Zamiro to protect everyone,' he said softly.

I was stunned and sat down on the floor where I stood.

Aya was nodding now too, and then explained more about yesterday's events including the part about the Carrion Tug. It has an operating camera on the front that views everything, and it would not be long before other Represents would come looking for answers. Between them, they had realised that the AIC would not have any overhead vision of The AIC and The Carrion destruction, and we had not seen this either when we watched the vision at the jewellers, but I can remember the screen going blank the closer we got to the facility.

I had thought it was the cut-off for the tracker, but it was likely that The AIC were controlling the information, the vision, and the view, so no one could see what or where The Carrion departed from. I still didn't like what I was hearing though.

'Can I come too?' I said defiantly.

'No you can't,' Carlyle said holding up his wrists. 'I have just re-set my chips, and this will give me about twelve hours to escape, to go somewhere else, to leave everybody safe. Marty will take me on the boat.' He then explained about the re-set chips, and the ability to break away from The AIC and be tracked.

It was all Creedence's idea. Aya had thought of it too as Kilby had given his chips to her yesterday. We thought of all of this on the shuttle trip home last night.

'I will still have four of them to keep me invisible for a while at least'.

No wonder he could not look at me in bed last night, I thought, it was just not the guilt from Kilby's death, it was this too. I had to concede it was the right thing to do, for my safety, for my family's safety, for normality but my life is never going to be the same again. We beat The Carrion, but I lost Kilby and now I have lost Carlyle too.

I looked at him. 'But you can't get access to anything, buy or sell anything, can't do anything or use anything,' I suddenly realised the impact of the situation with his wrist chips being removed.

All he said was, 'I will manage.'

There was then another knock on the door and I knew it was time that Carlyle left me. This time it was Hawke. 'It's time,' he said looking at me and then to Carlyle. I couldn't believe it, losing Kilby and now Carlyle. I went up to Hawke, but he was still very guarded, so I hugged him, then said, 'Thanks for this. I understand I think,' and he smiled.

I then watched them leave. Marty, Hawke and the love of my life, Carlyle.

After about twenty minutes Aya and I made our way out onto the balcony, and she pointed out to me a boat in the distance as it was just leaving the port I could just make out a man standing at the bow, and a one-armed man in the wheel-house, and they were heading west, off into the unknown.

Marty had said that the boat would be going west to the other side of the bay, but it would not be able the berth any-where as the tide was too low, so Carlyle would have to swim or float the rest of the way to the shore, whichever shore that was.

I turned around and moved back inside and Aya slid the glass doors shut behind us so I stood there staring out through the glass, watching as long as I could as the boat was now getting smaller and smaller in the distance. I asked Aya what she was going to do now. Still working at the AIC? She said that she was going back to ER work instead, explaining that she was already a qualified midwife, but was now going into obstetrics to become a qualified Doctor.

'I want to help people live life and not be around the death stuff anymore.' And then clasped her right hand into my left hand as I held up my right palm and pressed onto the glass. '

'Bye Carlyle,' I said softly. Aya looked at me, 'He will be back. He is a Flighter.'

I nodded in agreement trying to hold back the tears. 'And he is also a fighter. He fought The Carrion and won. We won.'

'Who is he going to fight next then?'

I said still staring into the glass and she replied quietly. 'The AIC.'

Chapter 64 Aya

It is two months later; Monday 29ᵗʰ February: 'How is he?' I asked Zamiro as I was with her again today and I was again in her Apartment, 1103. We had been spending a lot of time together and whilst Carlyle was keeping himself scarce it was good for the both of us to keep together after everything that had happened. I still live in my Apartment 503 downstairs, so we were always able to easily visit each other.

I was looking down at Carlyle lying on a plastic stretcher. He had been carried to 1103 from the beach below us by two other ERs and was softly lowered onto the matted floor. I took a breath. 'How long has he been away? Have you noticed his wrists are no longer bandaged? He must have cut out his wrist chips, maybe he does not need them wherever he has been living.'

Zamiro nodded. 'Two months. He must be managing without them.'

'You still don't know where he goes then?'

'I have an idea,' she replied but didn't elaborate.

'So what's happened just now then?

'He said he was swimming off the breakwater and that

something attacked him. Not someone though, something,' she further clarified.

His injuries were much worse than we first thought, but he had been stoically fending off suggestions that I should attend to his wounds. I was concerned that he might exsanguinate, so I leaned down to him and tried to roll him over to get a better look, fortunately, as the other ERs had not yet left, they were able to assist to turn him onto his side.

We then saw that there was a copious amount of blood seeping through his swimming shirt. It was beginning to stain the matting on the floor underneath him. Zamiro pointed out the three large and bloodied raked scratches along his back. He was now lying prostrate on the floor, so she moved to cradle his head in her hands.

Carlyle whispered to her. 'I told you not to fall in love with a Flighter. Flighters and Ground-dwellers should not get acquainted' and he took a deep breath, 'And I didn't reach forty to celebrate my death day.'

A single tear fell on his left undamaged eye and I watched as Zamiro leant into him, softly kissing his forehead, He opened his eye and looked up smiling. 'You are so beautiful. Do you still miss me?' again whispering to her.

'And you are a hero,' she said in return, then added, 'You are my hero, too.'

He closed his eyes and was now sleeping, or was he unconscious? He can't be dead. I will not let him die, not now, not yet, as he is not yet forty summers.

Zamiro looked at me. 'It is true. It is dangerous to love a Flighter isn't it?'

Chapter 65 Marty

I miss Kilby even though it has been about two months since we defeated The Carrion, and I am clearing his possessions from the apartment he shared with Aya. She had collected them for me and placed them in her storeroom, and I still can't understand how he managed to convince her to live with him, but it seems so irrelevant now. He knew what he was doing, always did and as they say, the pain of loss lessens eventually, but love continues forever.

My arms still give me phantom aches from when The Carrion took it from me at the arena, and has it been that long already? There is talk that I may qualify for a prosthetic forearm and as Fata is on The GOD Panel says he might be influenced as there has been development in this field by the Emergency Responders.

I am hoping today is the day that Aya lets me know of my good fortune.

I heard a knock at the door and was surprised at this as was not expecting anyone other than Aya, but she can access the apartment anyway so maybe it is Hawke, as he has become a good friend since changing his opinion on life. I opened it and a man and a woman were standing there. I think I know the man from somewhere, but am not sure who they are. Represents maybe? Are they looking for Carlyle?

'Hello, can I help you?' The man leant forward, and I can see he is having trouble standing. He clutched at his knee area. 'Sorry, I am not used to my new leg. It's still new to me having this,' He rolled up the trouser leg to show a prosthetic leg.

'I am Mitchell, and this is Dana, and we are looking for Aya. We thought she lived here, in Apartment 503?'

I nodded. 'Well, yes this is her Apartment, but she is not here at the moment. I am clearing out my brother's stuff.'

'You're brother was Kilby.' Mitchell said. 'So, sorry for your loss.' Then Dana added 'Everyone knows what you guys did. Defeated The Carrion.'

I nodded to her, 'So, what can I do for you?'

'We have come to thank Aya for saving my life. Is she around?'

I considered this and knowing that Carlyle is most likely still upstairs with them in Apartment 1103, however, I am a little reluctant to offer to meet with them, then I realised that I could ring them as there is a telephone in both apartments, so I moved over and made the call.

Aya answered and said it would be OK.

As we were going up there I asked them about the latest at The AIC facility. I have been able to watch from the farm next door and wondered how The AIC dealt with the carnage and the destruction of The Carrion. Dana said she would rather explain it to all of us together, and I acknowledged this as a good idea. As we reached the apartment door I knocked loudly, then I called out.

'Make sure any packages are out of sight,' alluding to the fact that Carlyle may be in the apartment somewhere. Aya let us in and greeted Mitchell and Dana with a warm embrace. 'So good to see you again Mitchell, you're looking better. How is the leg?'

'It's good, still a bit wobbly, but it's good.'

I watched as Dana walked over to Zamiro and hugged her. I didn't know that they knew each other. 'It's been a long time, Zamiro.'

Zamiro stepped from the embrace. 'Have we met?'

'Yes, a long time ago as we went through our Wrist Installation Day together at The AIC. I have been looking for you for seven years. I didn't know that Marty and Kilby were your brothers. I'd met them on that day too.'

Zamiro sat quickly down on the sofa. 'I had almost forgotten all about it as it was so traumatic for all of us. After all of this time, I wanted to find you too, wanted to thank you for helping me get through it. I would have never managed it without you either.'

Aya asked them what it was all about, as everyone knows the Installation Days are a celebration, nothing ever traumatic about them, never has been, so when they told us, we were horrified.

Dana looked at us. 'That was the day it all started for me and my mistrust of The AIC,' Dana went on to explain why she decided to work there. I could tell that Mitchell had no idea about her history with The AIC.

Dana then asked; 'Have you seen Carlyle?'

Aya and Zamiro looked at her, and with that comment, he

hobbled out from the spare bedroom, obviously still in pain, but was able to stand.

'Hello Carlyle, good to meet you again after all these years too,' she said to him. He looked at her and smiled. 'Hello, Dana. Yes, it's been a long time.'

Aya, Zamiro and I looked at them both, as we didn't know that they knew each other either. 'I still miss Mel.' Dana said.

'Me too, and she was a Flighter too,' he said softly.

I looked over at him, wow, he said that someone else was a Flighter. I had never heard anyone call someone else a Flighter, and he mentioned Mel. I knew that was a name from his past. Dana did not react to Carlyle saying Mel was a Flighter, perhaps she didn't know.

'I didn't know that.' Dana said confirming my suspicion.

Zamiro had told me about Carlyle having lost his family and his girlfriend when The AIC brought down the planes all those years ago, and I recall that Mel was her name. Dana, is her sister?

Then they all moved closer together, and Dana went on to explain that Mel was indeed her sister and she too had lost her family that day, all except for her youngest sister Frankie, but she had no idea where Frankie was now. 'Have you ever been back to Anidak and your farms since?' she asked him.

Carlyle smiled again, 'I am living there now, as my grand-parents have returned from their long sojourns around the world. They have been harbouring me and without my wrist chips. The AIC cannot track me.'

'How are Lennon and Julia then?' Dana then asked him.

Then it all came out, their history, the farm at Munta,

losing their families but she said nothing about Carlyle being a Flighter. Perhaps Dana does not know that of him either.

Meantime, Mitchell had sat down at the dining table filling us in on the latest at The AIC and went on to say that it was Dana who had let Aya, Kilby and Carlyle in on the day of the fight and she had given us access to all the areas and it had nothing to do with the Mitchells AIC maintenance bag.

'So, it was you that let us through all the doors too? Aya asked her and she confirmed this to us again. How was that possible? I thought.

Dana then went on to inform us that The AIC had since scooped everything out of the cement channel including Kilby and dumped it all away, most likely into the sea.

'No repercussions from The AIC yet? I asked.

Mitchell responded solemnly, 'No, nothing yet but they are up to something as they will not go down without a fight.' he then stood up and came over to me with something in his hands.

'Here, you might like this,' He presented me with Kilby's AIC pass - it was relatively unscathed from the borax/ethanol slurry. I was surprised at this but was very thankful too. We all were.

We then stayed there talking about everything for hours and I saw that Carlyle, Dana and Aya were standing so close together now, and Dana was prodding at his wrists.

Were they all plotting something? A plan to defeat The AIC perhaps?

I overheard Carlyle saying that he had removed his wrist chips on the boat trip when he had left Edi-Aleda after The Carrion was defeated, and he explained he didn't need to have the wrist chips to maintain a lifestyle as the farm was self-sufficient. The Munta/Anidak community knew him and had welcomed him back.

Maybe there was a lesson in there for us, and maybe The AIC could not track us.

I went up to Mitchell and we started talking about his new prosthetic leg. Aya then joined in with the news that I was hoping for and although it has been a long time to wait, told me that I will qualify for a robotic forearm. She mentioned they are providing them with an extra strength function. I was looking forward to it, as it will make me whole again, and much stronger than I ever was before. I decided to rest momentarily from all the conversation and moved out onto the open balcony. It was a beautiful day, and it was a beautiful golden dusk.

We no longer fear The Carrion.

I could see from here children playing below me on the sand and their sounds as squeals of excitement wafted up from below as they ran from the incoming waves. I saw another group fishing off a rocky groyne. Life is good, life is better.

I could see one of the men had caught a fish on his line. He was straining with the effort, the rod was bent, and the twine was pulling. I then saw the fish. It was big and dark in the blue water.

He made his way down the rocky breakwater with his net and looked back at his friends and family. I then saw what he had caught, it was Cobalt Blue, but it was not a fish.

It was a Water Carrion.

He dropped the fishing rod in horror, but his reaction was

too late, and he was too slow. The Water Carrion propelled itself out of the water and took the man in its giant metal maw, and with one slick movement slid gently back into the sea.

When is the beginning of the End?

The FLIGHTERS - Genesis
BOOK I
Coming December 2024

It is the year 2031. Gil Andersson is the chairman of The AIC (Artificial Intelligence Corporation). We told him we were not ready for the machine to take complete control of Edi-Aleda. We told him they needed more time to set up the fail-safes – the machines might never stop learning. He told us that he knew better, but the machine knew better than him. The AIC can now control everybody, everywhere and everything.

The FLIGHTERS - Requiem
BOOK III
Coming December 2025

It is the year 2045. It has been twenty-one years since The AIC (Artificial Intelligence Corporation) went live. Can The Carrion be finally defeated? Can The AIC be overthrown? Has it been long enough for humanity to learn from its mistake – to rely on artificial intelligence to keep us completely safe? Humanity learns from its mistakes, after all, it is in our nature. What if continues to humanity rely on artificial intelligence not to make the same mistakes? The AIC has learnt we are not a threat, but does it know everything about us?

Author's Biography:

The author is a former long-term banker by profession and worked within the Bank's Credit Card Fraud Team, where he obtained a Private Investigators Licence. He resides between Adelaide, South Australia, and the Sunshine Coast, Queensland.

In November 2022, the author won an award from Wakefield Press, Adelaide for his short story: 'Car on a Hill'.

Other published titles include: 'One Tricked Phoney', 'Two Hurtled Gloves' and 'Three French Bens' from the Nic Thorn & Associates Investigations series. These books are set in modern-day Australia and investigate scams, frauds, and genuine misunderstandings. They are littered with humour, music and pop-culture references. They are available online or in paperback.

www.ingramcontent.com/pod-product-compliance
Lightning Source LLC
Chambersburg PA
CBHW070050120726
47909CB00002B/338